Southwyck

Book 1 of the Villages of Wyck Series

Christina Waymreen

LOCCN: 2015915119

BISAC: Juvenile Fiction / Fantasy & Magic

Cover art by John Nikolouzos

SouthWyck

ISBN-13: 978-0-9960132-3-9

To all my girls

Contents

South Wyck

KAR

KAR Homely leaped out of bed, positive that he was late for school again. He looked at the huge grandfather clock relaxing on the wall and sighed with relief. It was half past five in the morning. He didn't know what it was about that clock, but today the elaborate woodcarvings, surrounding the clock face, curled up to one side and smirked at him. He glared back at it. Despite all the paper he jammed underneath its legs, it never seemed to be enough to make it stand upright. The next day, the wad of paper would disappear and the clock would lean contentedly against the wall again. He had finally given up. He figured that it must be one of those really old grandfather clocks—a tired, wizened, and cranky one. His father had fiddled with it one day and now when it struck six in the morning, an old man with a soft flowing white beard and bulging eyes would pop out, hobble along a plank of wood, bang a crooked cane, and holler "Get up, get up, you lazy bones!" His father had no idea how that happened. He had been trying to get it to whistle a merry tune or at least toll the soft chiming of bells.

His parents had, at one time or another, bought the rest of the furniture in his room at various estate sales. They were always able to haggle their way into a good bargain and they came home flushed and excited from those trips—often lugging huge but quirky pieces of newly acquired second-hand furniture. They just didn't see the sense in buying new, being that wood seemed to age so well. Even his bed was the same one he had slept in as a baby. One day he was sleeping peacefully, curled up behind bars, and the next thing he knew, the crib shook, made a few popping sounds, and expanded. It had continued growing with him each year. His mother thought it was the best piece of furniture she had ever purchased. Other pieces of furniture seemed to have a magical urge to redecorate the room every now and then. They would march around while he was in the room studying, reading, or hanging out with his best friends, Haylen and Jack.

1

Sometimes, while he was sitting doing homework, his chair and desk danced around the room like rascally kids. The pair would eventually wear themselves out and settle down into some corner of his bedroom. During those events he would just fling himself on his bed and finish his studies. The desk and chair would take too long to find another spot to settle, at times.

He loved the chest of drawers the most. He would throw in his socks, shirts, shorts, underwear and just about anything else and the next morning they would be folded neatly, in separate drawers. He was happy to take care of this chore for his mother and she always smiled gratefully at him when he carried his pile of clothes off into his bedroom. Once there, he would grab a pair of socks, ball them up, and happily fling them at the chest of drawers. In turn the drawers would open up like the mouths of hungry predators and gobble up anything he threw at them. Having practiced through the years, he never missed a hungry mouth. Once finished, they would slam shut and reopen for inspection, clothes folded to perfection.

Kar was too excited to laze in bed that morning. It was his birthday. At last he was thirteen years old. He walked up to the full-length mirror and scrutinized his face. His father promised he would look just like him once he turned thirteen. He couldn't see any difference in his features since he tumbled into bed the night before. His almond-shaped eyes, framed by thick dark lashes— too long for his taste—peered back at him. With a shake of his head, his silky black hair always fell into place. He still thought his mouth was too big. No, he did not look like his father at all. His eyes did not become small and beady, nor was his nose snubbed like his father's, and he definitely did not have a receding hairline. He was a disgrace to the Homely name. What was worse, his eyes changed to match the color of the clothes he was wearing. If he wore a red shirt, his eyes would display flaming pupils. His favorite chocolate-brown pajamas turned his pupils the color of the mud on his father's boots after a hard day at the quarry. He had certainly eliminated orange from his wardrobe altogether because the resulting eerie eyes had terrified strangers in the market (and everywhere else, for that matter). He'd seen people scurrying away from him and his mom in the vegetable section. He once bet Lillian Bigfoot that he had more whispers of *funny eyes* behind his back then she did about *funny foot*. He sighed when he remembered winning that bet, as he pulled out a pair of brown shorts and a blue sweater from the depths of the chest of drawers. Blue eyes would not frighten anyone.

But none of that mattered at the moment. In just a week, it would be *What's My Magic?* Day. Excitement mingled with apprehension made him suddenly break out in a cold sweat. What would *his* magic be?

Last year somebody had shape-shifted into a mouse, while someone else had the ability to transform into a cat. Chaos erupted and his father had pulled poor Henre Lisp from the cat's mouth just in time. Henre never dared to turn into a mouse again; but Kar would occasionally see the cat wandering around the street, sometimes with a contended look on its face.

Kar didn't care much for shape-shifting, unless he could change into a lion or a tiger. Now those were really big and powerful animals. On weekends, the zoo was filled with shape-shifters of every imaginable kind. His father did not think there was much of a career in shape-shifting into strange animals so that others could stare at you. He was sure that Mr. Lance, who shape-shifted as a rhinoceros for the zoo on the weekends, did it to supplement his income. It seemed that teachers were not paid enough.

Kar washed his face and dressed slowly. His mind was shuffling through all the possibilities that his soon-to-be magical finger could possess. His father worked at the quarry levitating huge boulders and moving them to their requested destinations, sometimes miles away. Very few people had the magical ability to levitate large, heavy objects. He was so proud of his dad. Even his mother had a rare magical ability. She could lift her hand into the air and write a message in the sky. Every one of the skywriters had their own unique handwriting. His mother's,

3

though, was the neatest and tidiest of them all. She had a fun job at the Department of Sky Advertising, and sometimes she would leave him embarrassing notes. *Don't forget to buy bread on your way home.* Sometimes she'd get sentimental. *Thinking of you, sweetie, on this beautiful day.* The kids at school never knew whether messages like that were for Mr. Homely or for Kar, but they still snickered behind his back (and more often, to his face) whenever they noticed a *sweetie* floating across the sky. He couldn't lift his head up at school for the rest of the week without everybody cooing at him. He knew he'd have *Happy birthday, Sweetie* floating across the sky today. But it was an important day and he wanted everyone to know, even if Lucas Nosty, who had also turned thirteen a month earlier, would laugh at him about it.

He heard his mother calling. At the same time a small round door opened up near the top of the ancient grandfather clock and a wooden plank shot out. From within its dark recesses, a carved figure of an old man, back slightly bent and wearing a crinkled pirate costume, stepped out with a tiny parrot sitting on his left shoulder. A black eye patch covered one of the bird's eyes. The old man's mangy white beard almost covered his shiny black boots, and what remained of the hair behind his ears stood out like cotton balls. The pirate marched across the length of the plank, striking it six times with a crooked cane, while the parrot flapped its wings and squawked, "Get up, get up, you lazy bones!" It hollered the wake-up call another two times for good measure. The old man then scampered back into the clock before Kar could find something to throw at it.

"Kar, sweetie, breakfast," yelled Mrs. Homely from the kitchen.

Kar ran down the stairs and greeted his mother with a hug. He loved hugging her. When nobody was looking, of course. She always smelled of freshly baked bread.

"Mom, you're squeezing the breath out of me." Kar's voice sounded muffled and far away, his head firmly straddled by her hefty bosoms.

4

"Sorry. Happy birthday, darling," she said, releasing him and smacking kisses on his cheeks. She pulled him back at arm's length and stared at his face for a few moments. "I always liked the color blue for your eyes, sweetie. You should wear that sweater more often."

"Mm, thanks, Mom," he said, taking in a gulp of air and giving her a quick peck back. He wiped his wet cheeks quickly with the back of his hand before she noticed. "What's for breakfast?"

"Best pancakes in all of Wyck," she said, planting a plateful of pancakes on the table, "With lots of blueberries and strawberries - a special treat from Mrs. Swoonzy. She gave me these for a discount on some cloud advertising. What do you think of this?" she asked, spreading her hands. "Get your blueberries and strawberries here—fresh pickings every day at the Swoonzy farm."

Kar nodded enthusiastically. He was too busy tucking into his breakfast to voice his opinion. His mother's ads weren't usually very catchy but her messages were always clear.

Mrs. Homely beamed, her face sprinkled with beads of sweat from hovering over a hot stove. Her broad shoulders strained under her flowery housedress like planks of wood under pressure. A small yellow kerchief was tied around her head to keep her hair out of her eyes, but somehow her curly brown bangs had escaped their prison and they danced around on her forehead whenever she moved.

Digging into his special pancakes, Kar looked around to see if his birthday present was anywhere. Usually there was a gift wrapped and waiting for him on the counter, but he couldn't see anything unusual in the room. Was the special breakfast of strawberries and blueberries his gift? He hoped not.

"Where's Dad?" he asked, piling more of the pancakes onto his plate.

"He's out in the yard. His broomster died out on him last night. I told him the Fixit shop could do a better job and he should have sent his in. But you know your father. He can fix anything, or so he says." Mrs. Homely rolled her eyes and Kar snorted in agreement. "He's trying to see if he can get it started again. I say we need a new one, large enough for the whole family. A three-seater would be nice."

"Can't wait to have one of my own," exclaimed Kar between bites. "The Triple Alpha broomster. Sleek, shiny, and flies like the wind." He gestured wildly with enthusiasm. His fork slipped out of his hand and hit the side of the kitchen wall.

"Kar!" Mrs. Homely frowned at him. "Stay, I'll get it." She picked up the fork from the corner of the kitchen where it fell.

"Sorry, Mom." Kar smiled sheepishly. "Anyway, I wish they had accepted Lillian Bigfoot's idea about the padded broomster seats instead of those hard grooves. That would have been a lot more comfortable."

"That'll be the day when Karl Wasster takes anyone's advice," said Mrs. Homely. She shoved a clean fork into his hand. "And you still need to be sixteen until you earn your license to fly, young man. 'Till then ...'"

"Till then you'll have to make do with this," boomed Mr. Homely as he walked into the kitchen, pulling a bicycle. "Happy birthday, son."

Kar stood up quickly, his eyes flashing brighter than the color of his shirt. It was not just a bicycle. It was a red Classic Two Wheeler. What the Triple Alpha Broomster could do in the sky, the Classic Two Wheeler could do on the ground. He gave his dad a huge hug and grabbed the bike by the handles.

"Wow," cried Kar, his voice almost hoarse from excitement. "Wow! Wait till the guys in school get a load of this. Can I go now?" He beamed over his shoulder at his parents as he maneuvered his bike out the back door.

Mr. Homely nodded happily. Mrs. Homely sniffed hard and wiped the corner of her eyes. Kar hopped on the bike. It fit him as if it were custom made. The stretch of the pedals met his stride as he felt it glide forward effortlessly. He was giddy with happiness. For the moment he forgot all about *What's My Magic?* Day. As he cycled merrily to school, he was blissfully unaware that the color of his eyes was slowly changing to match the flaming red of the Classic Two Wheeler beneath him.

LILLIAN BIGFOOT

LILLIAN BIGFOOT swung her skinny leg over her secondhand broomstick and hoisted herself onto the padded bicycle seat she had strapped on for comfort. When not in use, the broomster usually hovered two feet off the ground. She bounced up and down to check the comfort level of her seat and adjusted it for balance. She couldn't understand why no one had yet developed comfortable seating. The thin broomsticks they churned out these days (and sold at such gigantic profits) were streamlined for speed—not comfort. She'd never trade her old Alpha Broomster for one of those new cheaply made models. She leaned forward and grasped the handles jutting out from the sides of the front end and twisted the left one. The broomster sputtered once and died. She twisted the handle again, placed her feet in the straps that hung off the sides, and waited for it to warm up. The straps were customized to fit her because she had one foot larger than the other. It was a proud family trait, but she had never been especially fond of it. She knew it always came in handy during the winemaking season; otherwise, it made her limp and it was just a nuisance. She wore very long skirts to cover it up. That morning she had on her best outfit: a dull brown corduroy skirt and matching jacket. It was her mother's, but she didn't care. She loved vintage clothes.

The broomster was finally ready to fly. She pointed it upwards and it lifted off the ground. She didn't want to be late for her first day at work. She had been accepted for the job of bunny at the daycare center. When she hired Lillian, Madam Dripster, the owner of the only daycare center in SouthWyck, had reminded her that she expected all her employees to arrive at least an hour before the children.

Lillian climbed high into the sky, away from all the noise. Everything below seemed so tranquil. Four straight paved roads met in the middle, connecting the four villages in one big square. The dewy forest surrounding them all seemed to protect the villages from unwelcome strangers. But Lillian often wished she had the chance to see what someone who wasn't a Wyckian would look like. Realizing that she had a little bit of spare time, she circled the villages. The homes in EastWyck, the oldest of the villages, had tattered roofs and crumbling chimneys. Her parents had forbidden her to visit EastWyck. "Nothin' there but a bunch of hooligans," her father often muttered when news of EastWyck reached him. Those who could afford to leave EastWyck moved to either SouthWyck or WestWyck.

"More hooligans," her father would say, shaking his head, when he saw some of those former EastWyck villagers move into their neighborhood. "There should be a law against that!"

The richest of the Wyckians built their fancy mansions in NorthWyck. Lillian could see the sparkling windows of NorthWyck from her broomster as she slowly flew over the houses. She wished she had friends there just so she could take a peek inside those homes. The oldest of the village folk said that once upon a time a Queen ruled the Wyckians, and she hailed from NorthWyck. Imagine, thought Lillian, royalty among the Wyckians! Now that was laughable. The Councilmen would not have liked that for sure. She dropped down over SouthWyck, her hometown, still grinning at the thought.

She spied Mrs. Beadlepoof's wide frame plodding along the street: she was already up and about and poking her nose into everyone's business. Those who caught sight of Mrs. Beadlepoof quickly skipped across the street. It would have been difficult to slide past her unnoticed because she took up most of the sidewalk. She would virtually capture anyone who passed her by. Lillian's grin erupted into a burst of laughter when she saw Mrs. Beadlepoof snag unsuspecting Mr. Nooza before he turned the corner on his way to school. Short, bald, and absentminded, he was definitely no match for Mrs. Beadlepoof as she tightly clamped onto his elbow. Too bad, thought Lillian, zooming over roofs and treetops, as she was sure Mrs. Beadlepoof would wheedle some kind of information out of the poor man and spread it through town. She would probably hear about it during dinner.

She gunned the broomster and zipped over the village square. Shops were opening up all along the center of town. Lillian thought SouthWyck was beautiful. Everything in the village was in perfect harmony. Each cobbled street that wrapped around the tiny village had a purpose, as did the narrow lanes crisscrossing through them. They had built the school and day-care center just outside the town, by the fields. A river meandered through the forest and wrapped itself halfway around the village boundaries before turning east out of the region. The Wyckians never bothered to venture past those lines. On its way out, the river flowed under a bridge built by the members of the Survive Or Else scout camp. It was a boys' and girls' camp, which Lillian had once joined. She had barely made it through. Her one big foot had come in handy when she needed to defend herself. She could also play any kind of ball game that required a powerful kick to get it near the goal, through it, or over it, depending on the game. Her parents had designated a room specifically for all of her kicking trophies.

Mount Footsteps loomed ahead, large and foreboding. On clearer days it looked like a giant upside-down cone with vanilla ice cream oozing and dripping over the flattened tip. Most of the time it was covered in clouds. No one knew what lay beyond Mount Footsteps and no one cared to find out. Even if anyone felt brave or suicidal enough to attempt it, they would have to pass the nine councilmen's cave just halfway up the mountain. The councilmen didn't like anyone flying their broomsters near the cave. A NO-BROOMSTER-ZONE sign had once been etched into the side of the rock, but erosion had erased part of it and now it just read NO-B-OO-ZO. It was still enough to keep the most adventurous of spirits nearer to terra firma.

Lillian hoped her first day at work would liven up what had been a very boring seventeen years of life. Other than the Grape Stomping week and the yearly celebration of *What's My Magic?* Day, there was nothing to anticipate. Yes, there was the Gift Giving day and the occasional birthdays and holidays here and there, but she would give it all up if something exciting would happen in her life. She yearned for something thrilling—something to bring excitement into her day-to-day existence.

She could remember vividly when it was her turn for *What's My Magic?* Day. She had stood on that stage with the rest of the excited thirteen-year-olds, hoping and praying that when she pointed her finger and wiggled it about, that her bit of magic would be the best ever. Instead she had turned into a bunny with one ear humiliatingly longer than the other. She had hopped up and down the stage for what she thought was a torturous hour (but her mother said it was at least a minute) until she could figure out how to get herself back to her normal shape again. For a moment, she thought she would be able to shape-shift into any type of animal, but every time she wiggled her finger she turned into the bunny with the funny ear again. Her parents had said that she should be grateful she still had her one big foot. Grape stomping was an art and, until now, no one had the magical ability to turn anything into wine. At least the Bigfoot family livelihood was secure for the time being. They had their vineyards to tend. If only Lillian would just interest herself in the family business. But Lillian had bigger and brighter things in mind for her future, if she could just figure out what they were.

Her parents had discouraged her from shape shifting into a bunny. There were too many strange creatures (and even stranger Wyckians) running around that would have no qualms about making a stew out of her. They often reminded her about poor Henre Lisp's experience with the scruffy cat. She would nod and shudder.

But last week she finally had her shot at her only magical ability. Miss Laxern had retired from the daycare center and there was an opening for a furry animal that the children could play with. Miss Laxern could only shape-shift into a lizard that was no longer than six inches and could easily fit into a child's hand. Sometimes, on really strange occasions, a lizard with two heads would appear, freaking out the teachers. The children didn't mind, but Madam Dripster did and she hired Lillian immediately, happy to find something softer and furrier for the children than the cold and clammy reptiles of the past twenty years.

Madam's Dripster's magical ability was to make it snow. She didn't care for it and, in fact, hated the winter months. If she had her way, she would skip winter altogether. The councilmen had disagreed and declared that it was important the villagers experience the full four seasons; and winter was definitely one of them. There were at least five more villagers who could make it snow and were happy to do so, as it was a steady job, albeit seasonal. Madam Dripster was asked to help out when one of the snowmakers was sick. She agreed, only to oblige, but would not allow the snow to cover the ground; at least, not while she was on duty.

Lillian dipped the broomster towards the parking lot of the daycare center. The air felt nippy. The tip of her nose was sore as the wind tore at her clothes and practically slapped her face. Her thick, long, strawberry-blond pigtail stood straight out behind her, almost pulling her head off. She always hoped the force of the wind would tear the freckles from her face, but they only seemed to be nourished by the beating, and after she dismounted from her broomster, they looked even bigger and healthier.

It was difficult to fly the broomsters when the weather department decided high winds were in accordance with the spring season. As she neared the parking lot of the daycare center, the bicycle seat loosened and she flipped to the side, her skirt falling over her head, blocking her view. She dangled precariously but was forced to let one hand go to pull her skirt up over her head, her feet still strapped to the pedals, but it was too late and the broomster crashed into the parking pole, denting the front end. The padded seat finally tore off completely, dumping her unceremoniously flat on her back on the ground; her feet still strapped to the pedals. She got up, freed her feet, and, leaving her mangled broomster where it fell, limped towards the daycare center. She was glad that those who saw her limping expected it because of one foot being larger than the other, and not from the fact that her body ached from head to toe.

Above her a cloud advertisement began to form. *Blueberries—Strawberries—fresh pickings everyday at the Swoonzy farm.* A couple of seconds later she saw *fresh bait at Masters Bait Shop—for all your fishing needs.* Her father and grandfather would probably be first in line for that.

Madam Dripster stared down at her from the thin turquoise monocle she held over one eye. She deemed it necessary to scrutinize all new recruits for tidiness. Lillian could tell from Madam Dripster's frown and head shake that her outfit, now a wrinkled mess, had generated disdain.

Madam Dripster's nose was thin and the tip extended outwards to a point in space that forced others to stand at least a foot away. Every other day it dipped to a different consonant. Today her nose dipped every time she pronounced the letter d. On better days, it would dip to the q's and the z's. She could usually avoid having to say words with q's and z's, but the rest of the alphabet was difficult. Every morning she woke up reciting the ABC's while screwing up her eyes, trying to look down at her nose. The second her nose started to vibrate, she would note the letter down in a little notebook. She soon became adept at avoiding the troublesome letters.

Hers was a magical mishap of the worst kind. Not even the councilmen had a cure for it. Many of these mishaps occurred throughout the villages. Sometimes they would disappear as quickly as they came. Madam Dripster, however, had been suffering from the malady for the past two years. She was at her wits' end. She had to spend her weekends just getting over the headache that her errant nose gave her throughout the school week.

Madam Dripster always wore tight black outfits that reached just above her ankles to show off her high-heeled boots. She loved to wear boots no matter what the weather. Today she had on her new shiny, ruby-red leather boots with fake diamonds studded on the pointy tips. She had shoved and pushed her way through the weekend sales extravaganza and finally purchased them after she had roughly pushed aside a few other Wyckians who got in the way.

"Goor' morning, Miss Bigfoot," said Madam Dripster. Lillian had gotten used to Madam Dripster's letter dropping and no longer felt the urge to howl with laughter when it happened. She nodded back but was treated to an added bonus today when she heard a slight "boing" in the air as she stopped short of the letter d. Madam Dripster had to improvise with different letters sometimes. In this case an r was substituted with a d. It didn't make things sound better, thought Lillian. Except for the fact that Madam Dripster was standing steadily on her feet, her speech reminded Lillian of the way Grandfather Bigfoot sounded after he had been sampling the wines in the cellar.

"Mornin' to you, too, Madam Dripster." Lillian gave a short curtsy and almost tripped over her foot.

"I hope that you are 'reary for your first 'ray at work?" asked Madam Dripster, glaring at her and ready to pounce if Lillian even dared to tilt one corner of her mouth upwards in the hint of a grin.

"Oh, yes, definitely. Can't wait," replied Lillian, crunching one side of her lip as a precaution.

"Excellent. The chil'ren will be here soon. The first hour you will have class A at the en' of the hall. Please be gentle with the chil'ren. They are quite upset about Miss Laxern's retirement. They were use to the lizar' although I was not very fon' of this type of animal for the chil'ren. You know," she said, bending slightly towards Lillian as if taking her into her confidence, "nobory else has come forwar' to apply for the job."

Lillian jumped back just in time to save her right eye from the pointy tip of Madam Dripster's quivering nose.

"I know for a fact that Mrs. Fromangy cour' change into a puppy." Madam Dripster's nose reverberated slightly with displeasure. "But she claims she has lost the knack for it. 'Oubtful, I say, but a bunny? Why, it's a 'ream come true for these poor chil'ren. When you finish with class A, go to A1 an' then take a break. See me afterwars', Miss Bigfoot."

"Yes, Madam Dripster," said Lillian, about to curtsey again. She pushed the ends of her mouth down with her fingers and let out a forced cough. "I can't wait. I just love kids."

"Wonnerful. Now go 'own the hall and get reary." Madam Dripster dismissed Lillian with a nod and turned to greet another new teacher.

Lillian ran down the hall, stifling giggles, and opened the door to Class A. It hadn't changed since she was a little girl. Examining the blackboard for old times' sake, she noticed it still had the same scratch marks on it. She had added to that collection way back when. The room certainly looked smaller but she knew it just seemed that way because she had grown.

Twenty minutes later, eleven children flew, screeching, into the room; and each one headed towards their favorite toy. Nobody paid attention to Lillian, who was sitting on one of the tiny stools in the corner. Madam Dripster had told her during the interview that the new kindergarten teacher, Miss Dropsy, would tell her when it was time for her to shift into a bunny.

An already frazzled Miss Dropsy followed her students into the classroom and nodded towards Lillian. Her eyelids sagged heavily over her black beady pupils, giving her the appearance of someone on the verge of either dropping off to sleep or just about to wake up. For an hour Lillian watched as the children played and ignored Miss Dropsy's constant requests to stop hitting each other with toys. Miss Dropsy was new to teaching and had no idea how to control the children. After doing her best to wipe tears and trailing snots from tiny faces, she herded the children into the center of the room and clapped her hands for attention. Everything flew towards her, including the children. She had forgotten that she could magically lift and bring all small objects towards her with three successive claps of her hands. She normally would clap twice, but today she just plum forgot. Lillian's stool slid away from under her and she fell painfully onto a toy broomster. Her yell blended with the children's shouts of surprise. With help from Lillian, the teacher finally settled the startled five-year-olds back onto their seats in the center of the room.

"Now, children," said Miss Dropsy, dabbing at the faint imprint of the letter Z from the small alphabet block that had smacked into her right cheekbone. "We have a special treat for you today!" She held her hands stiffly behind her back to remind herself not to clap or gesture too wildly.

The children cheered.

Lillian gaped at her in alarm. She was suddenly terrified. Did she have time to change her mind?

"This is Miss Bigfoot. And guess what?"

"What?"

"She can change into a bunny!" cried Miss Dropsy. The children scrambled off their seats and surrounded Lillian.

"Change! Change! Change!" they chanted.

Lillian obliged and wiggled her right index finger. Instantly she shriveled down in front of their very eyes to a fluffy white bunny with one very long ear. One of the boys reached over and grabbed her by the hind leg. He swung her around his head. She slipped out of his sweaty fingers and flew across the floor, crashing into a wall. The children charged towards her and another grabbed her by the ears before she could escape. Miss Dropsy intervened when one of the children grabbed the frightened bunny by the throat and dunked her head into a glass of water.

"But bunny wants a drink of water," wailed Charlie Tweetle in protest.

Miss Dropsy carefully placed the frazzled bunny carefully on top of her desk and tried to keep the children at bay. For a moment the bunny sat there, drenched and stunned. Finally, with a shake of her head, Lillian brought herself back to normal. She was dripping wet and her thick strawberry-blond braid had come undone and fell loosely, covering one side of her face.

She was shocked at the treatment she had received from the children. She had never expected them to react in such a way. She'd been expecting them to pet her gently and coo with excitement. Her skirt was wrinkled and torn. She took one look at the children around her and made a mad dash for the door. Little Cindy Wasster grabbed her by the ends of her skirt, but Lillian managed to pull herself free. She fumbled at the doorknob before jerking the door open. Her big foot caught on the torn hem of her skirt and she flew into the arms of Madam Dripster, sending both of them crashing to the floor. Madam's monocle flew out of her hand, and skidded across the marble floor, finally rolling down the front steps of the building. Mr. Swan, the gardener, happened to be walking by at that exact moment. Oblivious to the small piece of glass that rolled in front of him, he stepped on it. The crunch echoed through the corridor.

"Miss Bigfoot! I never!" The tip of Madam Dripster's nose showed its annoyance. She pushed Lillian off and managed to get herself into a sitting position.

"Help me up, please," she said, extending her hand to Miss Dropsy, who looked as if she was about to faint.

"Madam Funnynose go boom!" The children giggled hysterically from the doorway of the classroom.

Miss Dropsy rushed to help her up. Lillian was still dazed and on all fours. The past five minutes she'd spent as a bunny were making her ears ring and she couldn't resist the urge to hop to freedom. Charlie Tweetle ran after her and jumped on her back.

"Go, bunny, go!" he yelled in childish glee.

"Miss Bigfoot!" cried Madam Dripster as she watched Lillian try to hop her way down the hall and shake Charlie off her back at the same time. "I will see you in my office immediately!"

Madam Dripster clamped her hand on her mouth. The dreaded d letter bounced off the corridor walls like a dazed bumblebee. To her horror, and to the horror of those who were witnessing it for the first time, her nose started to dip slowly. It forced her head down and then slowly up until her neck was stretched to the limit and she was staring at the ceiling. Suddenly her long nose whipped her head back into place and then slowly swung from side to side. Holding onto her nose, Madam Dripster quickly spun around on her tall ruby-red heels and raced down the hall to the safety of her office. The sound of a lashing whip echoed through the hallways as she slammed the door shut.

LUCAS NOSTY

WHILE LILLIAN was being reprimanded by the headmistress, who was also trying to control her wayward nose, by holding it steady with one hand, Kar was pedaling his bike as fast as his thin legs could go. He dropped his hands to his sides and shifted his body for balance. The bike moved gracefully along the road. He was certain this was just as good as flying. As he turned the corner to the school, he could see Principal Larity leaning out of his office window. The principal could magically open and shut any door. Kar knew he was waiting for the second when he would shut the giant gates of the school. Anybody coming late would have to ring the huge bell to get in and would automatically receive a one-hour detention after school. Kar had given up counting the number of hours he sat with Lucas Nosty in the detention hall, but today, with the help of his nifty new bike, he might be able to kick his detention habit. He might even be able to play ball with his friends after school.

He parked his bike in one of the parking slots designated for bikes and stepped back to admire it again. It stood out from all the others. Kar swelled with pride.

A voice dripping with sarcasm interrupted his thoughts. "Hey, look at that. Somebody's got a new bike."

Kar turned slowly around; he already knew who was behind him: Lucas Nosty and the twins, Allen and Avery Squint. The whole school called them the Nasty Boys. The twins weren't identical, but they shared their big build and the same vacant expression. One had brown curly hair that needed constant trimming and the other just shaved it entirely. Avery loved the feel of his shaven head and could often be seen smoothing his scalp with the palm of his hand.

Lucas Nosty, on the other hand, seemed to take the art of bullying as a birthright. He especially enjoyed tormenting Kar. Lucas was taller and stronger than most of the children at the school. No one could determine the color of his eyes because of his perpetual squinting, and his perfectly straight blond bangs covered the rest. Although Principal Larity wished he were in some other school, he had to admit that Lucas was far superior in intellect than any of the other students and maybe even some of the adults in the community. If asked, Kar considered Lucas Nosty a cruel and dastardly magical mishap all by himself.

Kar watched in trepidation as Lucas walked up to his bike and circled it, letting out a slow, clean whistle.

"A red Classic Two Wheeler. So, whaddaya know. Did Sweetie get a new bike from mommy?"

Kar quickly looked up at the sky, just in case. It was cloudless. "Leave me alone," he retorted, turning his back and starting to walk across the schoolyard where his friends were playing ball while waiting for the school bell to ring. It was the wrong thing to do, Kar knew, but staying would invite even more trouble. It didn't matter in the end. There was no right answer when it came to the Nasty Boys.

"Hey, I'm talking to you," Lucas said. "Where're your manners?" The Nasty Boys surrounded Kar. Lucas poked him in the back. "I said I'm talking to you."

"And I said, leave me alone," Kar shot back, keeping his eyes on Lucas' hands, which at any minute could ball up into fists. Kar was no match for Lucas and he knew it. Lucas poked him in the shoulder. Kar's patience evaporated and even though he knew it was the wrong thing to do, he poked Lucas back. Lucas grabbed Kar's head and twisted it under his armpit.

"So," Lucas said, his voice dripping with false pleasantries, "whaddya say you sell me your bike for a couple of dragons and I'll let you go?"

Kar kicked with his feet but only managed to graze the kneecap of one of the twins standing behind him. "Make it a hundred," he gasped, trying to pry Lucas' steel grasp from around his neck. A crowd soon surrounded them.

Jack, Kar's best friend, lunged at Lucas and grabbed a hold of his left arm. "Let him go!"

Lucas easily pushed Jack away with his free hand while still keeping his grip on Kar. "Look who's here to save you. Little Jack Boldilocks."

The twins grabbed Jack and held on to his arms. Jack squirmed between them, kicking air. They only laughed at his attempts to free himself.

Kar's breathing was now getting labored and he felt he was going to pass out. The grip around his neck felt tighter and tighter and a ringing sound filled his ears. Just as his vision blurred, he heard a loud booming voice and felt Lucas release him. Kar fell to the ground, coughing and heaving.

"Enough!" Principal Larity's voice blared out from a large brass horn pressed to his lips. All the children in the playground turned to stare up at him hanging out of his office window on the second floor.

"Lucas! I will see you and Kar in my office immediately." When he spied the twins trying to melt casually into the crowd, he added, "Also you, Squinty Boys."

The heavy steel gates were slowly grinding to a close behind them as the Nasty boys shoved each other all the way to the principal's office. Kar regained his color and followed them on wobbly knees, up the two flights of stairs.

Principal Larity was waiting for them behind the huge oak desk that took up most of the office. Like the rest of the room, he looked very intimidating. He was a thin man with gray tufts of thinning hair and a face that seemed to melt with age. His suits were always tailored the same way: a short, stiff cloak over a white shirt and black trousers. Except for the fashionable emerald-green color, the cloak and dagger outfit was as outdated as the pointy, white-tipped shoes he wore and the auburn mustache that surprisingly met his graying sideburns. The mustache was the only part of his body he did not allow to age, and keeping it trimmed and dyed was an essential part of his meticulous daily grooming.

"If there was another school to send you to, Lucas, I would have sent you to it a long time ago," he said, drumming his fingers loudly on the black leather pad covering most of the desk. "Since I witnessed the whole thing from the window, I will not entertain any excuses. Lucas, Allen, and Avery, you will have two-hour detentions after school for a whole week. During that time, you will complete your homework and hand it in before you leave for home."

Lucas shrugged.

Homework was not a big deal to him, thought Kar. He might be the biggest bully the school had ever known, but he was the smartest student they had ever known, too. Kar eyed Allen and Avery. They were smirking stupidly. Lucas always did their homework for them.

Principal Larity leaned towards the twins with a glint of power in his eyes. "Allen and Avery, you will not be with Lucas in the detention room. You will sit in my secretary's office to do your homework."

The twins' chests deflated. A tiny piercing sound of surprise and disappointment emitted from their lips.

"And Lucas," said Principal Larity, turning all his attention back to him. "If I see you so much as lay a hand on another student again, I will simply throw you out of school."

Kar's eyes widened in surprise and hope at the very thought of it. He also did not realize that his pupils had quickly changed to the color of the small green chalkboard to his right. There was always a list of student names on the board. Nobody could ever understand what they had done or what was in store for them, but no one wanted to find their names on the list. He quickly scanned the list and was relieved to see that his name did not appear.

He turned his attention back to the principal, who was still lecturing Lucas. Clearly bored, Lucas had tuned him out. Kar realized there was no record of a student ever being thrown out of school. This would probably be the worst thing anyone had ever heard of happening in the quiet village of SouthWyck. (EastWyck had a reputation for being noisy and for kicking its kids out of school on a daily basis.) Kar secretly hoped that Lucas would get the boot or that, even better, his family would move to EastWyck.

Lucas shrugged his shoulders and glanced at Kar, his lips curling in a sneer.

Kar knew that look. Years of side-glances and lip curling read like a bestseller on Lucas' face: *I'll get you*. And Kar knew he would. But only Lucas knew when and how.

Principal Larity asked Kar to stay and he dismissed the other three with a wave of his freshly manicured left hand.

"I need to ask you something," said Principal Larity when they were alone. "It seems that we have never received your birth certificate. Could you kindly ask your parents to send us your birth certificate before *What's My Magic?* Day?"

Kar nodded, relieved to discover that he had avoided detention this time.

"We need to verify that you officially turned thirteen today. The councilmen need all the birth certificates at City Hall before *What's My Magic?* Day commences. It is your birthday today, isn't it?"

Kar nodded again, his throat still sore from Lucas' tight grip. A red welt had appeared around it.

"You may go now, Kar, and take care of that mark around your neck. Check in with the nurse."

"Yes, sir," said Kar hoarsely, and turned to leave.

"And make sure you keep out of Lucas' way. I would hate to suspend any student from my school, good or bad." He sighed and turned to some papers at his desk, completely absorbed.

On his way to class, Kar visited Nurse Faloola, who gave him a cold pad to put across the welts on his neck. He knew he would spend the remainder of the day figuring out how to keep his distance from Lucas. Even if he hid, Lucas would find him anyway. It was scary. They were in the same class and took the same subjects and while Lucas excelled at them all, Kar earned enough good grades to keep his parents happy.

The bell rang for the second class. Kar was still rubbing the painful spot when Jack and Haylen joined him. They looked at

Kar's flushed face and the red marks that were still vivid and sore looking.

"That nasty, nasty Lucas and those twin monsters!" cried Haylen. A tiny frown appeared between her soft white eyebrows.

"Don't worry about it," said Kar, looking nervously over his shoulder. He watched the Squinty twins shuffle along towards the next class and then turned back to his friends. He described what took place in the principal's office.

"Well, at least Lucas was caught in the act for once," said Haylen.

"It doesn't matter," said Kar. "There are more important things than Lucas."

"Yes," said Jack. "It's your birthday today, isn't it?"

"Happy birthday, Kar," said Haylen shyly, handing him a birthday card.

"Thanks, you didn't have to."

"It's from both of us," Jack said with a huge grin as they walked down the hall to the next class.

As he ripped open the card, a ten-dragon gift certificate to their favorite soda shop fell out.

"Ah, thanks guys: my favorite place!"

Haylen and Jack just nodded and smiled.

"Have you tried, you know, wiggling your finger, lately?" asked Jack, changing the subject.

"You know we need the magic powder first for anything to happen," answered Kar, putting the gift certificate between the pages of his Wyck history book.

"There hasn't been any interesting magic for a long time. Most of it is lifting things or changing into boring animals. I'd like to be able to shape-shift into a lion and scare the pants off Lucas. That would be interesting," said Jack, snapping his fingers. "Better yet, I'd eat him."

"I wish I could be an elephant and just crush him," added Haylen, pounding her fist into the palm of her hand. Her short hair, which was as white as the advertisement that was slowly appearing in the sky above the school building, swished around

24

her face. The Nasty Boys often teased her about the luminous glow that emanated from it. They'd ask, "Hey, Haylen, can we borrow your head for a moment? We need some light." Her solemn, piercing black eyes gave her childish features a look of wisdom far too old for her age. There were times that one look from her could make a grown adult shiver.

"I wish he would just disappear and forget how to come back again," said Kar, his voice still raspy. They all laughed and filed into the classroom.

Principle Larity stood waiting for them in the front of the class. "Sit down, please. I need to speak to all of you for a moment."

The children plunked their books down on the top of the desks and noisily settled into their seats.

"As you know, *What's My Magic?* Day is next week. All those who have turned thirteen before this great day will be the center of attention. As you probably know by now, we Wyckians consider the twelfth year of life to be the turning point of our lives. Granted, it is very early to acquire such a hefty burden when you are mere children, but it takes time to hone the magic skills that will be bestowed upon you. This is the only time of the year when Wyckians from all four villages will be present at the ceremony. We must all be on our best behavior."

Principal Larity looked down at a piece of paper he was holding in his hand. "Six children from this school have turned thirteen before this event. I would like all of you to attend a short rehearsal on how to conduct yourselves at the ceremony. It will take place this afternoon at two. I will see you all at the gymnasium then. We don't want things to get out of hand - or, shall I say, out of finger." Lucas hissed a nervous sneer, but no one else laughed.

All six of the thirteen-year-olds lined up in the gymnasium at precisely two o'clock. Principal Larity was standing in the middle of the auditorium, rocking back and forth on his heels, talking to Mr. Nooza, the math teacher. Miss Varnus, the home economics teacher, was using a small compact mirror to re-apply her lipstick. She drew on a new face almost every morning. If it weren't for her bright auburn hair and the medal around her neck, nobody would recognize her.

"All right, boys and girls," said Principle Larity, finally looking up. "I want you to stand in line alphabetically by your last names."

Everyone shuffled around, quietly reciting the alphabet and trying to determine their places in line.

"No, no, I will call out the names," said Principle Larity, laughing. "Michelle Ablelord. Angela Beaster. Jack Bold. Kar Homely. Lucas Nosty and Haylen Roc." The children lined up to face the teachers. "Memorize your places in line."

"Ahem," Mr. Nooza said, stepping in front of the children. "*What's My Magic?* Day will probably be the most important day of your lives. It can be the best day," he paused for a moment, "or the worst day." Six panic-stricken faces metamorphosed before him. He continued after calming them down.

"I'm sure you've already been to a few ceremonies and know exactly what I mean. Sometimes what we want simply does not happen." Mr. Nooza wiggled his finger, shape-shifted into an enormous turquoise-dotted butterfly, fluttered his wings, and reappeared again. "And we end up with magic that does nothing to further our careers. I want you all to keep this in mind. It's not the end. Many of us, like myself," and he bowed his head slightly, "continue to lead successful, productive lives. Thankfully, being a teacher has been the most fulfilling job I could ever want."

Kar's anxiety upped a notch. What would he do if he had no magic worth anything, like Mr. Nooza? Become a teacher, too? Not if he could help it.

"Those lucky few who have something worthwhile to point your career towards will be assigned to special instructors to hone your new skills. But I'd like to warn you: if your magic is considered dangerous, you will have your fingers wrapped for good; unless, of course, the councilmen deem it necessary to use it when the need arises." Kar's classmates fidgeted. He could almost hear the pounding hearts coursing down the line, matching his own.

Miss Varnus stepped forward to show the children the proper way to wiggle their fingers. Kar could only stare at her right index finger, which was wrapped in black velvet and adorned with a stunning ruby ring. For safety reasons, the councilmen had assured the townsfolk when they wrapped her finger tightly on that fateful day.

"It's very easy," she said. "Not back and forth, but up and down."

Miss Varnus was proud of her ability to hurl objects at great lengths; and every four years, the councilmen permitted her to enter the Villages of Wyck games. She had a gold medal for hurling a spear with such force that it had imbedded itself on the surface of the moon. Nobody yet had the ability to remove it and she had never let anyone forget it, either. She wore the large gold medal around her thin neck every day.

The afternoon passed pleasantly enough. Lucas did manage to trip Kar by putting his foot out like a cat pretending to stretch. Kar simply got up, dusted himself off, and ignored him.

They practiced how to walk across a stage, state their names politely with a small bow or curtsey, and wiggle their index finger. Kar thought it was an extremely silly way of doing magic but did not dare voice that opinion aloud. He knew it was just for ceremonial reasons. His father lifted things with a wave of his hand and his mother wrote out advertisements on a piece of paper and just blew on it. She could even point at the sky and write.

Before they left, Miss Varnus showed them how to exit the stage quickly if something major happened that was hazardous to their health; which was known to happen often when new magic was created from the fingers of the very young.

The bell rang and interrupted the session. They trouped out together to gather up their belongings before heading home. Lucas stole off to the detention hall but not before he glanced back at Kar with a sick smile.

Kar hurried out of the school building and bumped into Jack, who was looking up at the sky. Along with other assorted advertisements, another cloud message floated above the school building. A *happy birthday sweetie* trailed behind a sale at the Masters Bait shop.

"Oh, no," Kar moaned, and covered his face with his schoolbook. "I should have told her not to do it this time."

The chubby Squinty twins were standing in the middle of the playground chanting, "Sweetie, sweetie."

Kar and Jack just walked past them.

"Haven't you forgotten something?" Kar asked the twins.

"Yeah, whaddidweforget? Maybe this?" Allen flashed a fist at him.

"Detention?"

"Oh," said Allen, with a seriously frightened look. He grabbed his brother and they plodded up the stairs towards the secretary's office.

"Magic words, eh?" said Jack, laughing heartily. As they reached the bike rack, Jack's brown eyes widened in surprise and delight when Kar pointed out his new bike.

"Wow," Jack exclaimed, "a Classic Two Wheeler! Aren't you lucky? Can I try it?"

"Yeah, sure," said Kar. He pulled the bike out from the stand and his face fell. Someone had scratched the word *Swetee* on the cover of the wheel and the front tire was flat.

"Those two can never spell anything right," said Jack, shaking his head. "Sorry, buddy." He ran his hand through his messy brown hair, making it look even worse.

Kar succeeded in holding back his tears, but he could not hold back his words. "I'll get them all one day."

"Yeah," said Jack, smiling at Kar to lighten the mood, "hopefully, next week when you turn into a lion and eat them or Haylen turns into a big ole' elephant and stomps them flat."

THE MISSING BIRTH CERTIFICATE

THE BROOMSTER kept circling. Lillian tried to fix the dent and correct the broomster's trajectory, but she failed and had to limp all the way back to the village center, dragging the broomster behind her. She usually avoided walking as much as possible. She hated hearing "poor Lillian" and "tsk-tsk" from Wyckians who, like cowards, would dole out their false pity and then dash into stores to gossip about her as she passed. She dropped the broomster off at the Fixit shop and reluctantly continued home on foot through the center of town. She noticed a *happy birthday Sweetie* floating in the sky. It must be Kar's birthday, she thought, grinning. With nothing to do with the rest of her day, she decided to swing by and visit Mrs. Homely. Lillian had been Kar's babysitter since he was seven and even though Kar's mother was much older, she and Lillian had become very good friends.

As she walked towards the Homelys', Lillian wondered if anyone in the history of SouthWyck had ever been fired on their first day at a job. She hadn't even lasted a full day. Just one lousy morning. She found it hard to stomach the memory of it but she couldn't help thinking about it still.

Madam Dripster hadn't been able to concentrate on Lillian's face at all. Her face whipped from one side to the other as if an invisible hand was continuously slapping one cheek at a time. She held on to her nose with one hand but the magic was just more powerful than she could control. She had been able to shake her finger at Lillian, however, and the resulting blizzard forced everyone to evacuate the building. It was a catastrophe that was sealed by Madam Dripster's final words to Lillian: "I will see to it that you will never work as a bunny again!" Lillian had promised herself the same thing as she dug her way out from the snow in the office and finally exited into the street. It had been a horrible experience and it had given her a newfound respect for Mrs. Laxern, who had transfixed the preschooler's as a lizard for the past twenty years.

She spied her friend, Margaret Taxor, standing outside the bread shop holding a small flat stone. Lillian was always envious of her friend's natural beauty. Margaret's cheeks seemed in a perpetual blush and her thick dark eyelashes curled up so high they almost touched her perfect eyebrows. Her alabaster skin was flawless and her dark glossy curls bounced with the slightest movement.

"Hey, Maggie!" cried Lillian, making those curls bounce and swing in alarm. Margaret's bright eyes widened when she noticed Lillian's crumpled clothes. "What happened to you?" Lillian was a sorry sight. Not only were her sleeve and hem torn, but also she was dripping wet from the waist down and missing her broomster. "Have you been fighting again?"

"Worse. I was at the daycare center."

"Oh, bunny for the day, I see," said Margaret, grinning.

"Just for an hour," said Lillian, grinning back. "You should try it. Maybe they'll do better with you. You can shape-shift into a pony and give them rides."

"Oh, no, not me!" She shook her curls vigorously. "I'll just stick to sewing and the occasional pony rides on the weekends for extra money. Hate that horsy smell. Scrub myself for hours afterwards."

They pushed their way into the bakery shop. Margaret handed the stone she was carrying to a pudgy bald man behind the counter. He weighed the stone on a large bronze scale hanging from the ceiling. "That's one and a half pounds," said Mr. Tweetle, whose son, Charlie, had been one of the children at the daycare center. His feet made little tapping noises on the tiled floor of his bakery shop. On most days he tap-danced back and forth to work. Recently, however, the town council had approached him and instructed him not to wear his dancing shoes with the metal tips during the day. The tapping was grating on the town's early morning nerves. Now he silently did the shuffle behind the counter. His was no magical mishap. The whole family loved to tap dance.

"Anything else?"

"Yes," said Margaret. "I'll also take some of the chocolate butter, please."

"Excellent." Mr. Tweetle touched the stone with his right index finger. It glowed for a moment, wobbled, and changed into a hot loaf of bread. He cut a thick slab of chocolate butter and wrapped up both items, tapping, twirling, and humming all the while, and then handed the package to Margaret.

"Anything for you today, Lillian?" asked Mr. Tweetle, smiling deeply. Two dimples appeared on each cheek.

Lillian shook her head. "No, not today, thank you." She turned to Margaret and sighed quietly, "Lucky Mr. Tweetle."

"Yeah," replied Margaret, "he's got a great magic finger. Who wouldn't get rich turning stone into bread?"

"I was thinking of his feet," said Lillian.

"Oh, you," said Margaret, shaking her head at her friend's misery. "Why don't you go to his dancing classes? That would be fun."

Lillian shook her head. "No, it's not for me. I tried it once. If I wasn't stepping on my own foot, I was stepping on someone else's. After a while, everyone stayed clear of me."

Margaret turned away for a moment and managed to control her face, as she had herself tripped over her foot once. She paid for the bread and butter and they stepped out into the street.

"Why don't you try the employment agency? They may have some openings for you. Petting zoo might hire you."

They were now walking up the street. Busy shoppers rushed by the pair, only stopping for a moment to catch a glimpse of and snicker at Lillian's appearance. She turned to glare at them. "I'm through with being petted," said Lillian. "I never want to be or see a bunny again."

"Well, you still have your big foot," said Margaret, patting Lillian's torn sleeve. "Like your father said, nobody can change water into wine."

"Yeah, right," said Lillian, making a sour face. "I hate wine. I hate grapes. In fact, I hate all kinds of fruit."

31

"Well, here we are at the employment agency," said Margaret. "Just go in and try. You don't have anything to lose, you know."

Lillian shrugged her shoulders. "I guess. Wish me luck," she said. Stepping first with her large, right boot, she walked into the employment agency. If it didn't work, she thought, she might approach Mrs. Homely and ask her if she could squeeze her in somewhere at the Department of Advertising, doing some filing.

After filling out some paperwork at the employment agency, Lillian quickly picked up a present for Kar and headed towards his house. She tapped at Mrs. Homely's kitchen door, opened it slightly, and saw her sitting at the kitchen table weeping into her apron.

"Oh, what's going to happen to us," Mrs. Homely wailed, not noticing Lillian. "What are we to do? They're going to find out; oh dear, they're going to find out that there is no birth certificate." She blew her nose loudly.

"Now, now, Mrs. Homely," said Lillian, patting her on the back. "Who's going to find out what?"

Mrs. Homely jumped a few inches off her chair. "Oh, Lillian, you gave me the fright of my life!" She wiped her nose again with her apron. "What am I to do?" she continued. "I know they will be asking about his birth certificate soon."

"Whose? Kar's?" Lillian dropped the package wrapped in blue paper on the table and, dragging over a chair, sat next to Mrs. Homely.

"Oh, thank you, Lillian. You never forget his birthday, do you?"

Lillian knew she would have forgotten if it hadn't been for the birthday greeting splattered across the sky, but she remained silent.

Lillian could guess Mrs. Homely's fears. While babysitting for them a few years ago, she'd overheard a private conversation between Mr. and Mrs. Homely. When they had discovered that she'd been in the next room during that conversation, the Homelys had begged Lillian never to repeat it to a living soul.

She had promised with all her heart. Since then she hadn't given it another thought until she walked into the kitchen.

"What am I going to do?" cried Mrs. Homely. "They will surely find out and it will be all over for us."

"What makes you think that?"

"Principle Larity will need the birth certificate before the ceremony." She twisted her hands in dismay. "We don't have one. You know he's not our real son. What if Kar finds out? He just asked me the other day why he doesn't look like a Homely. He's too beautiful to be our son. Nosey Mrs. Beadlepoof's been asking me questions about him all year. That horrible woman. She just can't leave things be."

"Why don't you just tell her the boy takes after your side of the family, the Browmers?"

"Oh, that doesn't work. Everybody knows our family is hefty and muscular. Kar is tall and slim and couldn't beat a fly even if he tried."

Lillian's mouth twitched at the thought of Kar fighting a fly and possibly losing.

"Kar is neither plain nor strong," Mrs. Homely continued, sniffling. "A bit of wind could carry him away. How could anybody leave her newborn baby out in the cold like that?" She raised her apron and blew so loudly into it that Lillian thought Mrs. Homely's ears would pop out of her head.

"If we hadn't opened the door to shoo that noisy cat away, we would not have even seen a baby on our doorstep. He would have never made it through that cold night. I just can't stop thinking about it. Who was she and why did she leave her baby on our doorstep? She didn't even leave a note. Only a piece of paper pinned to the blanket with his name on it!"

"You've been asking that question all these years," said Lillian, feeling sorry for her. "It's not going to do you any good at this point. Let's just forget about it. As far as I'm concerned, Kar is your son and always will be and that's that."

"I guess you're right," said Mrs. Homely, removing her soiled apron from around her waist. "She hasn't shown up all these years to claim him. Maybe she's dead?" She shrugged her massive shoulders and looked hopefully at Lillian.

Lillian sighed. It definitely wasn't an appropriate time to ask Mrs. Homely for a job. Instead, she resolved to take Mrs. Homely's mind off her worries for now. It was the only way she could help. So, as Mrs. Homely pulled a cake from the oven and set it aside to cool, Lillian told her in detail what happened at the daycare center. Mrs. Homely shook her head and made small exclamations of sympathy, even though once in a while she let out a loud chuckle.

Still listening to the tale of daycare mayhem, Mrs. Homely opened the door of the burner in the back of the oven and poured coal into it. Coal was cheap. There seemed to be at least ten people who could magically transform small stones or pieces of wood into coal. They kept dropping their prices and competing for each other's business.

She then added some ingredients into a glass bowl, still laughing at the antics of the children at the daycare, and with a few powerful strokes of her arm turned it into a sweet icing delight. She would soon spread this on the cake as well as the finger-shaped cookies while Kar's favorite meal of chicken and potatoes slowly baked in the oven.

Lillian was glad she brought the smile back to her friend's face. Before she let herself out the door, she turned back to Mrs. Homely and said, "If there is anything that I can do for you, Mrs. Homely, you know I would."

"I know, dear. You're the best friend this family has." Lillian returned the tiny smile with a big one. She really would do anything for a family that never once mentioned her one big foot.

Kar walked in as his mother finished the final decorations on the cake. He hoped his mother wouldn't notice his bad mood.

"Hi, sweetie how was your day?"

"Fine, Mom," said Kar. He forced a smile. "Mom, can you do me a favor?"

"Sure sweetie."

"I don't mean to hurt your feelings or anything, but could you not write *sweetie* all over the sky anymore. The kids laugh at me."

"Oh, sweetie, I'm so sorry," said Mrs. Homely. "I didn't know."

"Yeah, well, just don't write anything anymore; and from now on, just call me Kar."

Mrs. Homely looked at her son. She had forgotten how cruel kids could be. Kar had never complained. "I'm sorry, sweetie … I mean … Kar. I didn't realize …"

"That's okay, Mom, really. I'm just too old for that now."

"Yes, I guess you're right. I'll just use it for emergencies. I'll come up with a secret code between us or something." She waved the icing-covered spatula.

Kar rolled his eyes. "As long as …"

"I know, I know. I promise you. No more sweeties. Maybe something mysterious."

"I guess I can live with that," Kar laughed.

Mrs. Homely smiled at her son. "You have to pick one word, honey, or it will be sweetie again."

"Alright, alright. I have to think about it. How about python?"

"Python?"

"I learned all about snakes today and the python was the most interesting."

"Okay, I guess, but it sounds creepy."

"That's why I like it," piped Kar.

Mr. Homely walked into the kitchen before Mrs. Homely could reply. "What happened to your bike?"

"Just some kids," said Kar. He pulled the collar of his blue shirt up to his chin to hide the marks still visible around his neck. If he told his father what really happened, he would be off the next day to demand an explanation and embarrass him in front of the principal and probably the whole school.

"Which kids?"

"I didn't see them. I can fix it," Kar said, avoiding their eyes. "It's just a few scratches and a flat tire." He picked up a finger cookie and took a bite. "Mm. Lemon icing. These are really good."

Kar noticed the look that passed between his parents.

"I'll fix it myself tonight," said his father wearily.

The rest of the evening passed pleasantly enough. Kar had a few more presents to unwrap before he excused himself to do homework. As he left the room, he mentioned again to his parents that he needed to give his birth certificate to the principal.

Mr. And Mrs. Homely stared at each other from across the dining table. Dishes were left helter-skelter on the table. Mrs. Homely did not have enough energy to pick up anything. Mr. Homely got up and piled the dirty plates on top of each other. As he was about to head to the kitchen, Mrs. Homely stopped him.

"Leave them, Karl. I'll clean up later."

"I can easily do them," said Karl. He added a few more to the already precarious pile and headed to the kitchen. Mrs. Homely could hear him clunking them down into the sink. She did not have the energy to do a thing. Worry sapped it all. She followed Karl into the kitchen and sat down at the breakfast table. She looked deflated.

"What are we to do? If the councilmen find out, they'll take him away from us. No adoptions are allowed in Wyck. You know that."

"Hush, my dear." He placed the last dish on the rack and turned to put the cutlery away. "We'll think of something."

Mrs. Homely started crying.

AMOS FOUNTAINE

THE NEXT morning Lillian Bigfoot stood outside Mrs. Homely's back doorstep. She had received a note from Mrs. Homely early that morning asking her to come over as soon as she could. Lillian knew it had to be something important because it was very expensive to have a courier drop a letter anytime after dark. Only a few people could shape-shift into carrier pigeons and they were usually occupied. She wished she had a cushy job like that. Number one, she would be flying, and number two, it made a lot of money.

"What's wrong?" asked Lillian, hoping that Kar had not found out about his heritage and skipped town in anger.

"Oh, my," said Mrs. Homely, dragging Lillian into the house. "What're we going to do? We have no birth certificate. Nothing. They'll find out he isn't our son and take him away from us. I'm sure he turned thirteen. He was only a few hours old when we found him on the front steps. We have to run away. Leave the village." She wrung her hands.

"Now, now, Mrs. Homely, enough of that; we'll think of something." Lillian's brow wrinkled as she concentrated on the problem. She was desperate to help her friend. She couldn't bear losing the Homelys.

"We have to think fast. They need it soon." Mrs. Homely's plea was urgent. She sat down at the kitchen table and rubbed her face.

"We could go to Amos Fountaine in EastWyck," Lillian suggested slowly. "Maybe he can help us? I heard he could forge anything."

"I heard he's in jail."

"Who told you that?"

"Mrs. Beadlepoof."

"I should have guessed," said Lillian. "Maybe it's a family business?"

"I heard from Mrs. Beadlepoof's sister that he has a brother living somewhere on the outskirts of the EastWyck Village.

37

Some place called the Greenfields that nobody has yet dared walk through. It's full of snakes," added Mrs. Homely with a grimace.

Lillian shivered. "Ugh."

"Doesn't matter, I'll walk through anything. Tomorrow, would you be able to get some more information out of Mrs. Beadlepoof? She takes a walk every morning around seven."

"Don't I know that!" Lillian snorted. "She has the whole street to herself. Nobody wants to be anywhere near Mrs. Beadlepoof when she takes her daily morning stroll on Padding Lane. She grabs a hold of you and doesn't let go until she squeezes as much gossip out of you as she can and then some."

"I'm sure she does," said Mrs. Homely, chuckling with her. "I heard Miss Varnus' elbow was black and blue once and if she hadn't had her finger wrapped, I think she would have sent Mrs. Beadlepoof to the moon."

Lillian laughed, imagining Mrs. Beadlepoof shooting towards the moon and wishing it could really happen.

"I would go and meet up with her but I have the early morning shift tomorrow at the Department of Cloud Advertising," Mrs. Homely said.

Lillian agreed to go and consult with the town's infamous busybody to help the Homelys. She promised to go the next day. She had no job, no prospects, and the employment agency never got back to her. It seemed that her future was tied to her family's grape stomping. A very depressing thought.

By six-thirty the next morning, Lillian was already up and walking out the front door. She wore a heavy sweater to protect her elbows from Mrs. Beadlepoof's iron fingers. She had told her parents she was getting an early start on finding a job. She was normally an early riser, so it didn't dawn on them to suspect her errand. If they knew she was about to place herself in harm's way, they might have locked her up in her room for her own protection and to make sure that the silly notion never crossed her mind again.

Lillian knew Mrs. Beadlepoof always finished her morning stroll on Padding Lane. Most people avoided that street at dawn, but Lillian was determined, albeit frightened, to bump into her. It wasn't long before she found herself caught in the woman's strong grip.

"I see you're up early, Lillian, just like myself. An early riser always gets the benefits of the day. Keeps the body supple, the blood flowing, and one's weight normal." Mrs. Beadlepoof propelled Lillian along the pavement by the elbow. She had not gotten any larger but she had not gotten any thinner either, through the years. She still reminded Lillian of a large wine barrel with arms and feet.

"Yes, I decided to take your advice and get some exercise," Lillian, replied, twisting her arm away.

"Why don't we take a walk together? It's nice to have company," said Mrs. Beadlepoof, grabbing Lillian by the elbow again just in case she refused.

They walked together down the street. Mrs. Beadlepoof took up the whole sidewalk, forcing Lillian to walk on the cobbled road with her elbow extended painfully upwards.

"So, I heard you got fired from your first day at the daycare center for starting a fight or something? What a shame. Hope your parents weren't too disappointed in you."

Lillian gritted her teeth. "I didn't start a fight. The children got a bit out of hand, and Madam Dripster threw out the wrong letter and things just happened." What was the use of explaining, thought Lillian. She would probably draw her own conclusions anyway.

"Well, and what was this about starting winter way before its proper time? I heard that Madam Dripster had to order two bags of salt just to clean up the snow from the horrible blizzard you started."

"I didn't start any ..." Lillian began to say before she reminded herself that it was no use explaining. Mrs. Beadlepoof would concoct her version of what happened and peddle it to the villagers as the truth. She had better keep her story short and sweet. The villagers liked Mrs. Beadlepoof's versions anyway, since they were more entertaining.

"Kicked out of the daycare center for starting a fight. Tsk tsk." Mrs. Beadlepoof continued shaking her head. "I thought you were better than that, Lillian."

Lillian sighed. "Sorry, it won't happen again."

"Good, dear," said Mrs. Beadlepoof patting Lillian's hand. "Yep, yep, they had to evacuate the building because of a snowstorm. Imagine! A snowstorm in the month of May! I heard it was in the building." Mrs. Beadlepoof was breathing heavily by now. Walking and talking was taking its toll on her, but she pushed on with both pursuits still in mind.

"Well, the air feels somewhat crisp these days don't you think? We haven't warmed up a bit since the storm. Better not be any snow on my sidewalk. I need my early morning walk. It's a fitness thing, you know. I won't have all this slipping and sliding about." She glanced at Lillian and switched the subject. "I wonder what kind of job might suit you. You do have that big foot. You should keep to grape stomping."

"Yeah, just my luck, I guess." Lillian spoke softly under her breath. The sheer weight of Mrs. Beadlepoof's tirade was depressing.

"What do you mean 'just my luck'?" asked Mrs. Beadlepoof, who could hear a leaf drop.

"I meant just what you said." Lillian laughed nervously. How could she have forgotten those ears? It was known far and wide that Mrs. Beadlepoof could literally hear a baby cough two blocks away. "Some people should just leave magic well alone. My family traits are good enough for me," Lillian lied. "I feel sorry for those who only rely on their one bit of magic to make ends meet."

Mrs. Beadlepoof nodded vigorously in agreement.

"I mean ..." She just realized that she never knew what Mrs. Beadlepoof's magical ability was. Bear? Mountain lion? Great big steaming loaves of bread from stone to keep her fed all her life? She glanced at Mrs. Beadlepoof's fingers. No, there was no black ribbon on any of those sausage-like fingers to show she had any magic that could be deemed dangerous. Think, think, she said to herself. What was it? Snake? Worm? Caterpillar? She knew her parents had once mentioned something about Mrs. Beadlepoof's ability that had made them all burst into laughter.

"Take myself for instance," Lillian continued, her curiosity about Mrs. Beadlepoof growing. "What is a bunny good for? Probably a good stew, but that would not be a skill that I would want to put on my resume."

"Yes, yes," said Mrs. Beadlepoof, still huffing and puffing with exertion. "It would be a one-time thing. Don't be too hard on yourself. Grape stomping must help overcome your family's lack of any worthwhile magical abilities."

Lillian kicked a pebble down the street and thought it was the perfect time to weasel information about Fountaine. "Well, I guess you're right. Take Mr. Fountaine, in the next village. His family skills just land him in jail. All he can do is forge documents. I heard he does a good job." She peered sideways at Mrs. Beadlepoof, who had pursed her lips at the mention of Mr. Fountaine's name.

"Yes, he's in jail."

"See, some family traits just land you in jail." Lillian sighed dramatically. "I wonder where the rest of his family is now? Are they all in jail?" She held her breath, hoping that Mrs. Beadlepoof would soon divulge some information. She wasn't disappointed.

"I know for a fact that his brother built a house in the Greenfields," said Mrs. Beadlepoof, giving her a curious look.

"Really? How interesting. Must be a nice house."

"No. It's a vile-looking thing with a red roof. Imagine that? A red roof! It sticks out like a sore thumb. It is almost as if he wants people to know where he lives. Who would want to go through that snake-infested field to get to him, anyway?"

"Well, they can fly over it."

"Sure you can, if you want to get caught by the police."

Lillian stopped walking, Mrs. Beadlepoof tugged her onwards. "What do you mean?"

"Who would want to visit a Fountaine unless you wanted something to forge? The authorities would be bound to catch up with you and ask you questions." She stopped and looked down at Lillian suspiciously. "And why are you so interested suddenly in Mr. Fountaine?"

"No reason at all. No, really: just making conversation," said Lillian, gulping painfully.

Lillian had to endure another half hour of gossip and likewise had to dispense some of her own family's news. Mrs. Beadlepoof was especially interested in knowing why her grandfather had been seen tottering in and out of the bait shop yesterday and about what Lillian thought of Kar not looking like a Homely at all. In response to that question, Lillian just fixed her eyes straight ahead and mumbled some excuse about needing to get to the employment agency. Mrs. Beadlepoof picked up the scent of a secret. "I know you're hiding something," Mrs. Beadlepoof kept saying, shaking Lillian by the elbow.

Lillian tore herself away and for the second time in twenty-four hours, ripped her sleeve.

That evening she paid a visit to Mr. and Mrs. Homely and gave them the rundown of the morning's event. Kar was upstairs doing his homework with Jack.

"A red roof?" said Mr. Homely. "That helps, at least. I'll take the day off tomorrow. Got the broomster humming once again. It sputters loudly at take off, but I guess that doesn't mean anything if I get caught flying over the Greenfields."

"What're we going to do?" asked Mrs. Homely. Her lower lip trembled.

"What we have to do. Get a birth certificate for Kar." Mr. Homely banged the dinner table with his fist and sent a plate and a glass flying. "I'll think of something when I get there."

Mrs. Homely knelt down to pick up the pieces of plate, which had broken cleanly in two, off the floor. "How much is that going to cost us?"

"I took all our savings out, just in case," said Mr. Homely.

42

"That much?" gasped Mrs. Homely, bumping her head under the table trying to catch the glass that was fortunately intact as it rolled away from her.

Mr. Homely shrugged. "Better safe than sorry. I don't want to make two trips."

"Let me go instead!" Lillian interrupted. She even surprised herself at the bold offer.

"No, we can't have you doing anything so dangerous for us."

"It won't be dangerous for me as much as it will be for Mr. Homely. You know how suspicious everybody gets when somebody takes a day off and can't explain why." Lillian looked from one to the other. "Everybody tends to pass by just to see what the matter is. Such nosey villagers," she said, crossing her arms angrily.

"I'll just say I have some errands to run. It's easier for me. I have nothing to do and nobody even notices me much," said Lillian miserably, "up in the air, anyway."

Mr. Homely shook his head. "It's still too dangerous for you, Lillian!"

"She has a point, though." Mrs. Homely got up and paced the floor. "Right now I feel as if all eyes are on us, especially with Mrs. Beadlepoof asking so many questions lately."

"Okay, we agree, then," said Lillian, getting up and heading towards the door before Mr. Homely could protest. "I'll be here tomorrow before dawn."

As she tripped out the door and grabbed her repaired broomster by the handles, she could feel the rise of excitement surging through her. At last she was doing something worthwhile with her life and maybe even something dangerous. How thrilling! She went home and threw up.

Christina Waymreen

THE GREENFIELDS

LILLIAN SNUCK out of the house two hours before dawn broke. The newly repaired broomster jumped to attention at the first flick of the handle and she flew upwards and away from the village. The moon was hidden behind clouds Mrs. Homely had magically gathered for her. She promised to get rid of them the minute dawn broke and before the weather department realized that clouds were not scheduled on that particular day. Anyone wanting to modify the weather had to put in a request to the head of the department at least ten days in advance (with legitimate reasons, of course). Mrs. Homely assumed (correctly) that her need to forge papers wouldn't be a legitimate reason. She also told Lillian that any unauthorized magical weather changes resulted in finger bonding. Mrs. Homely could not afford to lose her job at a time when they might lose all their savings.

By the time dawn broke, Lillian had landed in a dark alley in a dreary and notorious part of the EastWyck village. This spot was within walking distance to the Greenfields, but Lillian was not set on foraging her way through tall shrubs that were crawling with snakes.

The street she had dropped into was lined with pubs. In the early morning hours, drunks were stumbling home from the bars. She looked around in horror and fear. Her father was right! These Wyckians *were* just a bunch of hooligans!

She mustered all her courage and shuffled into a pub called *Here's To Us*. The place smelled vile and the floor was so filthy and sticky that she had to pry her boots up with every step she took. It was almost empty that morning. The only patrons that remained were the ones unable to lift themselves off the floor. She looked around and spied someone who was actually sitting up and staring into space. He did not look pleasant, but he was the only one with his eyes open.

"Hey there," she said nervously, as she pulled herself forward and finally stood in front of him.

The man's eyes flickered into life and he gazed solemnly up at her from where he was seated behind a grimy wooden table, his back to a wall.

"Hey," he grunted back.

Lillian felt a momentary wave of uneasiness sweep over her but she pushed it deep down inside, somewhere in the pit of her stomach, where it flopped around, making her queasy. She pulled up a chair and sat opposite the gentleman. The smell of bad alcohol wafted around the man and she had to fight her instinct to gag.

"I need some information," she said, trying to sound as grown up as possible.

"We all do," the man replied. "Getting it is the problem." He wore a faded brown cloak that was frayed at the seams. A hat of the same color and age lay on the edge of the table. His face was lean and colorless and his tiny, cat-like eyes peered beneath thin black eyebrows.

"Do you know of anybody who can give me some information around here?" she asked again, holding onto her trembling knees.

"Like what? The weather?" He drank whatever was remaining from a chipped mug.

"Like, well, let's say I want to buy some, you know, *gribbich*," whispered Lillian, leaning towards the man. She held onto the side of the table with both hands. She looked around to see if any of the prone bodies on the floor were listening.

"It's *grippich* and you're too young to smoke. Do your parents know where you are, young lady?"

"They sent me," she lied. "Actually, I heard that this guy in a red house might have some to sell. He lives in the Greenfields. Do you know how I might go about getting there?"

"You can walk," said the stranger.

Lillian felt the room spin as she tried to lock eyes with the stranger. "I need to reach someone who lives in a house with a red roof in the Greenfields." She spoke rapidly before her courage ran out the door and skipped out of town.

45

"What do you want him for anyway? Everybody knows he doesn't sell smokes to kids. If your parents want any, just bring them here tomorrow, same time, and I'll be happy to get them some; for a price, of course." Lillian recoiled from his sour breath.

"He's my cousin, you see. I'm just fooling you. I want to pay him a visit and somebody told me that you might know something like a secret passageway through the forest." Lillian surprised herself at how well she could lie, even though she could hear her knees knocking.

"Everybody's his cousin," the stranger sneered, and looked towards the bar. "What does a guy need to do to get some service around here?" There was no answer. Lillian could see two legs poking out from the side of the bar.

Oh, my, Lillian thought. He knows I'm lying. "Do you know of anybody who can help me to get to him?"

"Yes," said the stranger, rubbing his chin, his thin eyebrows almost meeting as he stared intensely at Lillian. "I can. I'm getting tired of this conversation. Your lies are boring me."

Lillian felt the panic rising from her stomach and had to fight her small breakfast back down.

He looked at her again and sighed. "Why not? I'm getting no service here. Might as well leave." The stranger stood up and bent forward, practically touching Lillian's nose with his. "It'll cost you."

Lillian recoiled at his proximity. "How much?"

The stranger got up and threw his hat on.

"How do we get there?" asked Lillian excitedly, following him. "Is there some kind of hidden passageway or something?"

The stranger's lips curled, showing a gap in his upper front teeth, and he walked out of the pub. Even though he caught sight of Lillian's one extra large boot, poking out from under her long skirt, he did not glance at it a second time. Lillian followed him, feeling slightly impressed with the stranger who was at least polite enough not to stare in wonder like everybody else who saw her large foot for the first time. People usually gasped and pointed rudely until they learned to do it behind shop windows.

She followed him outside where he stopped next to a shiny black broomster. It was an antique and Lillian let out a slow whistle of appreciation.

"Get on," the stranger said, ignoring the compliment.

"But the police will see us." Her whispered protest ricocheted off the alley walls and she clamped her hands over her mouth. A few sleeping drunkards twitched in annoyance at the sound.

The stranger sat on the broomster and wiggled his index finger. Suddenly the air about him thickened and Lillian could no longer see the stranger or the broomster beneath him. After a few seconds both reappeared again.

Lillian cried out in delight: "Ah, what a very handy bit of magic!" She temporarily forgot her fear of the stranger and, eager to take a ride on the cool black antique, climbed up and sat behind him. "Let's go, then."

"Not until we get a few things straightened out."

"Like what?"

Silence spoke louder than words.

"Oh, money," said Lillian nervously. "I've got enough, I think."

"You better or you'll be walking back. And you know what that might mean."

Lillian nodded behind his back. Her fears reared up again like an angry stallion. She'd heard all about the snakes of Greenfield!

The weather department in EastWyck, Lillian noticed, was not as tidy as their own. The early morning fog enveloped them like a thick cotton blanket. Since the moon was hidden, she could hardly make out anything below. She figured that it was just as well and imagined all kinds of snakes slithering and hissing between the tall blades of grass.

It took only a few minutes before she felt the broomster dip slightly before it made a smooth landing. She was impressed with the old broomster's speed and agility.

47

She noticed through the dimness that they had landed in the front yard of the biggest house she'd ever seen. It was even bigger than the houses in the grand NorthWyck village. The early morning sun found its way through the fog for a few seconds and illuminated the crimson roof, doors and windows. In a flash the clouds sailed by and hid it again from view.

"The Greenfield snakes hate the color red," said the stranger before she could even ask.

It was good to know, thought Lillian, although she was not wearing any red in case she had to walk back. She couldn't bear to think about that possibility right now. She swallowed hard before stepping off the broomster.

The stranger walked up to the large double doors, opened them, and beckoned Lillian to follow him.

"You must know my cousin pretty well," said Lillian, unable to stop the lie from tumbling out of her mouth. She stepped into the foyer and stopped in amazement.

A mural adorned the large domed ceiling. Fairies tripped over flowers and men with long white beards looked down their noses in quiet repose. The Wyck Museum of Ages did not hold such wonders. She stood with her neck stretched back as far as it could go, admiring the scene.

"Wow." Her "cousin" lived very well, indeed.

The stranger ushered her into the next room. There was a large black desk in the back and the walls were covered in framed certificates and licenses. Lillian glanced at a few as she followed the stranger to the back of the dark room.

Certificate of High Breeding and Class, she read. Who would want one of those? Maybe the NorthWyck people were not what they seemed to be. She passed another. *This is to certify that the holder of this certificate has passed in all subjects related to Tomfoolery.* She thought that was just hilarious and almost burst out laughing when she noticed the stranger scowling at her from the depths of a deep leather armchair.

"So, what can I do for you?" the stranger said, leaning back into the armchair and putting his feet up on a small stool. Lillian was surprised to see that the soles of the man's shoes were red.

Embarrassed, she asked, "Are you who I think you are?" He was no cousin of hers.

"Angus Fountaine at your service," said Mr. Fountaine, bowing his head slightly. "And no, you are not my cousin, unless there is something I don't know about my family, which I doubt." He picked up a tiny silver bell that rested on the table next to the chair and rang it. A giant of a man strode into the room. His arms were so long that they dangled past his knees.

Lillian stared at him sympathetically. It must be one of those magical mishaps.

The tall butler glared back at her.

"You rang, sir?"

"Yes, some tea would be nice, Alfred, and light a fire, please, while you're here."

With a snap of his giant fingers the fireplace roared into life. Then Alfred turned and disappeared into another room.

"And now, miss, please come closer and tell me who might you really be?"

"Me?" Lillian asked, foolishly pointing to herself and taking a few steps back.

"I know everybody else here," said Mr. Fountaine, waving his hand about.

"Lillian." She was afraid to give him her last name.

"And what is it you want from me, Lillian Bigfoot?"

She sucked in her breath and let out a faint squeaky voice: "A birth certificate?"

"Interesting." Mr. Fountaine furrowed his thin eyebrows. He got up, walked behind the desk at the end of the room, and pulled out a giant ledger from one of the drawers. After flipping through the pages for a while he stopped and looked at her.

"Hmmm, very interesting: the second request in one week." He eyed her curiously. "It will cost you, you know."

49

"Yes, yes, I understand," said Lillian, nodding her head vigorously. "How much?"

"Two thousand dragons."

Lillian staggered slightly. "Why? Why so much?" she gasped. It was exactly the amount Mr. Homely had handed over to her the night before. But she hadn't expected to use it all. She hated the idea of using the Homely's entire savings.

"Supply and demand," said Mr. Fountaine. "I am the only one who supplies and I demand a high price." His next words made her spine shiver even though the heat of the fire hit her squarely in the back. "And that fee includes the cost of my silence, of course."

Lillian reluctantly drew out a scruffy leather money pouch, filled with silver and gold dragons, from a pocket in her heavy skirt and clunked it on the table. "That's just about everything he has ... I mean ... I have. Do I get a receipt?"

"Ah, so we are in business. I would have hated to see you walk back into town."

Lillian also hated that idea. But two thousand dragons? It would have taken her years to save that much, and poor Mr. Homely would lose it to a forger in a split second. At least he would give her a receipt to prove it to Mr. Homely, but she knew that Mr. Homely would have given his own blood for his son and, if he had to, his life.

Mr. Fountaine took all the information and stepped out of the room. Lillian walked around and read the rest of the framed certificates that hung in no particular order on the walls. *Grave Digging Certificate* as well as *Flower Arrangements* and *Broomster Repair of the Highest Order*. The one she liked the most stated that the holder of this license could drive any type of broomster. Maybe if she had the right amount of money she could ask for one of those. She could find a job delivering goods to and from the other villages. What money it would make! She would just ask how much and maybe she could save up for it.

When he re-entered the room, she had to ask: "How much is this one?"

Mr. Fountaine handed her a small envelope. "The certificate wasn't too difficult, my dear. It seemed I already had one set up. I just needed to change the name." He peered at the certificate she was pointing at. "That would be two thousand five hundred Dragons, plus sixty percent of all your profits, with a firm contract that you work for me for me at least the first two years. Want it?"

Lillian gulped. "Nope."

He grinned at her. "Nobody does."

She wondered, as she soared back to the alley on Mr. Fountaine's invisible broomster, whom he forged the other birth certificate for. It wouldn't hurt to ask.

"So," she said, screaming above the roar of the wind, "whom did you make out the last birth certificate for?"

"It'll cost you," he yelled back.

"How much?" she asked, rolling her eyes behind his back.

He landed the broomster next to hers in the alley and helped her off. "I told you already. My clients pay for my silence. Breaking it would be exorbitant."

MISS VARNUS

K A R R A C E D on his bike to school. His father had repaired it and it was just as good as new. The birth certificate was safely folded and tucked in his back pocket. The anxiety of *What's My Magic?* Day still made his stomach flip. He handed the certificate to Principal Larity and ran to the first class before the door closed. He barely reached it in time and had to squeeze himself through. Being late before the main gate closed was just a small detention compared to actually being late to class, which merited triple detention time.

Miss Varnus had the first class that morning. At the moment she had her back to the students and was staring at her image in the window. Kar noticed through the reflection of the glass that she had drawn her eyeliner in a way that made her eyes look slanted. She also drew eyebrows straight across her forehead. Quite hideous, he thought. She had her hair up in a ponytail that swung with every move she made. She waited for all the students to settle down before she turned and faced them. They sucked in air. She looked like a stricken feline about to attack.

She never paid attention to the terrifying effect her daily make-up had on her students or on the public in general. She turned back to gaze out the window. Just a few hundred yards away, workers were preparing the outdoor stage. Kar's mother had told him about the memorable *What's My Magic?* Day when thirteen-year-old Miss Varnus had stood there on the stage. A shy, awkward child, palms sweating, face melting from too much makeup, heart probably bursting with fear, she had wiggled her index finger and sent everything that was pointy and spear-like hurtling into space. The tall fir trees surrounding the school had been ripped from their roots. They had to bind her finger quickly before she was able to cause any more damage.

Miss Varnus twirled the ring that adorned the black velvety binding on her finger. At least they allowed her to enter the Wyck games, thought Kar. He noticed how she patted her gold medal, sighing. Instead of taking class, she sat back and retold glorious and somewhat exaggerated stories of bygone celebrations. The bell to the next class woke the students from the stupor she put them in. Eyes glazed from the endless drivel of her past, they pushed each other to get to the next lesson.

The rest of the day wasn't easy for the anxious thirteen-year-olds. They huddled in different corners of the schoolyard anticipating the worst, yet excited to the point of giddiness.

"What would you like your magic to be, Haylen?" asked Kar. They were in the piano room where Haylen was given a half-hour a day to practice, and where they often gathered when they wanted to be alone together. He bit into a ham sandwich. His black eyes, the color of his sweater, were half closed as he savored the taste. He loved the sandwiches his mother packed for him. Jack was thumbing through a music book, looking bored.

Haylen plucked at a key. "I want my fingers to be so nimble that I will be the most famous pianist in all the Wyck villages and beyond." She waved her hand and laughed.

"Well, you don't need magic for that," Kar teased. "Just practice."

"Anybody can play the piano with practice," said Haylen, huffing slightly. "But to be great at it; well, that's something else. That needs magic."

"Well, I've never heard of anybody being able to play any instrument by just wiggling their finger," said Jack. "Think of something else."

"Then I still would want to be an elephant," said Haylen.

"They'd bind your finger quickly," said Kar, finishing his sandwich.

"Hopefully, but not before I get a chance to squash the Nasty boys!" she yelled gleefully, banging her fingers on the piano keys.

It took them a while to stop laughing as they envisioned a mad giant elephant stomping on the Nasty boys during the ceremony.

"Kar," asked Jack, "really: what kind of magic do you want?"

"Anything that doesn't get my finger bonded." Kar sat next to Haylen and plucked at the piano.

Jack said wistfully, "I'd love to be able to fly."

Haylen played the scales as they thought about it for a while.

"There's the broomster," said Jack. "We'll all eventually be able to fly that. Not that I don't know how to already."

"Jack," cried Haylen, "have you been taking the broomster out without your parents' permission?"

"Oh, lighten up," quipped Kar. "Who hasn't?"

"Well, I haven't," said Haylen, disappointment showing on her face.

"It won't be the same as really flying, though," continued Kar, ignoring Haylen's frowns.

Again silence filled the room as they daydreamed.

"I'd love to be a real sorcerer," said Jack, pulling them out of their reverie. "I could conjure up anything. Not just with one finger, but with all of them."

"They'd probably bind all your fingers then," said Haylen. "But, seriously: what would you like to be able to do, Kar?"

"I don't know. Nothing, really," said Kar. He gazed out the window towards Mount Footsteps. "Maybe fly, like Jack, over the mountain top. See the rest of what's out there. I've never heard of anybody leaving the villages."

"I heard that somebody did leave but never came back," said Haylen, sweeping the keys with one finger and smirking.

"Really? How do you know that?" asked Jack, returning to the piano.

"Maybe they just thought it was better out there than here," said Kar quietly.

"Not really. They were banished. Exiled." Haylen played a soft tune, humming under her breath. She seemed proud of the little bit of secret she knew and they didn't.

"Why were they banished?" asked Jack, poking at the keys.

Haylen slapped his hand. "Probably defied the councilmen."

"The councilmen," said Kar. "Has anybody seen their faces? Who are they, really?"

Haylen went back to playing and humming.

"You know what, Haylen?" asked Jack.

"What?"

"You're probably right. Your playing does need magic."

Haylen punched him in the arm.

Suddenly the door banged open and Lucas walked in with his tubby entourage. "Ah, the threesome hiding as usual," he said with a sneer. It was always strange to hear a grownup voice coming from a thirteen-year-old body. "Leave, please: I need to practice."

Haylen gave him a look of disdain. "You don't play the piano, Lucas."

They all knew it was a lie. Lucas hated anything musical. It was just those two dorks of his who liked to bang on the keyboards because they thought it was fun. Sometimes Lucas obliged them too much.

Jack got up from where he was sitting on the piano bench and stood in front of Haylen, facing Lucas. "Wait your turn."

Kar stiffened. Jack always put on a brave front, but he'd never won a fight. It always seemed like a suicidal tactic to Kar.

"Let's go, Jack," said Kar, hoping to avoid a fight. "We can come back later."

Haylen jumped up. "I am sick and tired of being pushed around by the likes of you," she yelled, banging the piano lid shut. "I have another few minutes left to practice and you and your buddies will just have to wait your turn!"

"Tsk, tsk," said Lucas with a sick smile. "Always ready for a fight, aren't we?"

"And then they say it's all *my* fault," he said, rolling his eyes upwards and pretending to sigh. "Will you ever learn to obey orders? I think that you had better leave." His voice grew low and menacing.

Resigned to the fight on the horizon at this point, Kar stood up. "You don't scare us." Since they were all facing Lucas, he might as well, too. "We came here first and it says on the sheet that we have ten minutes left. Your cronies just want to bang on the piano. They'll ruin it soon."

Lucas spread out his hands. "My friends here are really serious about their music; right, guys?"

The twins sniggered, their bellies jingling up and down. "Yeah, Lucas, we like playing the piano."

Lucas walked over to the piano, pushed Haylen aside, and lifted the lid. "It's all yours, boys, unless one of you here wants to fight us for it? I'm able, willing, and ready, you know!"

Haylen tossed her head in indignation and stomped out of the room. Kar and Jack followed a few seconds later. It did not take them long to realize that another nasty fight with Lucas might get them into more trouble with the principal. *What's My Magic?* Day was looming near and maybe one of them might be able to magically shape-shift into something that would make Lucas shake in his boots. Kar hoped so, anyway.

LILLIAN'S NEW JOB

THE SOUTHWYCK population was two hundred and thirty-two plus, but during *What's My Magic?* Day, it rose to over seven hundred. They came swarming in from the North, East, and West villages of Wyck. All the children participated on one stage. It started from late morning and continued past sunset. Mr. Tweetle's students performed their tap dancing routine in the morning, to the embarrassment and anguish of their parents.

There was only one day in the year when the Serpent Moon aligned itself with the Dragon Star. When that happened, the councilmen had advised the villagers, new magic was able to reveal itself. Some Wyckians argued that the councilmen ruling the villages today were the same ones who first ordained *What's My Magic?* Day, centuries ago. Others disagreed vehemently, claiming that no one could live that long! As long as anyone could remember, villagers looked forward to the day when the star poked into the moon and, with a little help from the magic powder, thirteen year olds learned to unlock their one magical trait.

The stage was almost completed. It was a long and tiring process, and all those who could use their magic to lift and levitate heavy objects, bang large nails with the flick of a finger, and decorate the stage were asked to help. Mr. Homely was allowed to take the day off from the quarry. By mid-afternoon, the job was complete and everybody let out a collective sigh of relief, which almost toppled the construction. Magic had funny ways of showing up when least expected. Eventually the workers went home to dip their burning fingers into a cool glass of water and relax before the festivities began.

Lillian Bigfoot stood atop a hill looking down at all the commotion in the field off of the school grounds. She was holding a staff in her hand. Sheep were bleating all around her and Taff Peabrine, in the shape of a sheepdog, sat panting beside her. This was her third job in a week. The daycare center fiasco had marred her resume, even though it was the very first job she had ever had other than smashing grapes under her bare feet. Her second job at Piglet Farm of Bacon did not go well, either. Her job was to tend to the barn animals. Horses and chickens were okay, but Lillian had found it nearly impossible to feed the pigs. Some of them were so large they practically ran her out of the pigsty, and in order to avoid the giant sows, she had stepped on the piglets. There was a sudden dramatic increase in pork prices. At least she had held the job for a couple of days. The employment agency cautioned her that if she came back a third time, they'd have to warn potential employers about her history before they could take her on for another assignment.

But that was three days ago. She did have to walk a lot on her new job, but she solved the limping problem by wearing the same shoe size on both feet. Only she had to stuff straw in the smaller left one, which made walking a bit difficult, but not as bad as before. Her snickering siblings told her that she walked like Grandfather Bigfoot after a night in the wine cellar. Some meaner people mentioned the clown from the circus, but even his feet were smaller than her one big one.

She had asked her employer, Mr. Sincher, if she could take *What's My Magic?* Day off, but since she had barely started on the job, he refused. He did tell her that she had enough time in the evening to see the end of the ceremony, and anyway, it was always better at night. She'd be able to see the sparks flying from the children's shaking fingers.

Taff barked. She turned to see him herding some wandering sheep back to the fold that had taken off down the hill to investigate the ever greener pastures. In their case, it was true. Taff returned to her side.

"They're clearing the sky of all clouds for tomorrow. It will be pretty hot with all that sun shining down on us," said Lillian.

Taff barked twice.

"It will be too hot for the sheep, too." She looked down at Taff who had sprawled over her shoes.

"I know where we can get some shade," Taff said. He had resumed his natural form, which wasn't too far of a stretch from the shaggy sheepdog he could shape-shift into.

"I hope it's not too far. I want to get to the ceremony after work." She wanted to see how Kar would do. She knew he was anxious.

"There is a crevice near the edge of Mount Footsteps where a small brook runs. There is also some plant life and it'll be a lot cooler," said Taff.

"We can have a picnic," said Lillian excitedly. She shifted her shoes to the side a bit.

Taff grinned.

"You're pretty smart for a Peabrain—sorry, I mean a Peabrine," said Lillian, patting his head and forgetting that he had shape-shifted back to normal.

"So I've been told."

There were no clouds to hide the glare of the morning sun as Lillian flew over the village the next day. The sky was full of broomsters of every make and color. Everybody wanted to get an early morning start on the ceremony and a good parking space and seat. Lillian wished she could be there with them from the beginning, but the sheep needed tending to and Taff would be waiting for her. She had strapped a large picnic basket to her broomster.

It took a while to get the sheep herded down the hill and away from the blistering heat of the day. They walked along the shade of the mountain and down towards the running brook where trees and long savory grasses grew in abundance. She hoped the sheep would be content. She wanted to take her shoes off and dip her feet in the cool running water, but was too embarrassed to show them to Taff. It was one thing for her to go barefoot during the grape stomping season when she was the envy of the town folk, then to bare her feet when the size disparity would be so evident and so clearly out of place. Taff was busy herding the sheep into a small area to graze and joined her when the last of them had found a spot of grass to munch on.

"Have you ever made any use of your bunny abilities?" asked Taff, after shape-shifting back to his original form.

"Other than the business at the daycare center? No. Why?" Lillian asked He'd heard Mrs. Beadlepoof's rumors about Lillian's experience at the daycare center. Lillian had given him the true story on her first day.

"Nothing really, but when I'm a sheepdog, I smell things, hear things and see things differently. Sometimes I wish I had been born a dog."

"You don't mean that?"

"Sometimes I do," said Taff. "But this is the next best thing, anyway."

"Well, my parents scared me so much when they found out I could transform into a bunny. They convinced me some horrible creature could eat me. So other than the time I shape-shifted at the daycare center, I really never cared to do it." She shivered when she recalled the experience at the daycare center. It had been such a nightmare. "And I still don't care to."

"Really? Why don't you do it now with me? I'll protect you."

"Now?"

"Yes," said Taff, giving her a big smile of encouragement.

Lillian looked around her. Other than the sheep grazing in the distance, there didn't look like there would be anything dangerous in the vicinity and she had never asked her parents what those bunny-hunting creatures were anyway. She smiled tentatively at Taff. He was being so kind to her. It was such a refreshing change for her. "I'll do it."

On the count of three, they both shape-shifted together. Taff changed into the shaggy sheepdog and Lillian transformed into the fluffy white bunny with the tip of one ear just barely touching the ground. What she hadn't realized before—because she had never shape-sifted around other shape-shifters—was that when she became an animal, she could actually read Taff's mind.

"This is very strange," she said. "I can read your mind."

"It's because we still have human minds," he said. "Beware of the animal mind you can't read."

"Why?"

"Because if you can't read its mind, it's a real animal and you better get out of its way."

"Oh, I see. All shape-shifters read each others' minds?"

"It keeps us from eating each other," he explained. "Well, I'm going to hop over to the brook and stick my hot paws in. Care to join me?"

"What about Henre Lisp, who almost got swallowed by the cat?"

"Oh, that. The two of them were always fighting each other anyway. That cat wasn't really going to eat him, silly. It was just to scare poor Henre."

Taff ran, splashing into the gurgling brook while Lillian hopped her way over. The water was cool and delicious to her rabbit tongue. Her bunny ears heard sounds she never knew existed: even the sound of ants marching through the grass. Her furry nose wrinkled in delight as the wind carried every tantalizing smell. She hopped away from the brook, shaking off the excess water. A feeling of inquisitiveness overwhelmed her. She wanted to know everything about this place. To find its hidden secrets. She hopped away from Taff, who was still dashing up and down the stream, barking in pleasure.

She sniffed at pebbles and wild flowers and hopped over beetles and slugs until she found herself near the mouth of a cave. Her bunny ears heard no sounds, but the stale odors of a long forgotten cave made her wrinkle her tiny pink nose. She hopped her way into the darkness. The cave was icy cold compared to the heat of the day and her rabbit's eyes quickly adjusted to the low light. Towards the rear of the cave a circle of small stones seemed to hold ashes where once somebody might have lit a fire to keep warm. Alongside a wall, somebody had written something with the burnt end of a stick. She couldn't make it out in the gloom of the cave.

"There you are," said Taff loudly.

Lillian jumped at the sound of his voice piercing through her mind. "You scared me!"

"I sniffed you out," he said, laughing. "Wow, what a cool cave. We could have our picnic in here."

"Good idea," agreed Lillian. "But can you make out what it says here on the wall?"

Taff padded closer to the wall to see. "Looks like somebody wrote a poem on the wall."

"Can you read it?"

"I'll try." Taff licked his lips and squinted.

"Hear ye, hear ye, this we say
Thirteen years shall pass this way,
And when those thirteen years are done,
The fall of Wyck will have begun."

"How awful," Lillian exclaimed. "Who could have written this?"

"There's more. Listen."

Hear ye, hear ye, this we say
Thirteen years shall pass this way
And when the final day has come
Beware the magic of the young.

"It still doesn't sound any better," said Lillian. "There's something else here, written on the side." She hopped nearer to the cave wall. "I think it says 'Lunate Marcel'. Who's Lunate Marcel?"

"No idea, but it seems very obvious to me," said Taff. "It's a prophecy."

"It looks more like a curse to me," grumbled Lillian. "And, anyway, I thought the councilmen forbade fortune tellers and prophets?"

"They might have. But somebody seems not to have paid any attention to them." He turned his back to the wall.

"It's very ominous. *The fall of Wyck will have begun.* It gives me the creeps." Lillian hopped out of the cave. "Let's get out of here. I can't enjoy our picnic with this creepy prophesy on the wall."

"Me neither," said Taff following her.

"Maybe the thirteenth year has already come and gone? Everything seems pretty peaceful to me."

"You're probably right," Taff said, scratching his side with his hind paw. "It's probably just a bunch of nonsense."

"Ready for that picnic now? Let's go find a new spot." Lillian resolved to dismiss the poem completely from her bunny mind.

"Woof. I'm right behind you." They ran and hopped out of the cave, determined to find a new picnic spot that would keep them cool.

WHAT'S MY MAGIC?

THE WYCK Security Patrol was out in droves that same morning, keeping the sky traffic as clear as possible while they helped the stranded Wyckians off of treetops and roofs. A demonstration was taking place through the main streets of SouthWyck as well. Faded signs reading *Free the Finger! Binding is Unjust! Digit Freedom for All!* waved above angry heads. Black-bound index fingers rippled in unison as angry chants of "unbind us" filled the late morning sky. These disgruntled citizens marched every year on this day and eventually wound up standing behind the seating area to watch the ceremony take place. They were curious to see which of the youngsters would have magic deemed too dangerous and get their fingers bound. They would soon be joining their ranks.

Those participating in the ceremony slept fitfully the night before. Many participants woke in a cold sweat, wishing they were a year younger. Some woke up screaming from nightmares and praying they would be gifted with some simple bit of magic, like curdling milk or shape-shifting into some household animal that would only be fit for the petting zoo. Others, however, like Lucas Nosty and Kar Homely, woke from those sweaty dreams hungering for more than the ordinary.

Alone in his room the morning before the ceremony, Kar wished he had never been born. He felt almost sick with anxiety. His room had changed a few times during the night and he had to move some things around before he could find his chest of drawers and some clothes for the day. He threw them all out on the floor of his room and tried on one shirt after the other. He wanted to get his eyes the right color for the ceremony. He didn't want to stand out among the crowd of teenagers. He wanted, above all else, to look more like a Homely. Ultimately, he chose a brown shirt with beige shorts that were held up by a brown leather belt. He had never felt so much inner turmoil in his life and hoped he never would again. He had no idea what was in store for him that day. The combination of excitement and dread bred panic in his mind. He was frantic. He wished he could find a place to hide until it was all over, and at the same time, he couldn't wait to dip his finger in the magic powder and wiggle it like he had been practicing all week. He wanted to know his destiny, but he was also horrified about what it might be. He felt like he had swallowed a rock. It was difficult to breathe.

His parents would never let him skip breakfast, especially on an important day. He practically shoved the eggs and bacon down his throat with a fork. All the parents of the children participating in the ceremony had reserved seating, so his parents didn't need to rush over and grab a good spot. Mrs. Homely tried to keep a pleasant banter going to cheer everyone up, but her husband and son's strained smiles were painful to watch and she eventually gave up and acknowledged their shared anxiety. Finally, after they had washed the breakfast dishes, they stepped out of the house and began their trek down the main street among the demonstrators and the rest of the town folk who chose to avoid the heavy sky traffic.

Mrs. Homely gave Kar a mighty hug before he stepped behind the stage. His ribs ached slightly from it, and Mr. Homely patted him on the back, trying to reassure him; but he was just as nervous as his son. Then they left to find their seats in the crowd.

Kar's classmates were seated on small stools behind the large stage curtain and he joined them The electricity in the air was almost palpable. They all shifted uneasily on their tiny seats. Between the four Wyck villages, there were quite a few thirteen-year-olds present for the ceremony. Their teachers were doing their best to boost the youngsters' spirits, but the participants' faces remained pale, their mouths dry, and their eyes shifted about fearfully. Even Lucas Nosty looked drained and was biting his lip, but he still couldn't resist needling Kar.

"Well, if it isn't sweetie. You better like cheese, 'cause I heard that's what rats like."

"And I bet you have a taste for flies," Kar fired back.

"If you're lucky, you might get to be one!" Lucas said as he curled his fingers into tight fists and stepped closer to Kar.

"Boys," cried Miss Varnus, pulling them apart. "Please, enough! Kar, find a seat until your name is called. It's going to be a long wait because the SouthWyck village will be last on the list. I don't want to hear another word from either of you. There is enough tension without anybody adding to it." She peered at them from under thick, black lashes that were so heavy she could hardly keep her eyes open. The rest of her face was painted in such cheery shades that she looked like a polished red apple.

Lucas gave Kar one of his famous nasty looks and turned his back. Kar walked over to an empty stool near Haylen and Jack. They squirmed nervously and could only muster a squeaky 'hello' to him. Suddenly the soft rumbling of the audience fell silent and the children rushed to the sides of the stage to watch. There was always entertainment at these events.

Mr. Tweetle tap-danced onto the stage and introduced the first segment. The wooden boards shook violently as his students pounded their way across the platform. The family members in the audience clamped their hands over their faces and moaned in embarrassment. Finally, after a brief moment of terror, when the first row in the audience was certain the pyramid of tap dancers would fall on them, the dance ended in a heap on the floor. The enthusiastic applause that followed was more of an indication of relief than of praise for the performance.

Sorenta Opus was next, and her voice scaled to the top of the musical notes. She was accompanied by howls from the forest. The show continued. The most amazing was Handel Kwaker. Packs of playing cards seemed to move fluidly between his nimble fingers. The audience couldn't keep up with him. Everyone knew that Handel's own magical ability was turning milk into cheese. He worked for Mr. Manarde down at the dairy farm. His one true love, though, was making cards disappear and reappear where they were least expected. The final moment came when Handel pulled out a whole pack of cards from the mouth of a volunteer. Kar whispered to his friends that he looked as if he was vomiting cards. They all giggled nervously.

After a short interval, a gong sounded and the nine councilmen of the Wyck villages appeared on stage. They were shrouded in long thick, purple robes, their heads covered in hoods with only small round openings for eyes and mouths. From underneath the hoods, silvery beards flowed to their waist. They wore white leather gloves that sparkled in the sunlight like they were covered in diamonds. They stood side-by-side, identical in height and in every other visible feature. No one in the village had ever seen their faces.

The councilmen drifted towards a long table where nine elaborate chairs with very long backs had magically appeared. They sat down and the councilman in the middle produced a sealed ceramic urn from the folds of his purple robe and placed it in the middle of the table. It was a simple design with a thick neck and a rounded bottom. The shape of a strong blue index finger glowed on its side. Everyone in the audience knew that urn, and the sight of it brought back hundreds of flashbacks. The last of the councilmen to be seated pulled out a roll of black velvet ribbon and a small sharp knife and placed them carefully on the table.

Kar stared anxiously at the glowing urn. There were many theories in the village about the origin of the urn and its magical contents. Some people believed that the great sorcerer, Anatolis, had molded the urn and that the magic powder was his very own ashes. Those who could not fathom having dipped their finger in the ashes of a dead sorcerer claimed the ashes came from the last real dragon killed in battle and that the urn itself had been crafted from the dragon's scaly hide.

The fifth councilman stood up, raised his hand, and spoke with a deep, disembodied hollow voice. Everyone in attendance heard it clearly.

"This year we have an exceptional number of children who have turned thirteen - almost twice that of last year. We hope that this new generation will reward the villages of Wyck two-fold." He waited until the typical applause died down before continuing.

Kar looked out into the crowd. It was only at this time of the year that all the councilmen would gather together with the villagers. He could see fear in the eyes of the audience and could feel the tension pulsing through the crowd when the councilman spoke. It was probably for the best that the councilmen visited so rarely.

"As you know, not everyone is blessed with magic that is beneficial to one's way of living." Kar could see Mr. Tweetle beaming from the opposite end of the stage while many in the audience nodded with understanding. Those who came to demonstrate against the unjust bonding of tiny fingers dared to boo loudly in the back. The councilman stopped and swept his eyes across the anxious audience. Then he continued using that same disembodied voice that was so low and hollow, yet all Wyckians heard it as if he was speaking in their own ears. "And that magic which is dangerous and not of any use to our peaceful village must be, for the safety of us all, bound." More jeers erupted from the back of the audience, where angry citizens waved defiant signs furiously above their heads.

"Let us begin." The councilman raised his hands, ignoring the hissing in the back. "Bring on the children of NorthWyck!"

Five children filed out onto the stage, each being pushed forward by the one behind. The last student, a girl, was prodded out onto the stage. Kar noticed their knees wobbling uncontrollably as they stood facing the councilmen.

The audience was ready for the action. Ancient warrior shields, used exclusively for this occasion each year, were raised to fend off any dangerous new magic. Those who did not own such relics relied on umbrellas, pots and pans, and anything that could protect them from sudden magical surprises.

Excitement ran so high that Kar could feel goose bumps rising all along his arms. He shifted his feet nervously.

"I don't think I can take this any longer," whispered Haylen. "What if we just refuse?"

"You can," said Jack. "But I'm going out there with or without you."

"We can't refuse," answered Kar. "I tried." He turned his attention back to the stage.

One of the councilmen took out a thick, round parchment and unrolled a few inches of it onto the table. A bottle of red ink and a long feathered quill lay in front of him. He picked up the quill and dipped it into the bottle of ink.

"State your name," he said to the first child in line.

She squared her tiny shoulders and stepped closer to the table. "Margeat Buttle." He wrote the name down.

"Margeat Buttle," he said, looking at the child with such intensity that her whole body began to shake. "You have nothing to fear." Yet his voice lacked compassion. "Please raise your right index finger."

Margeat did as she was told. Another councilman removed the top off the urn. "Place only your right index finger inside the urn." The councilmen's voices always sounded to Kar like the soft snarls of wild dogs.

Margeat almost fell flat on her face. She took one tottering step backward, then forward, and squeezing her eyes shut, dipped her finger in. She shuddered as if something cold poured down her back. After what seemed like a lifetime to Kar, the urn let go of her finger. She pulled it out and stared at it for a while. An ashy white powder covered her finger and gave off tiny glittering sparks. She then turned on her heels and faced the crowd. An overwhelming sense of alarm washed over Kar as he watched her standing, frozen, on the stage. She looked like she had turned into stone.

The audience was ready, though. Shields, pots, pans, umbrellas, and assorted protective paraphernalia covered frightened heads. Kar could hear Margeat's teacher whispering desperately from the side of the stage.

"Wiggle your finger, Margeat! Wiggle your finger!"

Margeat wiggled her finger slightly and stopped. She looked as if she wanted to run off the stage screaming.

Her teacher whispered out again. "Wiggle your finger, Margeat!"

She wiggled it again. Something odd was happening to her body. Her eyes rolled around in her head. She looked dizzy.

Kar stepped back so suddenly that he stepped on Haylen's feet. "Watch it, you clumsy …"

When he looked back, a golden horse stood prancing on the stage, its deep yellow mane glinting in the harsh rays of the sun. Its beauty brought tears to the eyes of the crowd. The audience roared with delight.

The horse shook its head and Margeat reappeared, giggling with happiness. The councilman with the quill wrote *golden horse with yellow mane* below her name. Then silence once again fell upon the crowd as everyone waited with bated breath on their decision. Would Margeat be allowed to keep this magical power? The nine councilmen conferred for a while, disappearing and then reappearing in a huddle. Soon they were seated again behind the table.

"To bind or not to bind," cried the middle councilman, standing up.

The man seated in front of the parchment paper stood up. "We, the councilmen, have agreed," he said; and paused for a few hateful seconds, "not to bind."

Pots and pans banged with enthusiasm and shields shook in jubilee.

Margeat skipped off the stage. The mood of the children lifted tremendously, and Kar seemed eager to dip his finger in that mysterious urn. Dead sorcerer, crushed dragon—it didn't matter. He hadn't realized he was holding his breath until he heard the sound of waves of applause exploding in his ears.

The urn was too high for the second child, Saff Swoonzy, to reach, and everyone waited patiently while a teacher brought in a stool for him. Again, the audience readied themselves.

Saff took another long, deep breath and dipped his finger into the urn. The urn released it immediately and Saff gave it a quick wiggle. A loud annoying crack broke the silence, and a bolt of lightning streaked across the sky. It hit a tree, splitting it in half and enveloping it in flames. The Wyck Fire Control was prepared for such incidents. A quick heavy shower by trained fingers in its vicinity stopped the fire from spreading, and the audience let out a collective sigh of relief before exploding into applause. They eventually settled down to await the verdict.

Five hooded heads nodded. The other four shook their heads in disagreement. The vote was cast. "We must bind!" Saff shrugged. What did he care, thought Kar? Saff was someone to be feared even if he was bound. Maybe one day they would need him and ask for his assistance. Start a bonfire or something. Burn down a barn. Help out at a barbecue. Kar smiled to himself. The first councilman in line stepped up to where Saff stood, grinning. He had snipped a black piece of ribbon and gestured to Saff to hold out his finger. He quickly wrapped it. The ribbon seemed to burn and melt, turning it black, although Saff did not look as if he felt a thing. Shouts of "free the finger" rang in the air but were soon silenced. Saff turned and left the stage, still smiling, with shoulders held as high as he could get them.

The third child turned into a frog and hopped down the stage before its webbed feet caught between the boards. They extricated the frog from the trap and everyone cheered. He left, unbound and embarrassed. The fourth student changed the pots, pans, shields, and anything metallic into bunches of sweet-smelling flowers. The audience squealed with delight, and Kar grinned at the sight of the parents who seemed to be already counting the money that a flower shop would bring. Sanatra Varnus, Miss Varnus' niece, skipped off the stage thrilled and unbound. She stuck her tongue out at Margeat, who was standing in the wings.

The fifth child did not fare as well. With a wiggle of his finger, hail rained on their heads and even the councilmen hastily disappeared for a bit until they could clear the stage. But the folks at the weather department couldn't wait until the child was old enough to work with them. Until then, his finger was hastily bound.

Next, the children from the village of WestWyck walked onto the stage. Having watched from the side, their anticipated fears lessened, and they were already breathing easier. There were six of them: three boys and three girls. One by one, they dipped their finger in the ashes of the urn.

Snow fell in abundance, followed by rain, and there was even another cloud writer. Another girl filled the stage with rose bushes of every color and size, making the veins in the neck of her predecessor pop with envy. One boy levitated the crowd above their chairs, and yet another sent their protective gear into outer space. The council folk brought everything back to normal before the children of EastWyck entered and took their positions.

The sun beat on their heads as the day wore on. The first child screeched in horror as she shot off the stage and flew above the crowd's astonished heads—much to the envy of Kar and Jack, who looked wistfully up at the screaming child. Another brought gasps of terror mixed with awe as the crowd cowered under their shields from a young fire-breathing dragon. The council folk quickly bound his finger. The rest slithered, hopped, and quacked, to the delight of the audience.

The day was not over yet and the worst was yet to come.

CHAOS

THE SOUTHWYCK children trouped out, almost stepping on each other, groggy from having to wait for their turn in all that heat. Kar wished somebody could magically conjure up a cool wind. There was only one person in the whole of the Wyck villages who could do that, and Arky Zerail's fee was always high. Cool winds were few and far between because the weather department could not always pay his outrageous fees.

But that was to end almost immediately. Michelle Ablelord conjured up the coolest wind anybody had ever felt before. Sighs of pleasure escaped the crowd. Kar searched the grateful faces for Arky Zerail and caught him sitting in the back, fuming. Kar couldn't help but smile. He was sure cool winds would be sweeping through the village more often, now. The weather department officials hooted with joy as Michelle exited, waving vigorously to the crowd.

The burning sun settled over the horizon. The fire-makers lit up the lanterns hanging on the poles above the crowds with a flick of their fingers. The stage looked eerie as the hooded figures cast huge shadows that mingled with the small shadows cast by the children in line for their destiny.

Angela Beaster stepped forward, smiling. She dipped her finger in the urn, pulled it out, laughed nervously, and waved it about with such enthusiasm that sparks flew from her finger like hundreds of tiny fireflies flitting into the night. She promptly turned into an apple tree—fruit and all. The crowed roared with laughter. Kar quickly turned to check her parents' reaction. They looked totally aghast at their daughter's wild behavior, but even the councilmen seemed to be shaking with mirth under their thick robes.

"Well," said Haylen, who was standing beside Kar and snickering. "There will be no shortage of apples in their home."

Kar felt sorry for the Beasters. "Yeah, I guess."

"What?" exclaimed Jack. "I think that's just great. I love apples. Maybe I'll …"

73

"I think it's your turn, Jack," interrupted Kar.

"Oh, right! Wish me luck, guys!"

Jack boldly strode to the center of the stage until he stood stiffly in front of the urn, its blue finger now glowing menacingly in the twilight. He bit his lower lip, stated his name loudly, and before he was even asked to do so, he plunged his finger in the powdery remains of the ancient wizard and pulled it out just as quickly.

Kar watched in awe as white sparks shot out slowly, than rapidly, from Jack's trembling digit. His body began to convulse, his back arching in pain as if a sharp knife had been plunged into it. His arms spread outwards to flap slowly.

"Oh, my!" cried Haylen.

A giant eagle soared into the night sky which was now alive with stars. Even the crowd seemed to have held its breath, and then, with a collective sigh of relief, it erupted into applause as the eagle flew back and settled on the edge of the table, almost toppling it over. Jack can fly! Jack can fly! What a lucky sod, thought Kar, envy brushing him slightly. He shook the bad feeling off and gazed at the sheer size of the eagle as it tried once more to perch on the table before missing it and landing heavily on the stage. It was like nothing Kar had ever heard or seen before. He couldn't help grinning at the thought of the zookeeper, Natter Kees, who was probably salivating at adding Jack to his list of birds. Even though they loved going to the zoo, he did not think that Jack would want to put himself on public display. Or did he?

The councilmen did not seem to share the villagers' enthusiasm, but in the end, Jack left the stage with his finger free of the black hideous ribbon.

Haylen Roc was next. Before she walked out, Kar could hear her desperate plea: "Please, let me be an elephant, please, or a horse, maybe a dragon. Not a mouse, please, not a mouse."

Kar clamped his hand over his mouth so that she would not hear the loud snort that escaped him.

Once more, the crowd cringed behind their shields. Haylen stuttered her name and, squeezing her eyes shut, plunged her index finger into the urn. Taking it out, she turned and shook it rapidly as if it was on fire. Sparks flew out and hit almost everyone and everything. The crowd shrieked and hid behind their shields again. Suddenly the ground beneath Kar shook slightly and stopped. Everything around him started to shimmer and fade from sight until everyone slowly disappeared. He rubbed his eyes and looked again. He no longer was standing behind a stage but on the hard ground looking at an empty field. What happened? Before he had time to panic, everyone reappeared. He was standing again at the back of the stage. The crowd looked horrified.

"Miss Roc," one of the councilmen barked, "you were not supposed to transport everyone onto the top of Mount Footsteps. It seems that your kind of magic is too dangerous and so, without further ado, please present your finger to be bound."

Sulking, Haylen shoved her finger into the councilman's face. "I think I would be an asset to this village," she grumbled, as he quickly bound her finger.

"She gave us a real fright," said Jack, running his hands through his hair.

"It was pretty freezing up there. I can just see her in the back of the crowd next year, screaming, 'Digit freedom for all!'" whispered Jack, laughing.

"Yeah, or," Kar replied, snorting with mirth as he raised his right hand into the air and wriggled his finger, "free the finger! Binding is unjust!"

They had no time to gather themselves before Haylen walked in. She saw them laughing, pushed them aside, and ran off the back of the stage in a huff.

Forgetting he was next, Miss Varnus had to come over and push the giggling Kar onto the stage. He quickly straightened himself up. There was no time to think about fear as he raced up to the center of the stage and stood before the councilmen.

But his heart gave a lurch as the brightly painted finger on the urn snuffed itself out like a candle. He looked around to see if anybody had noticed, but the crowd seemed like one dark mass to him. He moistened his lips, spoke his name as loudly as his trembling lips would allow him, dipped his right index finger into the gray powder, and turned to face the audience. All he could see were rows of metallic objects reflecting the moonlit night.

Kar waved his finger about rapidly, hoping the stage floor might just open up and swallow him. He was afraid he might just become some kind of buzzing insect. Lucas Nosty would get a thrill out of that! He waved his hand again. A very long moment of agony passed and still nothing happened. No sparks emitted from his finger. Absolutely nothing was happening.

The crowd looked around to see if they were still seated in their seats. Everything was still as it was. Kar waved his finger again. This time vigorously. No telltale sparks flew into the deepening night. The only sound he could hear was the rapid thumping of his heart, which seemed to cover the silence like the stampede of a thousand hoofs. He searched for his parents, finally meeting their white, stricken faces frozen in the front row. Where was his magic? The whole world seemed to swiftly twirl around him. He could feel the blood rushing away from his head and black spots appeared before his eyes. Suddenly the stage lifted and hovered above the crowd for a moment before coming back to rest in place as the crowd gave in to a warm applause. Kar stared at his pale, bloodless finger and then at his father. As if in extreme pain, he forced his frozen legs to move and tottered off stage, bumping into Lucas whose vicious smile almost cut his face in two.

"Just like your 'ole dad, eh? How boring," he said twisting his mouth in scorn. "Get out of my way." He shoved the weakened Kar aside. "It's time for real magic."

"Let's see if you can do better," Kar snapped back in anger, almost wanting to punch him right in the nose. At least Lucas hadn't noticed he had no magic. Shame covered him like a blanket of sweat.

"Just watch me, little boy," said Lucas, pushing him away, "and you will see what greatness looks like."

Kar felt that Lucas was up to something. He could almost smell it as he watched him pound the floorboards, with his heavy boots, towards the urn.

"Lucas Nosty, at your service," proclaimed Lucas with an exaggerated bow before the councilmen. He raised his head slightly and turned it towards Kar, who was still standing near the wing, the ugly smirk on Lucas' face stretching forever.

The urn shook slightly on the table as the turquoise painted finger reappeared and glowed even more brightly in the shadows of the night. His hands bunched at his sides, Lucas stood in the middle of the stage as if relishing the moment.

"Get on with it, young man," snapped one of the councilmen. "Put your finger in."

With a sudden swift movement, Lucas plunged his strong muscular hand down the urn's thick throat, holding it down as far as he could before the urn spat it out and rolled off the table, smashing into hundreds of pieces as if it were made of fine crystal. The councilmen leaped towards Lucas, but with one swift flick of his hand, he sent them flying off the stage, landing in a big heap on the ground. Turning to face the crowd, he waved his hand, flinging their makeshift shields high into the bright moonlit night. The crowd screamed in panic and Lucas laughed and clapped his hands like a delighted infant.

"Now I have all the magic in the world," he shouted, "and no one can stop me. Nobody will bind *my* finger." He aimed his hand again at the councilmen, who had reappeared onto the stage. They, in turn, had snatched off their white gloves and nine skeletal hands were now pointing at Lucas.

"Lucas," one of the councilmen thundered. "How dare you break the urn?"

"And what are you going to do about it?" Lucas bared his teeth at them. "Bind me? We'll see to that!"

With a flick of his wrist, Lucas sent a bolt of lighting coursing through the air. It hit the councilmen like a well-aimed spear.

Except for the last councilman, who disappeared just in time, they all exploded into flames, and in seconds, they were nothing but ashes blowing in the wind.

Lucas turned to Kar, who was still cowering with his friends at the side of the stage while pandemonium continued around them.

"You," he snarled. "How would this feel?"

Everybody was now on top of each other, trying to get away as benches snapped and children screamed in terror. Kar cringed and waited to feel the impact, but nothing happened. He looked up to see a bewildered look on Lucas' face.

"What's this?" Lucas screamed. "Why haven't you been destroyed?"

Kar shrugged his shoulders. He didn't know either.

"Stop this, Lucas," pleaded Kar. "You don't know what you're doing. It's dangerous."

"I do know what I'm doing!" Lucas roared like an angry lion. "I am taking what is mine!" Kar watched in revulsion, as, with every word Lucas spat out, he seemed to be aging right before his very eyes. The magnitude of what he had done rapidly showed on his face as wrinkles on his forehead and eyes materialized and magnified until he looked like an angry, wizened old man.

Once again, Lucas pointed his long (and now shaky) finger at Kar, who covered his head with his hands and cringed, waiting to feel himself engulfed in flames. After a very long moment, he looked up and saw a bewildered and still older Lucas staring at his hand.

"What? Magic's not working, Lucas?"

"I don't understand," Lucas said, his voice sounding as old as his body. He continued to wave his hand at Kar. "Why doesn't it work on you? What magic is yours? I thought you had none. You think I was fooled by your father's pathetic display?"

"None that I know of," said Kar, straightening himself up. "By the way, if you could just conjure yourself up a mirror and look at yourself, you might not be too happy with all this magic."

"Don't be stupid," said Lucas. "Maybe you won't be that cocky if I get rid of your friends first and deal with you later."

"I don't think so." Kar threw himself at Lucas, but fell flat on his face. He got up quickly, but Lucas had vanished. Not interested in waiting for him to return, he grabbed his terrified friends and dragged them off the stage.

The village folk were picking themselves up from the fallen debris, moaning in pain and feeling bewildered about what had happened.

Jack's and Haylen's clothes were plastered with dirt and ashes, and bits of wood stuck out from their hair. Their eyes were glazed and seemed to sink into the back of their heads.

"Are you alright, Haylen?" asked Kar, stricken with worry. The parts of her white hair that were not streaked with dirt stood straight out like glowing candles.

"Yeah, I'm fine," said Haylen, shaking her head, her eyes like big black saucers. She pulled out splinters of wood from her ears. "Of all things to happen, who would have thought Nosty had it in him?"

"We all did," said Jack. "It's just the thing that Lucas would do."

"Wish I'd thought of it," he continued under his breath to Kar. "Hey! What's with those eyes of hers?"

Haylen glared at him. "I heard that."

"Well," said Kar, "if he has taken most of the magic from the urn, he must be able to transport himself anywhere."

"Maybe he's hiding now on Mount Footsteps," said Haylen. "What's that?" She pointed to a pile of burnt cloth on the stage floor.

"What's left of the councilmen," said Kar. "You both had your eyes squeezed shut most of the time, I guess, and must have missed it. Lucas sent a bolt of lightening through them. One was left, but he disappeared in a hurry."

"Ugh," said Jack, shuddering. "What are the Wyckians going to do with only one councilman?"

"What's the difference?" asked Kar. "One or nine; they're all the same. Just a bunch of bones." Kar described what he saw.

"It was rumored," said Jack. "But I didn't believe it!"

79

"Hey," cried Haylen, "look!" She waved her right hand in front of their faces.

"Don't wave your hand," cried Jack, flinching.

"Oh, sorry," said Haylen. "I meant, look at my index finger."

"So? It's a finger," said Jack, nervously smoothing down his mop of untidy hair. "What do you want it to be?"

"I know it's a finger," said Haylen, stomping her foot impatiently and tripping on a broken board. Kar grabbed her before she fell. "It's unbound. My finger's unbound!"

They all stared in dread at her index finger. The black ribbon had disappeared, leaving in its place a red mark. They slowly looked up and met each other's horrified gaze.

THE SECRET MEETING

NOTHING WAS the same again after the ceremony. Haylen's truant finger wasn't the only one unbound; all the truant fingers of other Wyckians past and present were also free to wave about and cast their dangerous magic. The demonstrators' wishes had come true at last, although by means no one would have anticipated. The demonstrators were delighted; no less after spending most of their lives rallying against restricted magical digits. Lillian had arrived to the ceremony very late and could not believe it when everything suddenly erupted before her eyes.

In the days that followed, the villages of Wyck saw thunderstorms, hail, and sleet. Winter came full blast as those who never had the opportunity to wiggle a finger did so now with unrestrained zeal. The remaining councilman had not been seen again and no one else held enough power to set things right. The streets were filled with strange animals of the four- and (even rarer) three-legged kind. The young fire-breathing dragon had burned down a few barns by mistake, while the golden horse was last seen running into the forest. Bolts of lightning streaked through the skies as those who had never been able to enjoy the power (due to what they presumed as unjust binding) rejoiced in their freedom. Some who had demanded that their fingers be free of the binds soon regretted the years of protests and demonstrations. Others gleefully wiggled their fingers to pull trees from their roots, while still others flung them to the far corners of the world. It was not easy bringing order to the chaos that freedom brought.

Two days later, a few of the sensible inhabitants of the SouthWyck village gathered together at the Homely's to discuss the bitter outcome of *What's My Magic?* Day. Lillian helped Mrs. Homely bring the tea and small sandwiches into the living room, while outside the dark screaming sky seemed to press in on them.

"This, this unleashed magic has only brought us grief." Mr. Nooza was sitting near the fire, rubbing his chaffed hands. "By golly, a blizzard! We've never had a blizzard—and at this time of the year, no less!"

"We must think of something before they destroy the villages," said Principal Larity, shaking his head. "I hear EastWyck was practically burned to the ground."

Mr. Nooza grumbled something unpleasant in answer.

"Who among us is strong enough to bring any kind of order?" Miss Varnus brought her handkerchief to her eyes. She dabbed at the corners delicately. Today she had painted on a look of shock and horror, in keeping with the mood. "Only yesterday that little pipsqueak, Swoonzy, tried to burn my house down with a bolt of lightening. I sent him off somewhere. Don't know where he is now." A tear flowed down her painted cheek.

"There, there, Miss Varnus," said Mrs. Homely, bringing in another platter of sandwiches and setting it on the small round table in front of her. "You had to do it. We would have done the same in your position."

"But he was only a child! I don't know if he will survive beyond the village or I…" Her voice disappeared for a while. She took a deep breath. "Or I must have killed him. Nobody knows what's out there."

"We must go house to house and see who will stand with us. We must do something," said Mr. Homely, plopping his cup of tea down on the table. There are a lot of us with more power than these children. We can bring some kind of balance. For instance: Miss Varnus, since you can send anybody practically to the moon that is a plus for us. And you, Mrs. Beadlepoof: what magic is it that you have, again?"

Miss Beadlepoof stiffened in the huge armchair she occupied. "I'd rather not say."

Lillian knew that everybody had been sworn to secrecy about the meeting; but somehow, the village snoop had found out about it anyway. She made a mental note to learn more about Mrs. Beadlepoof and get to the bottom of the woman's wily ways.

"If I recall," said Mr. Nooza, wiping his mouth from crumbs, "you can change into a sparrow."

Mrs. Beadlepoof's expression of quiet rage had them shifting in their seats. Lillian fiercely stared back at her, smiling sweetly.

"Well," said Mr. Homely, trying to lighten the mood, "I am sure that will come in handy somehow."

Miss Beadlepoof looked over at Lillian. "What's wrong with your eyes, silly child?"

Lillian uncrossed her eyes and blinked.

"You can be our messenger," piped in Mrs. Homely.

"I beg your pardon?" said Mrs. Beadlepoof.

"A messenger," repeated Mrs. Homely. "We need to send a message to the remaining councilman. He hasn't shown up to help us with all this. Has anybody seen him?"

Everybody shook their heads. Lillian was concentrating on boring a hole through Mrs. Beadlepoof's head again.

"Why me? Miss Varnus can send anything anywhere." Mrs. Beadlepoof waved her hand in Miss Varnus's direction. "She can send him a note on a spear or something." She raised her teacup and sucked at it loudly until she was finished.

"What a great idea," said Mr. Nooza, beaming at her. "A message. We need him here to bind those fingers up again. That will set things in order."

Mr. Homely shook his head. "If he could do that, he would have already."

"What do you mean?" asked Mr. Nooza, picking up a finger cookie left from Kar's birthday and biting into it.

"Just what I mean. If he could have, he would have done it by now. I think with the demise of the eight other councilmen, he doesn't have enough power over anyone. Why do you think he has disappeared?"

"Well, he should know something we don't. Maybe he has some information that will help us at least," said Mrs. Homely. "More tea, anyone?"

Mrs. Beadlepoof was the first to lift her cup. "I don't see what I have to do with it?"

"You can fly, Mrs. Beadlepoof; you can fly," said Mr. Nooza, spitting cookie crumbs.

"I haven't changed into a sparrow since … since I was a young girl. Heights make me dizzy!" Mrs. Beadlepoof looked ready to faint.

"I say we take a vote on it," said Miss Varnus, ignoring her act of drama. "All who agree that Mrs. Beadlepoof be sent up the mountain to speak to the councilman, say 'aye.'"

"I'll go on my broomster," said Lillian, who had not spoken a word during the whole time because she was too busy trying to read Mrs. Beadlepoof's mind and hide her foot under the chair at the same time. She had already met the forger and lived to tell about it. What was the big deal about a frightened councilman hiding in a cave?

"You are only a child," scoffed Miss. Varnus. "He'll eat you alive." She quickly put her hand over her mouth and looked apologetically at Mrs. Beadlepoof.

"You are all trying to get me killed," cried Mrs. Beadlepoof. "You can 'aye' yourselves blue in the face, but I'm not flying up that mountain!"

"Yes, I guess you're right," said Mrs. Homely, sipping her tea delicately. "We need a braver person to deal with this." She avoided Mrs. Beadlepoof's glance and quickly looked out the window to suppress a smile.

"Yes," continued Principal Larity innocently. "I am sure there is someone else who has the guts to do this. As we recently discovered, young Mr. Bold can change into an eagle. Now, that is an impressive bird."

"Magnificent," said Mr. Nooza. "It takes the courage of the young these days."

Lillian leaned forward, raising her voice: "I'll do it."

"No, I'll do it," murmured Mrs. Beadlepoof between gnashing teeth. She sloppily sipped more tea.

They pretended not to pay attention to Mrs. Beadlepoof or to Lillian, who kept waving her hand in the air like a student trying to get the teacher's attention and failing miserably.

"Are you sure that Mr. Bold will allow his son to career off into the mountains like that? It has to be done at night," continued Principal Larity, ignoring Mrs. Beadlepoof's grip on his elbow and Lillian's flailing arm, "when no one can see him."

"They are the Bolds," said Mr. Nooza, throwing his hands up in the air. "They're known for their courage."

"I'll do it," yelled Mrs. Beadlepoof. "Alright, I'll do it!" She banged the teacup on the side table.

Lillian sat fuming while everyone pretended to seem surprised and pleased. She hoped the councilman would tear her tiny fat sparrow body into bits and feed it to a baby dragon.

"You don't need to, really; I mean, Mrs. Beadlepoof," said Mrs. Homely, breaking the silence. "You don't really have to. We understand."

"When would you like me to go?" asked Mrs. Beadlepoof, the frown on her forehead bunching up like a ball.

"When Nero Dowell stops playing blizzard," piped in Miss Varnus.

(The blizzard had subsided by the next day because Mrs. Dowell found out her son was the culprit of the terrible snowstorm. She had grounded him and wrapped his destructive finger in medical gauze).

They were to meet again to send Mrs. Beadlepoof off with a message. Lillian arrived at the Homely's first; but instead of going into the house, she quickly hid behind some overgrown bushes with her broomster. Mrs. Beadlepoof arrived next and the rest followed within ten minutes. They all stood outside on the front lawn feeling flushed and uncomfortable. Giant snowflakes swirled slowly, melting before they even touched the ground because another truant finger was causing a heat wave.

"I do not like anyone to watch," said Mrs. Beadlepoof firmly. Lillian pressed deeper into the bushes as Mrs. Beadlepoof unknowingly walked towards her. She held her breath, reminding herself that those ears could hear one lowly ant marching between blades of grass.

"Do you know where the councilman lives?" asked Mrs. Homely.

"I know where everyone lives," answered Mrs. Beadlepoof with a sneer that twisted her thin lips. "Up there somewhere." She waved her hand. "You can get rid of those ugly snow clouds for me. I don't think the weather department is going to bear down and ticket you for misuse of magic right now."

Mrs. Homely wiggled her finger and the clouds disappeared to reveal a crescent moon. "That should be enough light for you."

"If I'm not back by morning, then I guess I'll never be back," she said, trying to look as mournful as possible, which made her look like a bleary-eyed cow.

Miss Varnus rolled her dolled-up eyes. "You'll be back."

"That's easy for you to say," huffed Mrs. Beadlepoof. "You're not flying into the jaws of death."

"Now, now," said Principal Larity. "The councilman is the remaining head of the Wyck villages. He'll probably be happy to see you."

"That remains to be seen." Mrs. Beadlepoof inhaled deeply and let out a huge sigh. "Well, I guess it's time to meet my fate. You can go back inside now. I don't want anybody looking at me when I change into a sparrow. At least give me a little bit of dignity."

They silently trooped back into the house. Mrs. Homely turned and waved before shutting the door. "Good luck, Mrs. Beadlepoof."

Instead of turning into a tiny, fat sparrow, Mrs. Beadlepoof snapped her fingers and disappeared from sight.

By now, Lillian's face had practically turned blue, and she gasped in a huge amount of air. To her dismay, she began to hiccup. Quickly pushing her broomster from where she hid it, Lillian hopped on and, pointing it towards Mount Footsteps, took off as fast as the old, sputtering contraption could fly while sounds of popping wine corks escaped from her lips. It took her a few minutes to reach the edge of the cliff where the opening of the cave to the late councilmen's dwelling stretched wide like a yawning cat. Luckily no new snowstorms had started up.

Gently, she landed the broomster at the end of the narrow cliff and with her back pressed to the cold mountain, edged her way to the opening of the cave. She pushed forward, inching her way into the cave, feeling her way against the clammy walls until she could see the backs of two heads sitting in large armchairs facing a roaring fire. She fell on her hands and knees, her heart ready to pop out of its ribcage, and crawled slowly towards them.

"... And they thought I could turn into a sparrow." Mrs. Beadlepoof's laughter sounded harsh and evil.

The councilman laughed with her. "You have been a good friend all these years, Mrs. Beadlepoof, and we have rewarded you well, but now we need you more than ever. I mean—I need you *now* more than ever."

"Oh, how so?" asked Mrs. Beadlepoof, tittering happily. Except for the exploding sounds of burning pieces of wood now and then, there was silence for a while.

Lillian could not believe her ears. What was this? Mrs. Beadlepoof was nothing but a spy, a snoop, a meddler, and a host of other names she was too upset to recall at the moment. No wonder she knew what was happening around town before it even had a chance to happen. She was probably in and out of places before anybody noticed she was there.

The councilman tilted his hooded head closer to Mrs. Beadlepoof's large one. Lillian wished she could hear them better and suddenly realized that she could. With a tiny wiggle of her finger, she shrunk into a bunny, big floppy ears and all. The sudden roar of sound hit bunny eardrums like the crack of thunder. On soft padded paws she hopped closer, squeezing herself between the two armchairs, and settled down.

"It has been said that the birth of twins will bring our world into chaos."

"What do you mean?"

"I do not know yet, and with all the other councilmen burnt to a crisp, I do not have all the answers. I am too weak to even bind fingers. I mostly dealt with informing the others of any misbehavior among the villagers. Thanks to you, of course."

"Don't mention it. It was my pleasure."

Lillian's round furry tail trembled intensely.

"What we know is this," continued the councilman. "Lucas stole the powers of the urn; therefore, suffice it to say, he must have a twin. Does he have a brother, or maybe a sister?"

"Not that I know of," replied Mrs. Beadlepoof.

Lillian could hear a cup rattle and something like a biscuit breaking in half. She could never stop eating—that filthy spy! He must pay her a lot to keep her in food. I wonder how much he pays, she thought. No. I mustn't think of taking on such a horrid job.

"He has two siblings about four or five years younger. All the twins I know are the Squinty Boys, who are not really twins, and two older women in our village."

The councilman had gotten up and was pacing the floor now. "Lucas stole the power of the urn. The prophecy says he has a twin. His powers are weak now, but they will grow stronger every day. He has to learn how to handle each one before he can use it successfully. At least that will give us time to find the twin and kill him ... or her."

A teacup rattled. "Kill?"

"Yes," continued the councilman. "What I do recall is that if the prophecy were to come true, the only way to return to what we had is to kill the twin. When his twin is dead, Lucas' power evaporates. Do you have any information you can give me at the moment? Anything that maybe at the time seemed innocent, but now, after all this, might look suspicious, from the time Lucas was born?"

"Not that I can think of at the moment, no."

"Anything that looked suspicious to you this past year—month—week?"

"Well, the only thing I can think of now," she paused to slurp tea, "is that while I was taking my morning walk the other day ... or you might say ... my morning forays for neighborhood news, I came across Lillian. She chatted away like the fool she is until she asked about Mr. Fountaine. I took it as silly, idle conversation from her; but now, I don't know. She might have had an ulterior motive."

Lillian gritted her sharp tiny teeth and furiously twitched her furry ball of a tail. Who does Beadlepoof think she is, calling her a fool? The beastly spy!

"Well, she might have been interested in forging some kind of certificate. You've been saying she can't keep a job," replied the councilman.

"I guess you're right, but who would loan her such an outrageous amount of money? You know they cost hundreds of Dragons, if not thousands!"

"Hmm. You might be right." He paused for a moment. Lillian could hear him scratching something with his gloved hand. "I'm beginning to remember something. Let me tell you what I can recall. Remember the Marcels?"

"Yes, those fools with their stupid prophesies. I thought you got rid of that family."

"We were able to eliminate Mr. Marcel, but his wife eluded us. We knew later that she died; but not before she gave birth, and we could not find the child even though we tried for a year. We concluded the child died with her."

"Oh, I see what you are getting at. You think the child did not die?"

"No, I think she had twins and was able to hide them in this very village. If so, one of them is Lucas, if the prophecy holds true. He bears no resemblance to the Nostys and, without a doubt in my mind, looks the spitting image of his dead father. Why are you smiling so, Mrs. Beadlepoof?"

"I have an idea, but I need to check on something first."

"What is this idea that is making you so cheery suddenly?"

"There is another boy I know who also bears no resemblance to his parents in the least. I have often asked them why, but they have always scoffed at my questions and ignored me."

"Who is this boy, pray tell?"

"Kar!"

Lillian shook uncontrollably between the sides of the armchairs. The heat from the fire almost burned her whiskers and she badly wanted to sneeze. She squirmed uncomfortably as she listened to their devious plan. When she thought she had heard enough, she slowly backed out from between the chairs, but before she could control herself, she sneezed violently. At the same time, a log fell in the fire, cracked open, and expelled something foul.

"Did you hear that?" asked Mrs. Beadlepoof.

Every muscle in Lillian's tiny body hardened. She could hear Mrs. Beadlepoof turning in her seat.

"I guess it's just the fire," she continued. "I could've sworn it sounded like a bunny sneezing."

Lillian was amazed. Did she know everything? How would a bunny's sneeze sound different from another animal's sneeze? How did she do that?

"So, you think it's that boy, Kar, whose father thought he could fool everyone by levitating the stage?" Suddenly the councilman jumped up from his chair. "Yes!" he cried, "of course! That must be it. No wonder the urn shied away from Kar. It was not his destiny to receive any magic. Now we can get rid of Lucas!"

"How?" Mrs. Beadlepoof screeched, and Lillian's ears shot up.

"Like I just told you, Mrs. Beadlepoof, one destroys the other. To get rid of Lucas, we get rid of Kar."

Lillian had no idea of how she managed to scoot out of the cave without being seen. It must have been because they were too excited and engrossed in their plan to notice her. They were laughing gleefully at what seemed to them to be the obvious conclusion. Not if she could help it!

Lillian dumped the broomster in the front yard of the Homely residence, which had been ruined by the constant weather changes, and snuck inside. Everyone was still sitting in the living room, twirling their thumbs and staring at the ceiling in agitated boredom. No one noticed her as she slumped into a chair, trying to catch her breath. Her head ached with all that she had just heard and seen. She pressed her fingers against her temples.

Mrs. Beadlepoof was not only the biggest town gossip, but the biggest spy as well. Lillian could hardly believe it. Could she tell everyone that Mrs. Beadlepoof had guessed Kar's identity? Was Kar's mother the woman who burned the prophecy on the cave wall and scrawled her name at the bottom? Luna Marcel, who died trying to save her sons? And how could Lucas Nosty be Kar's twin brother? It was too horrible to be true. Lillian stifled a groan. Not even the Homelys knew where their son came from. She twisted in her chair, uncertain about what to do.

"Mrs. Beadlepoof has been gone such a long time now." Miss Varnus had nearly torn her tissue to shreds. "I hope she's alright."

Beadlepoof's just peachy, thought Lillian, trying to keep her face composed despite all the fury she felt inside.

"Oh, I'm sure Mrs. Beadlepoof's fine," said Mr. Nooza, not turning away from the point he was staring at on the floor now. It had started to rain outside and the winds were picking up. "She …"

A frenzied pecking at the window interrupted him. Mrs. Homely walked over to the window and opened it. A wet sparrow flew into the room and landed bottom first on the floor.

"I'm never, ever going to do this ever again," cried Mrs. Beadlepoof as she stood on the rug, wet and disheveled. "It was terrible. That, that, skeleton was going to kill me! Didn't I tell you that I was flying into the jaws of death? Didn't I? Didn't I?" Her bosom was heaving like a bull ready to charge.

Lillian's face turned purple with rage. Not only could she transport herself wherever she wanted, but she could actually turn into a sparrow, too. They must have paid her with more than just Dragons! And what a drama queen, pretending she was frightened. If only she could just blurt everything out, but she knew it would be more dangerous for everyone if she revealed what she knew. Lillian knew it was wiser to keep it to herself for now. She folded her arms and scowled deeply at Mrs. Beadlepoof.

Mr. Homely jumped out of his armchair next to the fire and helped Mrs. Beadlepoof into it.

"Oh, my, what happened?" cried Mrs. Homely, throwing a shawl over her shoulders.

It took a while for Mrs. Beadlepoof to pretend to catch her breath. After about four cups of tea and two platefuls of cookies, she related the false events of her perilous journey. Only Lillian, who hoped the intensity of her deadly piercing stare would somehow paralyze Mrs. Beadlepoof's tongue, knew that the woman was a lying, cheating, good-for-nothing spy!

"He wanted to kill me!" She wrung her hands as she recanted lies of how she pleaded for her life and how the councilman eventually agreed to help them. He couldn't bind any fingers yet, but he could help bring back the peace if the villagers agreed to help.

Mrs. Homely asked, "What kind of help does he need?"

Mrs. Beadlepoof took a moment to gasp for air. "He says that the only way to get rid of Lucas' power is to find the child who holds no power at all." She deliberately allowed her gaze to land on Mr. Homely. "When we find that child, Lucas loses all the magic he stole from the urn and everything goes back to normal again." She was practically chirping the last words.

All the blood seemed to have drained from Mr. Homely's face. "When we find this child, what do we do with him ... or her?" He could barely squeak the words out.

"Kill him," Mrs. Beadlepoof said, biting into another cookie, her gaze sweeping the room with suppressed glee, "or her." She lowered her head, but not before Lillian caught the tiny, evil smile that appeared for a split second.

Lillian couldn't believe that Mrs. Beadlepoof was even telling them that much. Would she tell them that it was Kar they had to kill? What could she, Lillian, do now? She had no power to stop anybody, let alone crazy Mrs. Beadlepoof.

Mrs. Beadlepoof's thin lips opened and closed like a goldfish gasping for air, seeming to want to say something more, but not managing to find the words. Lillian wished with all her might that she would go home before she added anything new. Maybe, Lillian thought, staring down at her big foot, Mrs. Beadlepoof might think it was too dangerous to mention Kar's name right now. Mr. Homely might not take the news too well, and Mrs. Beadlepoof was not the most popular person in the room. That would certainly be all she would say at this point.

Suddenly all heads looked up to the ceiling. There was a pounding on the roof. It was hail. They decided to leave things as they were for now and head home before the weather worsened. Lillian pretended to follow them out and hid quietly among the bushes again. She covered her head from the onslaught of the hailstorm with her flimsy jacket. She then slipped back into the house when the coast was clear.

NOT A HOMELY

WHILE HIS parents bade Lillian good-bye, it was already past midnight. Kar softly shut his bedroom door. He threw another log into the dying hearth and watched it catch fire, shooting sparks onto the woolen rug and up the chimney. Even the furniture in the room seemed to share his anxiety. The chest of drawers moved back and forth between two different corners every few minutes. The table just couldn't get comfortable, fidgeting and adjusting itself like a dog shaking water off its back after a bath. The grandfather clock seemed to have the hardest time figuring out where to stand and after a few failed attempts at finding the right corner, threw itself into the closet and slammed the door.

Kar, who usually had the habit of pacing around the room whenever he was nervous, was content to let the chair he was sitting on do it for him. He had previously sat like a mouse at the top of the stairs, unable to see Lillian and his parents but able to hear them loud and clear. They had forgotten to shut the living room door and all Wyckians had raucous voices: a pleasant 'good morning' could sometimes sound like an invitation to a fight.

What he had just heard was worse than standing on the stage wiggling his finger and finding he had no magic at all. All his life he felt he was different. The news that he was not a Homely ripped through his heart like a sharp arrow, leaving him with an aching hole in his chest. Now he knew why he did not look anything like his parents! Poor Lillian, she must have gone through such a fright. He had not been able to hear the rest of her tale because halfway through her story, his parents had realized the door to the living room was opened and quickly shut it. All he could gather was that the councilman did not have enough power to bind fingers, Lucas had stolen all the magic in the urn, and that to get rid of Lucas, they had to get rid of the one who held no magic—him. And what was worse—he was not a Homely at all! He heard them mentioning a twin and a woman called Luna Marcel but the door slammed shut before he could find out just who was Lucas' twin. The idea of Lucas having a twin was horrifying.

He threw himself on the bed, but failed to realize that it had just started to change position. He found himself lying flat on his back on the woolen rug (also bought from one of those estate sales but, thankfully, not a nervous wreck like the other pieces of furniture). It gently wrapped itself around him. He lay still on the wood floor, feeling snug.

After a few moments of feeling utterly sorry for himself, he looked up and saw a large, dark shadow fly past his window. He jumped up, flung the window wide open, and stretched out as far as he could to see what was out there. Something swooped past him, pushed him aside, and crashed to the floor in a jumble of giant gray feathers.

"I've been practicing," said Jack, grinning and getting up off of the crumpled rug that had slid all the way to the back of the wall. "But I haven't been able to land as well as I did that first time on stage. I keep landing head first or on my behind. It hurts the same if I am human or eagle." He spat a gray feather out of his mouth and rubbed his backside.

Kar's bed had just shuffled towards him, perhaps afraid of Jack's abrupt landing, so Kar sat on its edge and gave Jack a weak smile. "It's always perfect the first time around, they say."

"What's wrong? You don't look good," said Jack, grabbing the chair as it passed by. "Whoa, fella," cried Jack, as it continued to the other side of the room, "take it easy." The chair stopped.

"Wow," said Kar, genuinely surprised, "where have I been? I had no idea they would actually listen. Grandfather clock! Come out here!"

The closet door swung open and the clock eased its way into the room. "Stand there!" Kar pointed and the clock dragged itself reluctantly to the corner. "And stay there until I say otherwise!" As usual, the clock shifted to one side and leaned on the wall as if put out by the command.

"You and you and you," yelled Kar, pointing to the dresser, table, and bed. "I want you here, and you here, and you here: and stay there until I say otherwise!" With some reluctance, the rest of the furniture marched to where Kar commanded.

"Finally, a room I can call my own," exclaimed Kar. "Thanks, Jack! All those years wasted."

Jack grinned. "Don't mention it." He pulled the chair over to the dying fire, sat down, and stretched his legs. "It's a mess outside. A lot of people are frightened and worried. That dragon has been practicing his fire-breathing tricks on a few homes. They also say Lucas might come back."

Kar's bad mood came flooding back and he fell silent.

Jack eyed his long-time friend. "Kar, is there something wrong? Tell me."

"I can't." Kar tried to control his emotions, but failed and turned his face away from Jack.

"Why not? You know something, don't you?" Jack could not hide the excitement in his voice. "You have to tell me," he pleaded.

Kar looked at his friend. Would everything change if he told him what he just heard? Would Jack rat on him? Could he trust Jack?

"I have to leave, Jack," said Kar, finally.

"Leave? To go where?"

"I don't know. Somewhere, somewhere far away, maybe even tonight."

"I don't get it, Kar. Why can't you tell me?" Jack's feelings were hurt, and it showed in his voice. "I thought we were best friends."

"Maybe you won't be my friend after I tell you," said Kar.

Jack shook his head to deny the possibility. "I'll always be your friend. Always. Trust me."

Kar thought for a while. He needed a friend to confide in and Jack had been his friend all his life—all of his soon-to-be very short life. "I overheard something today," said Kar. Jack leaned forward eagerly.

The first words were difficult to say, but after that Kar poured out everything he knew, keeping his face down and his voice in a whisper. "And so I'm not who I thought I was."

Jack sat up straight and whistled low in disbelief. "I can't believe it."

"Believe it."

"What're you going to do now?" asked Jack.

"I was going to leave, but now I know what I have to do. It came to me while I was telling you about it," said Kar.

"What's that?" asked Jack.

"Give myself up."

Jack jumped off the chair. "No, you can't."

"Why not? The villages are in ruins. Lucas is loose with all that power and the only way out is—well—me." The last words were tough for Kar and he turned his head away to avoid looking at his friend.

"No!" cried Jack, marching over to Kar. "I won't allow it." The chair tiptoed after him and gave the back of Jack's knees a nudge. Jack sat down again.

"Mrs. Beadlepoof will get her way sooner or later," continued Kar. "It has to be done anyway. I have to die!" Kar couldn't bear for Jack to see his face twisting from the very thought of an early death. He didn't know what he wanted to do with his life but he'd always wanted the opportunity to figure it out. He wanted a life.

"Not if I can help it," retorted Jack. He was angry. Wings began to sprout on his back and flap wildly about the room knocking things over. "I'll be back. Don't go anywhere."

Kar sat motionless on the bed after Jack flew out the window. He wanted to stop Jack from doing anything rash. He wanted to barge in on his parents and demand the truth from them. But he couldn't lift his legs to get up. His life was draining away. All the happy memories, all the joys, were masked in lies. They could have told him. Why didn't they? And where did they get the birth certificate? It had their names on it.

Kar Homely, son of Mr. Albert and Mrs. Clara Homely of SouthWyck. Born on the twenty-seventh of May in the eighteenth century of Wyck. They even had the time of birth! Half past midnight. Maybe they were his parents. Maybe all of this was just a misunderstanding.

Kar stood up, raised his right hand, pointing to some books on the desk. He wiggled his finger. Nothing happened. He wiggled it again. The books did not rise and hover over his desk. He was doomed.

Kar walked over to the mirror and stared at his reflection. He seemed a lot older than he had that morning. His eyes were sunken and his mouth was stripped of color, blending in with the rest of his pale features and making him look grotesque. Like an old man. Like Lucas! For a while he stood in front of the mirror, hoping this was nothing but a nightmare and that he would be jolted awake, as usual. Eventually he understood that he wasn't going to wake from this nightmare. As his eyes re-focused, he was once again aware of the room around him. He decided that he was entitled to know the whole truth before he could make a decision.

Wearily, like the old man he felt he was, he walked out the door towards his parents' bedroom. Standing in front of the closed door, he wondered for a moment if he should demand an answer now or wait until morning. He should be furious with them, but he felt numb and weak. Just lifting his hand and knocking felt like too much of an ordeal.

The sound of weeping from downstairs broke through his bewildered thoughts. He looked over the banister. The door to the living room was slightly ajar and he could see the dying light of the fire. He tiptoed down the stairs and stood behind the door. He could hear his mother gently sobbing.

"Don't cry, Clara," said Mr. Homely. "We'll find a way out of this."

"I don't… I don't see how?" Mrs. Homely blew her nose.

"I told you. Nobody's going to find out he has no magic."

"Oh, you fool, Albert. It's obvious. Mrs. Beadlepoof will never keep what she heard on the mountain a secret. What if somebody asks Kar to show his magic and he can't? You're not always with him. Soon they will know and they will be pounding on the door for his head. Oh, Albert, we must save our little boy. We must."

"I'm sure Mrs. Beadlepoof is not foolish enough to tell anyone. She knows what is at stake here," said Mr. Homely with a calmness even Kar knew he must have not felt.

"But … but … but …" Mrs. Homely stifled her wails. "She's Mrs. Beadlepoof! It's her job to tell everyone! Her life is more important than our son's! She's nothing but the village spy and she's dangerous."

A sudden commotion from the direction of his bedroom interrupted his eavesdropping. Kar leaped up the stairs and quickly ran back into his room. Jack and Haylen stood by the window. Haylen looked worried, her eyes were puffy and red, and her glossy white hair seemed flatter than usual and dull.

"You didn't tell Haylen, did you?" whispered Kar furiously.

"Of course I did," said Jack. "We're all friends, aren't we?"

"Yes, but …"

"Kar we have to get you out of town before anybody finds out," blurted Haylen.

"I can't," said Kar. "I'll feel like a traitor if I leave. I can't leave this town to the mercy of Lucas' whim. We all know what that is like."

"This is not your fault and you shouldn't be the one to suffer," said Haylen. "We must find your real parents. Maybe they know how to stop this."

"They are dead, from what I've heard," said Kar, hardly opening his mouth. "What are they good for anyway?"

"They must have come from somewhere," said Haylen. "You might have relatives. We could find those people. Maybe they can save you. They should know something!"

Kar put his finger on his mouth to quiet his frantic friend. "Shh! My, uh, parents might hear you!"

"Sorry," whispered Haylen, clamping her hand over her mouth.

"How am I supposed to do that? I don't have a single clue as to who they are or where they came from," said Kar. His eyes flashed the color of his cardigan. Purple.

"We're going to help you," said Haylen. "Lillian mentioned the Marcel family. Remember in the piano room I said that I heard from my parents that they actually exiled a couple from the villages? Anyway, my mom said their names were Artimus and Luna Marcel. Maybe they are your real parents?"

"What if they are Lucas' parents instead? How are we to know?" Kar threw his hands into the air. He had not been able to hear all the conversation between his parents and had missed the part where he might be Lucas' twin.

"Well, it's a start," said Jack. "If we can find them, we can tell them to come and take their son away."

"Yeah, I'm sure it will be that simple, Jack," retorted Kar.

"Well, I think it's a good idea," piped Haylen.

It wasn't any use. Kar could not persuade them to stay. Haylen already had a plan set up. She would magically transport everyone to the top of Mount Footsteps, and from there, they could see where they needed to go next. Jack reminded her that her magical abilities would likely take the whole neighborhood with them to Mount Footsteps. "Remember how everyone in the audience and on the stage ended up on top of Mount Footsteps?" he cried. "You might take the whole house or even the neighborhood with us. I don't think Mr. and Mrs. Homely would be happy about that!"

Haylen refused to listen. She was certain it was just a matter of concentration. She had brought an ancient map from the school library that she had conveniently forgotten to give back. She spread it out on the bed.

"Somewhere here," she said, poking the map, "is the village of Yongtown. They are known for being very nice and helpful."

"How do you know this?" asked Jack, annoyed with her. "No one has ever left the villages of Wyck to find out how nice people are on the other side of the mountain."

"I read it somewhere," Haylen retorted. "You know. Reading? You should try it once in a while."

"Huh! I read just as much as you do," Jack spat back. "Hardly any!"

Haylen tossed her head and turned to Kar. "Now we'll go home and get packed. We want to meet here as soon as possible. We only have a few hours left until daylight. We should get out before everybody wakes up."

"I have to tell you something." Kar looked pained as he faced his friends.

"What?" Haylen and Jack looked up at Kar from where they were sitting on the edge of the bed.

"Remember when you got everybody on top of Mount Footsteps?"

"Yeah," said Haylen giggling slightly. "I was so scared."

"Well, I was left behind," said Kar.

"I don't understand," said Jack.

"Magic doesn't work on me. I can't do it, and it doesn't have any effect on me."

"What? You mean you really stayed behind?" Haylen's eyes suddenly took the shape of an owl's for a moment.

"Yeah," said Kar, grinning slightly. "It was creepy. There was just an empty field all around me and then everyone reappeared. Then Lucas tried to fry me. He was so upset when he couldn't throw a single spark my way that he just upped and vanished!"

Jack and Haylen looked at each other for a moment. She folded the map, trying not to make any noise. "I wonder what it all means."

"Since you might take the neighborhood with you and leave Kar behind," said Jack, making a face at Haylen, "and the mountain is too steep to climb, there is only one way left."

"And what is that, Mr. Bold?" asked Haylen crossing her arms. "You can't fly us all there."

"We'll take my dad's broomster. He has a three-seater. The Triple Alpha Broomster!"

Kar whistled.

"That's stealing," said Haylen. "We can't do that. They'll have the Flying Security Patrol after us."

"You don't think they'll have the patrol looking for three missing kids anyway? We might as well be getting away quickly," said Jack. "What's the difference? Can you think of a better plan?"

"None of us has a license to fly," added Haylen. "They'll put us in jail."

"Before or after they chop off Kar's head?" yelled Jack.

"Quiet!" cried Kar. "My parents will hear you."

"Ugh!" Haylen made a face.

"Not having a license will not stop anyone from flying," continued Jack, lowering his voice. "I've known how to fly that thing for a couple of years now."

"It's an idea," said Kar, feeling slightly better at the prospect. At least they had a plan that might work this time.

"Fine," said Haylen, "but I'm not happy about this."

"Great," said Jack. "Haylen and I will be back in a half hour or so. Make sure you dress warmly. It's going to be very cold on top of Mount Footsteps. I should know. I was there!"

OVER MOUNT FOOTSTEPS

IT WAS almost dawn when they met again. Kar and Jack hovered impatiently outside Haylen's bedroom window. She couldn't decide what to wear or how much she needed to pack in the knapsack she carried on her back. She eventually chose a pair of brown baggy trousers tucked into a pair of black boots. She had on layers of tops, knowing that the trip over the mountain would be cold, and topped everything with a black cape trimmed with black fur. She had no time to admire herself in the mirror. She left a short letter of explanation for her parents. If she was grounded for life after this, she told Kar later, so be it.

Kar kept gesturing to Haylen to hurry up. The sun was peaking over the treetops and a bolt of lightning appeared suddenly, streaking across the sky and hitting the ground with tremendous force. Someone was practicing again. At last, bag in hand, Haylen flung herself behind Kar. Jack gunned the broomster and they took off. Haylen screamed and grabbed Kar around the waist.

"Is this how you fly?" She yelled over the wind. "I almost fell off!"

"It's not me, it's the broomster! It has a little extra kick. Try strapping yourself in with the belt on the side," Jack yelled back. "My dad installed it there after my brother fell off once."

Haylen found the leather belt and tied it around her waist. The trip up the mountain was difficult, as strong winds buffeted the broomster. They had to make a stop once when Haylen screeched that if they didn't stop, she would throw up on them. Since the wind was blowing from behind them, they took her threat seriously. Jack found a ledge and landed clumsily.

"I thought you said you knew how to fly." Haylen's face was green as she ran behind some rocks. They heard the sound of retching.

Kar and Jack stood on the ledge rubbing their hands from the cold. Dawn had broken, but a heavy mist crept up the mountainside, obscuring their view of the villages. Kar pointed over Jack's head to a flute poking out from a small opening in the mountainside nearby. "I wonder what that is?" asked Kar.

"It looks like a flute," said Jack, looking up. "I bet someone lives here."

"Do you think?" asked Kar.

"Think what?" Haylen had returned. Her cheeks were flushed and strands of hair were plastered to her face.

Kar pointed to the pipe. "What do you make of that?"

"A flute," said Haylen. "Someone lives here?"

They walked a few steps along the ledge until they found a round opening into what might be a large cave. A soft glow emanated from within. They hesitated before entering the opening, uncertain what might be in store for them within.

"It must be the councilmen's cave. We have to leave," said Jack, turning back. "My dad says they live in a cave on Mount Footsteps."

"Wait," whispered Haylen. "We know that only one survived and maybe he's not here at the moment."

"Yeah," said Jack, eyeing Kar, "he's probably out looking for you."

"If so," said Haylen, "this would be the last place he would think to look, wouldn't it?" She strolled into the opening and looked back. "Coming, boys?"

Jack and Kar reluctantly followed behind, still unsure.

Logs smoldered in a large fireplace at the opposite end of the room. A black cauldron hung above the bright ashes. Haylen found a stack of fresh logs and threw them on the embers. Soon a fire was roaring again. Jack lit a few more of the candles that lay around the cave. Shadows sprung across the room like a colony of bats taking flight. Kar still felt uncertain about their safety in the cave. "Someone might see the smoke coming out of the flute."

"We'll be gone before the mist clears," replied Haylen. "Let's look around and see if we can find anything interesting to help us in our search." They wandered about the cave picking up objects and scrutinizing them. At the back of the cave, leather-bound books were piled in a corner, covered with years of dust and spider webs.

"It's been a long time since any of them read these books," said Jack, picking one up. A spider scuttled out of the way. *"Everything You Need to Know and Then Some."* He picked up another. "*How to Kill a Dragon in Ten Easy Steps.* Now this is something I would read."

"Let me find something, too," said Haylen excitedly. She picked up another book and wiped the dust off. *"What Your Teacher Doesn't Want You to Know."* Haylen laughed. "I wish we had these books in our library."

"Here's one that looks interesting." Jack handed a book to Kar.

"History Keepers. What does that mean?" asked Kar.

Jack shrugged. "History? How should I know? Maybe we can find a clue in it."

Kar opened the book. The handwriting was fancy with a lot of twirls and loops. The first page showed a sketch of a man in long robes standing on top of a mountain with his arms raised. Each of his upturned palms held a globe. At the bottom of the page was written one sentence.

"He who often writes of the past can see the future clearly," read Kar.

Haylen looked over his shoulder. "I wonder what that means."

"It's against the law to read any kind of book depicting prophesies or futuristic concepts in the Wyck villages," said Jack rattling off the law by heart. "I wonder why they have these books here? It seems they haven't touched any of them for a long time."

"That law is according to whom at this point?" asked Haylen with one hand on her hip. "With only one councilman left, there are no longer any laws. Not even binding ones. I say each one of us take a book before we go. They might give us a clue to something."

"I'm going to take the dragon book," said Jack, hugging it to his chest.

"That is a silly choice. There aren't any more dragons. That book won't hold anything relevant for us," snapped Haylen.

"Oh, yes, there are dragons again," replied Kar. "What's his name shape-shifted into a baby dragon. Remember?"

"What's his name is a Wyckian," said Haylen almost sputtering in exasperation. "We don't kill Wyckians in…give me that book." She snatched the book from Jack, "Ten easy steps."

"You never know," said Jack, grabbing the book back. "I'm taking it. We might meet a real dragon one of these days and then you'll thank me."

Haylen rolled her eyes. "Well, I'm going to find something more interesting than that." She rummaged through the rest of the pile. "This looks pretty good. Wyck history."

"Ah, why are you taking that one?" whined Jack. "We take that subject in school. We already have books on that topic."

"Maybe they have something in here that we haven't taken in school," she retorted. "This book looks different. Kar, what are you taking?"

Kar was holding open a book. "I guess Keepers of History. Maybe they have something on the Marcel family?"

"Good idea," said Jack. "Now let's get out of here."

Kar turned and dropped the book.

"It is so very kind of you to light the fireplace. It is a little chilly outside these days, don't you think?"

The last of the councilmen stood in his heavy purple robes, the gruesome hood still covering his face. Two piercing hot coals glinted where his eyes should have been. He rubbed his sparkling white-gloved hands over the flames.

"My bones get chilly sometimes. Haha—haha—haha."

His eerie laugh echoed around the cave. It had a distinct ring to it that sent chills like tiny spiders running up and down Kar's spine.

They cowered in the dusty corner of the cave and watched as the councilman turned the armchair to face them and slowly sank into the soft cushion. "Why don't you come and join me?" he asked.

Kar measured the distance to the opening of the cave from where he stood. If they made a run for it, could they make it? Could all of them make it?

"I said." The words crawled out from under his hood, "why don't you come and join me?"

All three of them took a step back.

His eyes flashed like miniature black stars. "Is that you, Haylen Roc?" Haylen nodded slowly, gulping for air. "You have an interesting bit of magic. Transporting practically a whole population from one place to another. Is that how you got up here? Oh, no, that couldn't be it. All of Wyck would have been crowded in here as well. Haha—haha—haha."

Kar looked over at Haylen. Her forehead was furrowed and her lips were pressed so tightly together that it looked like a line was drawn across her face.

"You must think, Haylen Roc." He tapped his gloved finger on his hooded forehead. A knocking hollow sound filled the room. "Think of *whom* you want to take with you. Not just *where* you want to go." The fire blazed suddenly. "But a broomster can do the trick as well, no?"

The councilman turned his head to look at Kar and Jack, who were trying to hide in the flickering shadows. "It's Jack Bold and none other than Kar Homely. Oh, what luck! Jack, you're the giant eagle, right?"

"Yes, sir," said Jack, slightly stuttering. He slowly stepped out from the shadows and stood in front of Kar. Kar pushed him aside.

"And you. Kar of the Homelys, I presume? I do not quite recall what it is that you are able to do?" The councilman tapped his gloved fingers together. It sounded like the dull knocking of drumsticks. "If my memory serves me well, you did stand awkwardly on the stage longer than normal. Haha—haha—haha."

"He can lift heavy objects," burst out Haylen. "Very heavy ones."

"Ah, lifting objects, yes. Why don't you show us, Kar?"

Kar stepped forward from the shadows and bravely stood next to Haylen. "I'm a bit clumsy. I might break something," he said. "Why don't I show you outside?"

"It is too windy outside. Why don't you just lift me up? I think I am heavy enough in this chair." He banged the armrests. Dust swirled.

With his hand behind his back, Kar beckoned Jack to stand next to him. The three of them now had their backs to the opening of the cave.

Suddenly the councilman stood up. "It's best you go home. Your parents will be wondering where you are."

Relieved, Kar turned to walk out.

"Only Kar stays."

They stopped in their tracks. Haylen bent her head towards Kar. "Make a run for the broomster. Take it to the top of Mount Footsteps. We'll follow you."

"I can't leave you alone with him," Kar whispered back angrily.

"Trust me. Just go." She frowned furiously at him.

Kar hesitated for a moment, then turned and ran towards the opening. He skidded, tripping again as he finally made it through the opening.

Kar edged his way on the narrow ledge towards the broomster, which was now covered in snow. Icicles dripped from the handles. Glad that he had an inkling of how to start it, he brushed off the snow that had accumulated on the seat, flung his leg over, and twisting the right handle, pointed the broomster upwards. With a twist of the left handle, the broomster shot up and almost collided with the mountain. Barely making the turn, Kar once again pointed the broomster towards the sky, and with another awkward twist to the left handle, he disappeared into the swirling mist.

Below him, the councilman stood, shaking his fist. "You cannot hide, Kar. There are other ways to get you."

Kar landed clumsily on the top of Mount Footsteps. Snow covered the top like a smooth white tablecloth. He hid his hands under his armpits for warmth while pounding his feet. Maybe he shouldn't have left them with that evil councilman. Just as he turned to get on the broomster, a fire broke out in front of him. Books, broken plates, and furniture appeared suddenly on the once-clean mountaintop. Half of an armchair popped up beside him and he stepped aside. He tripped over something very long and white and bony

Suddenly Haylen and Jack materialized together on top of the mountain holding hands, eyes squeezed shut.

"You made it!"

Jack and Haylen jumped.

"I thought you guys would never make it. What happened?" asked Kar.

"I just closed my eyes and concentrated on Jack and myself and…poof…we're here." She looked around in utter surprise. "Oh, no, did I bring the whole cave with us?"

Kar pointed to the wriggling skeletal toes of the councilman attached to one white leg bone that he had tripped over. "Are you sure you didn't bring him along for the ride as well? He might be here, somewhere." They looked around for a while. Except for that one part of his skeleton, they could not find anything else.

"He's going to be hopping mad." said Jack, grinning.

Half of everything in the cave seemed to be strewn on the mountaintop. It was a mess.

Jack pounded his chest in alarm. "Is there anything missing from me?"

Haylen looked him over. "Do you feel anything missing?"

Jack stomped his feet on the ground and patted his arms. "Looks like I have everything. Glad you concentrated on me enough to get me here in one piece."

"You were the only one I was thinking about," said Haylen. "Maybe that's why nothing is missing from you. Magic is really hard work. No wonder they wanted us to take classes and practice carefully."

"We better get going before he gets here. I'm sure he's going to guess where we are and come looking for us," said Kar.

"He tried zapping you with a couple of lightning bolts, but they kept fizzling and dying whenever they got near you," said Haylen.

"Then just don't touch me," said Jack, backing away. "I like changing into an eagle. Hope you don't un-magic us back into the cave, too."

"It's not happening, is it? It doesn't seem to work like that," said Kar, giving him a nasty look.

"Don't be silly," said Haylen. "It's all very plain and simple now."

Kar and Jack scratched their heads. "Huh?"

"I'm just going to see what books I brought with me," said Haylen, ignoring the boys.

She found the Wyck history book, but the trip had torn it into shreds. Kar could only find the cover of *The Keepers of History*.

"Yikes," said Jack, "I'm feeling more and more amazed and grateful that I arrived in one piece. At least my book came with me whole." He whipped out *How to Kill a Dragon in Ten Easy Steps* from the inside of his coat.

"I guess I have to practice more," said Haylen with a sigh, flinging her fur hood over her head.

"Well, next time, do it on your own," said Jack. "I like all of me. Second time around might lose me an arm or something." He patted his chest again just in case. "Let's get out of here. It's just too cold!"

Jack and Kar fought briefly about who should fly the broomster. Haylen left them to make up their minds as she picked up a few more books from the snow, but they were all useless. It was getting colder by the minute. Finally Kar took out a coin from his pocket and flipped it into the air. It fell in the snow and they both lunged for it. Haylen intervened and flipped the coin, resting it on the back of her hand.

"Dragon's tail or Dragon's head?" she asked.

"Dragon's tail," Jack quickly claimed.

Kar frowned at the outcome and wanted to try two out of three. But Haylen pushed them towards the broomster and Jack climbed into the driver's seat, a silly smirk of triumph on his face. They had to leave quickly before they froze to death. Their layers of clothing just weren't keeping them warm enough in the sub-zero temperatures.

The trip down the other side of the mountain was uneventful. They were surprised to see several large villages connected by roads. Even with the help of the map, Haylen couldn't determine which one was Yongtown. It was getting warmer and warmer as they headed towards the ground, and after a while they had to remove the extra layers of clothing they all wore.

The weather behind Mount Footsteps seemed to be better than the Wyck villages. The sun shone brightly and a cool wind whipped around them. They could make out a large parking lot filled with broomsters below and decided to head there. Old-fashioned brooms hung side by side on wooden poles. Jack spied an empty pole and landed quietly beside it. Picking up what was left of their belongings, they walked towards a small booth marked ENTER. A bent old woman stood up to greet them. Her chin was pointy and one eyelid drooped heavily. The other eye had no eyelid at all and the eyeball beneath her sagging, bushy white eyebrows looked like a large watery orb with a bright blue center. Gold and silver chains dangled from her neck and her head was covered in a kerchief as multicolored as the dress she wore. The trio was struck temporarily silent at the hideous sight.

Finally, the old woman spoke, ignoring their stares. "That will be one duck every four hours," she said loudly. "Give me your hand." Jack reluctantly held out his hand. She took out a small wooden stump, licked one side and stamped the back of his hand with it.

"Ew!" yelled Jack. "That's just gross!" Slowly a clock appeared on his skin and showed fifteen past four. "When you come back, show your hand to Pipper," she said, pointing to another booth at the opposite end of the parking lot with EXIT scrawled on a lopsided sign, "And pay her on your way out."

"Guess that stops people from cheating." Haylen rubbed the blue stamp on the back of her left hand and grimaced at the old woman.

She grinned back. Two golden fangs sprung from the upper sides of her black gums. "You bet your bottom dragon! Folks around here know the consequences. Now don't forget where you've parked."

Haylen turned quickly away, eager to avoid looking at the woman. "I think it was Q55. By the way, what's this village called?"

"Everybody knows Yongtown," said the old lady surprised at the question. "Everyone."

THE LAST COUNCILMAN

THE SKELETAL form of the councilman, bereft of his robes and one leg, hopped furiously around the remnants of his cave. Snatching a broken table leg off the floor, he stuck it clumsily into the empty socket that once housed his left thighbone. He continued kicking at the shattered glass and broken armchairs until he found what he was looking for. The skull bowl was cracked slightly but there was still a bit of a reddish liquid at the bottom.

He stood next to the fireplace swirling the contents of the bowl. The table leg suddenly popped out of his hip joint and clattered onto the floor. He lurched forward and fell. Suddenly his empty socket eyes transfixed themselves to the face of an aged Lucas, grinning at him.

"Why are you here?" he cried angrily.

"Surprise!" cried Lucas. "Not pleased to see me?"

The councilman grabbed the bowl and shook it. "I'll get you, you, you …"

Lucas rolled his eyes. "Yeah, yeah, yeah. I'm here because I've been hearing some interesting things lately. Something about, oh, the un-magical Kar?"

"When we get Kar, you fool, we get you!"

"If you get Kar - and a big fat *if* at that." Lucas' face loomed closer almost jumping out of the oily liquid. "I'd never have thought that the life of Kar would be so detrimental to my welfare. What a shame. But it seems there is nothing else to do but protect my welfare."

Lucas' full lips twisted in malice. "This magic thing is so easy when you get the hang of it." Lucas snapped his fingers, making the councilman jump straight up. He stood awkwardly on one bony leg for a few seconds and then, not able to balance well, fell flat on his skull. He dragged his rickety bones up to face Lucas again. But Lucas was nowhere to be seen.

"There is only one thing left to do," the councilman cried loudly. "I must find Kar first and wring his scrawny neck myself!"

YONGTOWN

THE FRIGHTENING woman in the parking lot pointed out the direction to the town center. The walk was pleasant, through tree-lined streets. Haylen remarked that it seemed that everyone they passed was female and as ancient looking as the woman at the parking lot. The boys tried not to stare at them, as they seemed to be just as hideous as the first one. It was an uncanny coincidence. After a while they found themselves in the town square. Booths selling odds and ends of things they had never seen before stood in a circle around the cobbled square. In the middle, a fountain spurted water every few seconds - sometimes left, sometimes right - hitting anyone near it. Nobody minded the occasional spurts of water and they even welcomed them. The heat not only came from above but also seemed to permeate from their feet. The three shed the rest of their clothes and bundled them up, stuffing them into the knapsack that Haylen had conveniently brought with her. Kar slung the bag over his shoulder and they trudged on.

As they tried to maneuver around the fountain, various old women who were just as hideous, if not more so, than the woman they saw in the parking lot, would jump up from behind the stalls and shout into their astonished faces.

"Git yer love potion here!"

"Never be bald again!"

"Wisdom, anyone?"

"Be beautiful forever," said another, popping up out of nowhere and startling them badly.

"They should use it on themselves," whispered Kar, stepping on Jack's shoes as he tried to escape ugly knotted fingers pushing bottles into his face.

"Where's Haylen?" asked Jack. They looked around. Haylen was not easy to spot among the crowd of white-haired villagers. They finally found her standing at a booth holding a tiny green bottle.

"What could you be buying?" asked Kar curiously, picking up a green bottle and shaking it.

"Don't do that," hollered the booth keeper, whose black grubby hair hung down over her face, thankfully obscuring most of it. She grabbed his wrist with a misshapen hand and gently took the bottle from him and placed it back in the booth.

"Oh, sorry," said Kar, quickly wiping his hand on his jacket and shuddering.

"You'll upset the secret ingredient," she said, patting the bottle gently.

Kar eyed the green liquid in the bottle. A tiny round face with woeful yellow eyes appeared from the swirling depths of the liquid and blinked at him. "What's that?" Kar asked, taking a step back.

"The secret ingredient, of course," retorted the old woman.

"Now, young lady," she said turning to Haylen. "Ten dragons. No more, no less."

"Three," replied Haylen with a smirk. "No more. Maybe less."

"Why, young lady, I'll have you know that this secret ingredient is the best of the whole lot and is worth twice that alone."

"Three dragons," said Haylen, putting on a serious face and crossing her arms.

"Five!"

"Sold!"

Haylen carefully pocketed the small bottle in her baggy trousers and, after getting her change, grinned at the boys. "Maybe this will help us," she said.

"What is it?" Kar asked. "What did you buy?"

The old woman raised her voice at another pedestrian passing by. "Lost? Can't find your way? Ask Secret Ingredient and it will guide you!"

"Do you really think that an imp in a bottle can guide people?" Jack snickered.

Haylen blushed. "Well, she did show me how to talk to it."

"Yeah, well, try it again. I'm sure she had somebody hiding under the table when it 'spoke' to you." Jack nudged Kar in the ribs.

Haylen pulled the bottle out from her pocket and carefully placed it on the palm of her hand. "Do you know where there is a good restaurant around here, oh Great One?"

The boys chuckled louder.

The liquid in the bottle swirled, changing from green to pale blue. Jack and Kar poked at each other, stifling their snorts of laughter. The top of the bottle snapped open and a small green head with big yellow eyes popped out and looked around. "Walk two blocks east. Turn right. Walk another block. Turn left. Edith Witchone has the best pancakes in town."

Two jaws dropped.

"Close your mouth, boys," said Haylen, closing the bottle and pocketing it. "You might catch dragonflies."

Silently they followed Haylen down the street. More booths loomed ahead of them. The boys walked in the center of the road, fearful of the colorful bottles lying in rows on the stands.

"Grow ten inches taller in only ten days!"

"Fascinate your family and friends! Read their minds!"

"Ever wanted to see through walls? Get your special potion here!"

Haylen stopped in front of a small restaurant. Tables stood outside on the wide sidewalk, each surrounded by four chairs. In the middle of each table there was a large pitcher of water, a vase with one droopy orange-colored rose, and one unlit candle that was burnt halfway. Only one table was occupied. An elderly woman sat sipping from a tall glass filled with a red liquid. Her eyes were closed and she looked like she was enjoying every drop.

"This is it," Haylen said, pulling a chair out. "Come, boys, sit down. I'm famished."

The boys dropped themselves into chairs and picked up menus.

"Pickled pancakes," Kar said, reading aloud. "Yech."

"Egg pancakes," exclaimed Jack. "More yech."

117

"Here's something interesting," Haylen said, pointing to the back of the menu. "Pancakes your way."

At that moment, the door to the restaurant opened and a tall woman stepped out. She was a bit taller than her own doorway and had to bend her head slightly to pass through. In one hand she was holding a pad and in the other a quill that was most assuredly plucked from the tail of a peacock.

"At least she looks like a real old woman and not like a crazy old hag," whispered Jack.

Kar and Haylen hid their faces behind the menu and giggled.

"What'll you have?" she asked, moistening the tip of the quill with her tongue. Black ink stained the middle of her lower lip.

"I think we'll all have the pancakes your way," said Haylen, "and a glass of milk."

"Wise choice," said the waitress, snatching the menus from their hands and heading back into the restaurant.

"Wait," yelled Jack after her. "You didn't ask which way we wanted them?"

The waitress rolled her eyes and returned. "All right, smart boy, which way you want them. Sunny side up or scrambled?"

"Huh? I want them with strawberries," said Jack.

The waitress shook her head. "Out of season."

"What's in season?" Kar asked, agitated. He felt the hunger pangs kicking at his stomach.

"Well, there's frogs legs, eye of lazy, witches wart, and oh, yeah, ice cream."

"Ugh," said Jack. "What choices! We'll take the ice cream."

The waitress left to get their order. The trio sat silent for a while watching the town folk of Yongtown pass them by. Jack took out a box of matches from one of his trouser pockets and lit the candle. The shriveled rose straightened up and bloomed.

"Hey," cried Haylen in astonishment, "neat trick."

"Strange bunch of people," said Kar, pouring himself a glass of water. "They all look as if they've risen from the grave." He picked up the glass and the water vanished before his eyes. He was stunned and turned quickly to Haylen. "Did you see that?"

Picking up the pitcher again, he poured more water into the glass. It overflowed onto the table and down the side. He stood up quickly not to wet his trousers.

"You already filled the glass," said Haylen, exasperated with him now. "You're making a big mess."

Kar picked up the glass again and looked at it. "It doesn't seem to have any water in it." He put the glass to his mouth. Water spilled down his chin. Although he could feel water flowing down his throat, the water in the glass remained invisible. The glass slipped from his hand and shattered. He quickly sat back down.

"Now look what you've done," cried Haylen. "They'll probably throw us out now." She looked anxiously towards the restaurant door.

"We're already out," said Jack, shrugging. He poured a glass of water for himself and stared into it. "It's trick water." He slowly put the glass to his lips and drank. "Tastes like water even if you can't see it."

The door to the restaurant banged open and the waitress, head bent, rushed out. She bore a huge tray with three plates and three glasses of milk. She looked at the shattered glass on the sidewalk and grimaced. "Here you go." She did not mention the mess. After placing a stack of pancakes and a glass of milk in front of each one, she fished out a bottle of syrup from her pocket and plunked it in the middle of the table. "Enjoy!"

"It looks pretty good," said Jack, picking up a fork. He cut into the pancakes. "But I thought we ordered ice…" The plate rattled and screamed before he could finish his sentence. Terrified, Jack dropped his fork and pushed away from the table, almost toppling his chair backwards.

"Did you hear that?" he cried. "Oh, waitress!"

She came out with a broom and dustpan, sighing. "What now?"

"This plate just screamed," said Jack.

Kar and Haylen were still staring at Jack's plate with their forks frozen in the air.

"It's what you ordered," said the waitress. "I scream. We should have called it 'screaming plate,' but that just didn't sound right. I scream is a catchier name. Enjoy!" She proceeded to clean up the broken glass while mumbling angrily.

Kar dug his fork into the thick pancakes and took a bite. "It does taste good," he said shouting above the tiny screams coming from the plate. He picked up the bottle of syrup, turned his head slightly and closed his eyes, and with a bit of hesitation, squeezed some onto the pancakes. "Anything happening?"

"Nothing," said Haylen, leaning back in her chair just in case. "You can open your eyes now."

"Well, I ordered ice cream so I'm kind of disappointed with this, but I'm too hungry to put up a fuss," said Jack, stubbornly eating away. Those passing by paid no heed to the screaming plates and the three finally finished the meal. They ate with a fork in one hand and covering one ear with the other. It didn't eliminate all the noise but it helped them get through the meal.

"That was interesting," said Kar, wiping his mouth. "I wonder if all the meals here are as noisy as this one."

"I'm too full to care," said Jack, pushing his plate away. "Let's pay up and look around some more."

"Why don't we ask Haylen's, you know, 'Oh, Great One,' to tell us where we should go now?" asked Kar, biting his lip to keep from laughing.

"Oh? You believe me now?" replied Haylen with a slight upward tilt to her chin. She pulled out the tiny green bottle where it sat snug in her pocket and placed it gently in the middle of the now cluttered table.

"What do we ask him?" Jack asked. "We don't even know where we want to go."

"Well, we need to find Kar's people," said Haylen. She cleared her throat. "Where can we find Kar's people?" Haylen solemnly asked the bottle.

The bottle bounced a bit on the table and stopped. Haylen pouted. "Nothing's happening. That old woman swindled me!"

"I think you forgot the magic words," said Kar, no longer hiding his grin.

"Oh, yes," said Haylen sheepishly. "Where can we find Kar's people, Oh Great One?"

The lid popped open and the round green face with the big yellow eyes turned slowly around until it faced Haylen. "Haven't a clue, oh chubby cheeks."

"Oh, how rude," cried Haylen, shocked.

"Let me try," said Kar. "Oh Great One, where can we find someone who knows where the Marcel family lived or might still be living?"

The head popped out to face Kar. "Oh, magic-less one, past the bridge, across the water and up Teapot Mountain."

"Wow," exclaimed Jack. "That Secret Ingredient does know a lot."

Kar said nothing and pushed the bottle away in a huff.

"Another mountain?" asked Jack, exasperated. "I'm tired of mountains. And how do we know it's telling the truth? I bet this wasn't the greatest restaurant in town."

"Well, we have nothing else to go on," said Haylen, looking exhausted. "Oh, look," she cried. "Look up there." Everyone looked up to where Haylen was pointing. Up in the sky a cloud message was floating by. *Python run do not return.* The cloud sentence spread out and slowly broke up into wispy strings that eventually faded away. "Oh, there're probably cloud writers in Yongtown, too," said Jack. But then he paused. "It doesn't sound like an advertisement to me, though."

"That's my Mom." Kar explained the secret code they shared between them. "There's something very wrong happening in SouthWyck. We've got to get back and help."

Haylen argued that returning would serve no purpose. They would probably land in jail for stealing a broomster; or worse, the town folk would hand Kar over to the remaining councilman, who was certainly now bereft of a thigh bone and very angry.

By the time Kar agreed with her, Jack was already slumped over his empty plate, fast asleep. They asked a passerby if there were any inns and he directed them into an alley. There seemed to be some kind of event happening in town because every sign on their path flashed *No Vacancy*. Finally, they turned to Secret Ingredient for help. He pointed to the last Inn down a narrow lane.

The Inn's *Last But Not Least* sign creaked on loose hinges in the late afternoon breeze. They soon exchanged dragons with the innkeeper. Haylen was too tired to haggle and forked over the ten dragons for the night, but not before she gave the innkeeper a look of contempt. As soon as they had thrown themselves on their beds they quickly drifted off to sleep even though the mattress and pillow were the most uncomfortable ones they had ever slept on.

A PILE OF BONES

"SHOW ME your hand," ordered the woman with a face like a smashed pumpkin.

The councilman shoved his white glove in her face. He was completely covered from bony head to bony toe in purple robes. He had pulled the hood over his gray skeletal features.

The old woman stared at a bony jaw with her one good eye for a moment, shrugged, and took a hold of his hand. She spat on a wooden block and stamped the back of his gloved hand with it.

Without a word he swung the cane he was carrying forward and hobbled onto the main road. An old woman shoved him out of her way because he wasn't walking fast enough. Furious, he contemplated ending her days faster, but thought he'd better not attract any attention. He knew the children were there because he had spied the yellow broomster parked among the old washed-out brooms in the parking lot. They would not be hard to find among all the old biddies with their wrinkled faces and toothless grins. This was going to be easier than he thought. He continued along the main road until he came to the center of town.

"Lost? Can't find your way?" A green bottle was shoved in his face.

"Get away from me, you old fool," he said, pushing her hand away.

"Don't 'ave to be nasty, now," she grumbled. "Why you got yer face all covered up, missy? We're all ole' folk here. No shame in that. It'll all end soon."

The councilman growled and moved away. Stupid women with their stupid potions, he thought angrily. Their silly concoctions were no match for ultimate power. Soon he would be in control of all that magic. Of course, once he had gotten rid of Kar, Lucas would be nothing. A fly would have more strength than Lucas at that point. He smiled beneath his hood. Mrs. Beadlepoof was so easy to manipulate. Just a few dragons here and there and she hurried to do his bidding. But once he explained that the future of the Wyck villages was in her hands, she was eager to assume the role of the heroine, the savior of Wyck.

She was to notify all the villagers of the treacherous behavior of the Homelys. They must be punished. At least he had them up in arms against each other in the village. By the time he returned, they would welcome his rule, his control. After that, he would take one village at a time - not just all of Wyck, but everything beyond. He growled beneath the filthy hood. If he had a sense of smell, he would have reeled from its horrible stench.

"Have the power of ten men!" He shoved another hand away from him.

"You fools," he hissed, "you don't know what power is."

"Testy, are we?" mocked one woman. "You should go to old Gertie there in that green shroud she calls a gown." She pointed a skinny finger at a woman standing behind a row of red bottles wearing a long dress shimmering with green sequins. "She's got the potion for good manners." She stuck her tongue out at him as he turned his back and continued down the road. She squeezed the tip of her nose in disgust. "Shish, these women from across town. They're the worst. They absolutely stink."

He stopped at every corner to scrutinize the crowd. The children should have been easy to see amidst the haggard looks of the village folk. But they were not around. Could they have gone back to the parking lot while he was looking for them? He turned and, forgetting he had only one of his bony legs left (the other just a stick glued to his hip), he fell to the ground, knocking his ancient skull on the cobbled stones. He got up and tried to close his mouth but his skeletal jaw swung wide open. He tried clamping his yellow teeth together but they wouldn't meet. Nobody was paying attention to him as he slowly got up and adjusted himself. He pulled the hood over his face and hobbled down the lane searching for the three children, his bones clacking all the way.

OH, TO BE YOUNG AGAIN

NIGHT HAD fallen by the time Kar opened his eyes and stretched his limbs, more like a dog than a graceful cat. There was a lot of commotion going on in the streets. He jumped out of bed to look out the window. People were dressed in fancy attire, blowing horns and banging on small drums. The streets were lit with so many bright hanging lanterns that stretched as far as he could see, without straining his neck, that it wasn't hard to make out the details of people dressed in colorful costumes. Haylen joined him at the window.

"I wonder what's going on?" asked Haylen, yawning. "It looks like a carnival."

"I want to go and see," said Kar. "Let's wake Jack up."

After washing up and changing into clean clothes, they stepped out into the streets feeling refreshed. There was a lot of singing and dancing in small groups all along the main road. The restaurant where they had eaten was filled with customers. More tables had been brought out and plates screamed and cups jiggled amidst rowdy laughter. Jack was hungry again but there was a long line of people waiting for their turn. They stopped at a small booth where a woman with a bent back, breathing heavily behind a mask depicting a beautiful female face, offered them "Pigs-in-a-Blanket-Your-Way." More money changed hands and they set off happily down the road munching on buns that squealed with every bite.

Everyone wore masks depicting different beautiful faces of women. The noise of merriment was intense and no one seemed bothered by it. In the main square, the booths were gone and a band played a lively tune under the spitting fountain. Women danced together, twirling and lifting their long skirts. The music was so uplifting that Jack could not help himself and, grabbing Haylen, he pulled her into the dancing crowd before she could protest.

Kar looked on enviously. He never had the courage to do anything like that.

"Remember when we took dancing lessons with Mr. Tweetle?" screamed Jack above the noise.

Haylen giggled. "We were forced to be dancing partners. You kept stepping on my feet!"

"I did not," protested Jack. "*You* kept stepping on mine. I was just trying to get out of the way!"

"That was fun," said Haylen, slightly winded and flushed as the song ended. "I'm so glad they have such pretty masks on. I don't think I could stand to look at so many ugly faces."

"Maybe that's what they meant by their ability to stay forever young," joked Kar, joining them. He could hear the heavy wheezing sounds of the elderly women catching their breath.

Towards midnight the crowd seemed to grow restless. The music and noise faded away slowly until a clock from somewhere above their heads chimed loudly. Silence descended on the crowd. Everyone inhaled deeply and seemed to hold it until the last and final chime struck the midnight hour. A moment's pause and suddenly masks were flung high into the air. Gorgeous women appeared everywhere.

Kar turned to a lovely woman next to him and asked her, amazed, "What just happened here?"

The beautiful woman looked down at Kar and lightly touched his head. "Today is the day we grow young again," she said softly with a smile that could melt glaciers.

"Do you like it like that?" asked Kar, puzzled. "How long does it last?"

"For women it lasts, oh, many years."

"And men?"

"I do not know of any man who would want such a curse."

"You mean I'm going to be thirteen for years!" Kar's voice rose in dismay.

She laughed sweetly. "You have to be older than that for it to work. You are safe now. But never come back here after you pass the age of thirty. It does not bode well for men."

"I don't think I will ever want to come back here," said Kar, wiping the sweat that broke out on his forehead, relieved that he would not be frozen for life at the age of thirteen.

Kar was the first to wake up to the sound of the boring drizzle of rain beating against the windowpane. After the festivities the night before the rain seemed anticlimactic. By the time he finished dressing, the others were already up, their eyes still bleary from lack of sleep, yawning loudly.

They stopped by Witchone for breakfast again before heading to the parking lot. This time they made sure they ordered something that didn't make so much noise. They settled for Swicherroo eggs and bacon. Each time they took a bite, the plates switched places. By the third bite they got the hang of it and ate from each other's plates as they rotated around the table. It took Jack a while for his eyes to adjust from the constant movement of plates. He feared he was going to be permanently cross-eyed.

Pipper was standing by the entrance to the parking lot. She was wearing a dress that matched her violet eyes. Her golden hair was piled atop her head and her skin glowed.

"Show me your hand," she said.

Jack lifted the back of his hand for her to see. He couldn't keep his eyes off of her face. "Wow, you look just absolutely gorgeous!"

"Why, thank you, young man," she tittered. She peered at the image of the clock that had been stamped on the back of his hand. It showed ten minutes past seven. She calculated the amount of time the broomster had been parked and handed him a yellow receipt.

"It says five dragons," said Jack frowning. "According to my calculations, it should be four dragons and a duck or two."

"Never 'eard of a tip?" she asked. "You can't be cheap now."

"The way we're spending money," said Jack, grimacing, "we'll be broke in a couple of days."

"Just give her the money," said Haylen. "I have a lot saved up."

127

"I just hope so," said Jack, dropping the money into her outstretched greedy (and yet very youthful) palm.

They walked across the empty parking lot in silence.

"Do you remember the parking number?" asked Kar, interrupting their thoughts.

"Q55," said Haylen. "And anyway, I'm sure our broomster is one of a kind. We should see that yellow color from miles away. Everything around here looks old and tattered. I guess the day of everlasting youth doesn't work on their stuff as well," she concluded.

"Well, I don't see anything," said Kar, shading his eyes and looking around the lot.

They trudged around the parking lot for a while. Up and down the Q aisle at least five times until they realized that the broomster was really gone.

"Someone's stolen our broomster," yelled Jack suddenly. "My dad's going to ground me for life, right after he kills me!"

They went back to the lady at the entry booth. They found her sitting inside her tiny space, knitting. The years had also been wiped off of her face. It was flawless in its loveliness.

"Back so soon? Give me your hand," she demanded.

"No, no," said Jack, "someone stole our broomster. You said there would be dire consequences if anybody stole anything. You look great by the way!"

"I mentioned cheatin', nothin' about thievin'. Thieves are everywhere. Can't do anythin' 'bout that. But thanks for the compliment," she added, and blushed.

"Now what're we going to do?" whined Jack. "This is just our luck."

Haylen and Kar followed him back to where the broomster should have been parked.

"I know what to do," said Haylen.

"What?" Kar asked.

"Borrow these brooms that are still lying around," she said. "We have no recourse. We can't stay here forever."

"You mean steal? Why? We can buy brooms," said Kar. He had never stolen a thing in his life and was not about to start now.

"This is a life and death matter," said Haylen in a bit of a huff. "We can bend the rules a bit."

"I agree with Haylen," said Jack. "If they can't do anything about stealing," he mimicked the ticket lady, "then it should hold true for us as well."

Kar was uncomfortable about the whole thing but he had been outvoted. They were not in the mood to go from shop to shop looking for brooms. He followed them to some rickety old brooms that were lying next to where their yellow broomster had been parked. There were three of them on the ground. Haylen deduced that the owners of these worn-out brooms were probably the ones who stole the broomster.

"Do we have any idea how to fly these things?" Kar asked, picking one up.

"It shouldn't be that difficult," said Jack. He picked up another and straddled it. "Wish they had some padding on them. This is uncomfortable."

Haylen picked up the last one and scrutinized it for a while. "There is something here," she said, poking at a hole in the middle. The broom hummed and floated to her waist. "See? Easy." She sat sideways on the broom that hovered a few feet from the ground and poked at the small hole carved in the wood.

Haylen's hollers for help slowly died out as she disappeared into the sky. A few seconds later she returned, hands shaking uncontrollably and her frosty white hair was standing straight up like a porcupine ready for a fight, but she was none the worse for her ordeal.

"I told you, boys, it was easy." Her teeth chattered loudly.

"May I help you?" A young man stepped into their view. His abundant dark hair fell across his forehead in thick curly waves. A purple cloak fluttered around him in the morning breeze.

Kar stole a glance at Haylen. He didn't like the twisted smile on the man's face or the unnatural sound of his voice. "No, thanks," said Kar firmly. "We are not in need of any help." He hoped the man did not realize they were stealing brooms. He felt the nape of his neck grow warm.

"Ah, I thought you were having a problem," said the stranger. "It is my mistake." He bowed slightly, turned on his heels, and walked away.

"That man gave me the creeps," said Haylen. "Did you see those eyes? They were like two pieces of burning charcoal." She shivered in the growing heat.

"I had a feeling like this before, but I can't remember where or when," said Kar, trying to shake off the ugly sensation.

"Well, he's gone," said Haylen. "Let's get out of here."

They managed to hang their belongings on the end of the brooms. After a few practice runs they were able to fly side by side without bumping into each other. Kar searched for the bridge the green man in the bottle had mentioned and finally found three. Each faced a different direction. They chose the one facing a mountain that remarkably looked like a teapot. He pointed the way and they turned their brooms and flew behind him.

The wind tore at their hair and clothes. Kar almost fell off once but was able to grab ahold in time and wrap his legs around the thin broom. He could have sworn he felt an invisible hand give him a boost back onto the rickety broom.

Jack seemed to enjoy every moment of the unfamiliar flight. "Whew," he screamed above the wind. "This is fun!" He dove downwards like an eagle ready to pluck its next meal from the ground before swooping up again.

Kar felt his heart jerk as he watched Jack somersaulting.

"Stop it!" shouted Haylen hysterically as she tried to get her voice heard over the sound of the wind whooshing past her ears. "Just stop it!"

Finally, between the bridge and the mountain, a body of water loomed into view. The brooms dipped towards the ground of their own accord and they found themselves heading straight towards the lake. Kar could feel himself losing control. A young child was playing in the waves and ran eagerly towards them as the three landed painfully on the sandy shore.

"What happened?" asked Kar. "Why did we stop?"

"I don't know," said Jack. "Look at all the brooms on the beach." He groaned and rubbed his behind. It looked like a graveyard of old brooms.

Kar beckoned to the child. "Why are all these brooms stranded here?" he asked.

"'Cause they can't fly over the water, silly." The child screeched with laughter and dashed back into the waves. "They keep falling down from the sky!"

"It figures," said Jack. "Just when we thought we were getting close."

"What do we do now?" asked Kar, stretching out on the sandy beach. He was too embarrassed to rub his sore bottom like Jack and looked out towards the huge lake.

"I could go it alone," said Jack.

"You can't go," said Haylen. "You heard the little boy. Brooms can't fly over water."

"I didn't mean with the broom," said Jack, exasperated. "When will you remember that I can fly on my own?" Jack squeezed his eyes shut. A large eagle materialized, its wings flapping and blowing sand everywhere.

"Stop that. You're getting sand in my eyes." Haylen rubbed her eyes angrily.

"It might be dangerous, even for an eagle," said Kar, spitting sand.

The eagle flapped its wings and flew away. Just as it passed the tide it fell like a rock into the waves. Jack swam back to shore.

"I guess I can't go either," said Jack, shaking the water out of his mop of hair.

They paced the beach for a while, trying to think of a new plan. Nobody could swim that far and there certainly weren't any mermaids they could call for help; even if they existed (which, Haylen emphatically told them, they didn't). Haylen explained to Jack that the stories he had read of mermaids were just fairytales. At least it was proof that he had read something once.

Jack didn't appreciate her sarcasm.

Kar kept pacing the shore until he tripped on a broom and banged his head on another. He got up with a huge lump on the side of his forehead and the best idea yet.

THE RAFT

"A RAFT!"

Jack and Haylen looked at him with puzzled looks.

"A raft. Don't you get it?" said Kar, picking up the leftover brooms and piling them on top of each other. "We just need strong rope." "Hey, kid," he said, shouting out to the child still splashing in the water. "Where's the nearest village?"

"Where did you ever learn how to build a raft?" asked Jack, surprised by Kar's newfound skills.

"Survive or Else camp," said Kar. "Don't you remember? Had to get away from Lucas Nosty and ended up plunging down the waterfall."

"Oh, yeah," said Jack. "Now I remember. You were picked up by one of the older guys who could shape-shift into this giant vulture. Glad I refused to compete with you guys."

After trying to understand the child's directions and consulting Secret Ingredient in vain (he was taking a break, and told them so), Jack volunteered to bring the supplies from the village. Haylen handed him a long list. After what seemed like an hour, he returned with a large load in his beak. Before he could land gracefully, the bag fell. Food, rope, and other nautical supplies spilled out.

"What is all this stuff?" asked Haylen, shifting through a pile of things.

"Sailing things," said Jack, avoiding her look. "The salesman said I had to have them."

"What do we need a magnifying glass for?" asked Kar, placing it over his eye and making a face at Haylen.

"Or this," said Haylen, picking up a thick ball of string. "It says here it's specially made for kites. We need thicker twine to put the raft together. And what is this?" Haylen lifted a heavy black frying pan.

"The salesman said it was the most important thing we could bring," said Jack.

"Yeah, right, what do we do with it? Hit somebody with it?"

"And here is the kite. That at least explains the kite string." Kar waved a package at them and then continued rummaging through the sack.

"No, you cook with it, silly," Jack spat back at Haylen, ignoring Kar.

"What? With eggs we don't have? You spent my money on this?"

"You'll thank me one day!"

"Guys, just stop it!" Kar dumped a load of brooms and grabbed the frying pan from Haylen because it seemed she was about to use it on Jack. "You never know," he said, putting it in his backpack.

Haylen continued to rummage through the pile, picking small items up that might be of use. Jack had bought some rope, a box of matches, a compass (which they decided was a really good thing, which made Jack feel better), and more cheese then they thought they could eat in lifetime (which wasn't true, according to Jack. He said he could finish it off right there and then).

That night they camped on the beach. They had fun building the biggest bonfire they had ever seen in their lives and still there were plenty of brooms left over for the raft. Haylen was not too pleased at their enthusiasm about the bonfire, but they explained to her that it was a way of cleaning up the beach from all those dead brooms, and it made the chilly night more comfortable.

It turned out they did not need any type of rope to bind the brooms together. Whenever they placed one broom next to another, it stuck like glue. Try as they might, they could not even pry them apart. Towards the end of the day the raft looked perfect. They wondered if they would be able to pull it towards the water.

"I think it's too big," Haylen said, standing in the middle of the raft. Her white hair was frizzing from the heat and humidity. She looked like a dirty lamp emitting a weak flame.

"Sure we can," said Jack, pulling at one end. "The brooms are hollow and light."

"Hey, watch it," cried Haylen, trying to balance herself and failing.

"Oops, sorry," said Jack, helping her up.

"We should camp again, tonight," said Kar, wiping his sweaty brow. "I'm bushed."

Another bonfire lit up the beach. Jack entertained them with songs by making up lyrics as he went along. They all took turns making up their own songs to favorite Wyckian tunes. Eventually, though, their enthusiasm waned and they sat quietly together, staring at the crackling broomsticks.

Kar wondered what the others were thinking. Were they missing their families? Maybe he was a fool to look for his real parents when those parents had abandoned him. They didn't want him. Why should he sail unknown seas to find them anyway? Was it worth it? Then he remembered the real reason. Lucas Nosty. Lucas had bothered him all his life. Lucas constantly taunted him about his changing eyes and enjoyed circling them with bruises whenever he had a chance. Now Lucas was the cause of the burning, chaotic villages.

He wished he was home with the only parents he knew; the parents who cared for him. He even missed his rebellious grandfather clock. He smiled at the memory of it and looked around. Haylen and Jack had curled up next to the fire and had fallen asleep. He should get some sleep too, he thought, and lay down beside them.

The sound of something snapping brought Kar out of his light sleep. He strained his ears and looked around in the moonless night. The bonfire was crackling softly. After listening intently for a few more minutes, he convinced himself that it must have been something in the fire and dropped his head back again on his coat.

The sun shone brighter than they had ever seen it the next morning. It was so bright it stung their eyes. Kar squinted at the raft. "It's missing something," he said.

"What?" said Jack, shading his eyes from the glare.

"A sail," said Kar, before Haylen could answer.

They rummaged through their bags but could not find anything remotely like a sail.

"Now why didn't your salesman think to recommend that?" asked Haylen sarcastically.

He stuck out his tongue at her. "Maybe I asked and he didn't have any sails."

"I doubt it," retorted Haylen.

"Jack," said Kar, happy to interrupt their squabble, "I guess you have to go to the village again. Bring something we can really use."

"And no more cheese," said Haylen, quickly. "Try to bring some bread and water this time."

"Well, you better do it quick," said Kar. "We don't want to spend another night here."

Jack flew off, annoyed at his friends, and returned quicker than they had expected. He dropped a blanket on the sand with a bag full of bread and a jug of water. "That was real heavy," said Jack. "I dropped it a couple of times on the way."

"That's a blanket," said Haylen. "Not a sail. You could have found a bed sheet at least. It would have been a lot lighter."

"I looked," said Jack, truly annoyed now. "It was the best I could do."

Haylen picked the blanket up and spread it on the sand. "Well, I guess it'll do. It's made cheaply and is very lightweight."

"It better be," grumbled Jack. "I'm not going back."

They somehow managed to squeeze a few brooms upright and tie the blanket to a rope. Kar showed them how they would need to hoist the ropes up when the wind picked up so they could sail down the lake.

"So, what're we going to do now?" asked Jack. "Blow on it?"

Not even a slight breeze disturbed the air.

Kar snapped his fingers as a thought flashed through his mind again and without another word he searched again through the hundreds of broomsticks on the sandy shore. He picked out three of the thickest ones he could find and whittled the ends flat.

Jack sat beside Kar while he was concentrating on his chore, and decided to put the kite together. When Jack was finished, Haylen grabbed it and gave it to the young child they had met who had been looking wistfully at Jack while he assembled it. His delighted screeches loosened the tight grip on Jack's jaw, and he smiled as the young boy managed to fly the kite over the clear water.

By then Kar had tied the oars loosely to the sides of the raft. They dumped all their belongings on it and pushed the raft out onto the water. They rowed away, watching the kite swirl above them like a dancing bird.

TEAPOT MOUNTAIN

KAR JUDGED that Teapot Mountain was only a day away. A small breeze had started up and had eventually intensified. Soon they were gliding over the waves. Up and down. Down and up. Haylen sprawled face down on the edge of the raft, head hanging over, moaning, "I want to go home."

But even though the mountain did not look far away when they began their journey, by the time the sun was setting it seemed they had not come any closer. Haylen, seasick from the never-ending motion of the waves, refused to eat anything they offered her. Each time she watched one of them take a bite out of a piece of bread or cheese, she groaned and crawled to the edge of the raft.

Night soon covered them like a twinkling bedcover and Haylen, too exhausted to sit up, stared at the stars from where she lay near the edge of the raft. She had flung her hands out to her sides in a futile effort to steady her world. Her stomach heaved and her eyes rolled around so much, she thought stars were streaking across the sky. "It's beautiful out here," she said miserably. "The stars are so big and they move so fast. I wish I didn't feel so terrible."

Kar felt sorry for her as he watched her crawl over to the edge of the raft again and throw up the only bite of cheese she had taken just a few moments earlier.

Three days later, they finally realized they were not any closer to the mountain than they were the first day. They couldn't understand it. Jack said he could practically reach out and touch the mountain, but they just couldn't sail any closer. Every time they requested help from the Great One in reaching their destination, he had come out of his tiny bottle looking no better than Haylen. Groaning loudly and clutching his head, he tried hard to focus his big yellow eyes on them, but always failed. He would try to answer their request, but each time he opened his mouth, he would slap his hand quickly over it and dive right back into the safety of his bottle.

Food and water were running out, even if Haylen could only take a few bites at a time. Finally, trembling and exhausted, she pulled out the green bottle once again and placed it on the raft.

"Oh, Great One," she said, gulping down whatever seemed to want to rise from her empty stomach. "Please help us. Where are we?"

Secret Ingredient pulled his head out of the bottle and looked around. His yellow eyes had turned as green as his skin and with a weak voice, he whispered, "Lost."

Before Haylen could ask another question, he groaned loudly and popped back into the bottle.

Jack, who was never sick a day in his life, picked up the bottle and shook it angrily. "Lost?" he screamed. "That's all you can say?"

Kar took the bottle and laid it gently back on the raft. "Oh, Great One," he said, "I'm so sorry about that." He shot Jack a dirty look. "How do we reach the mountain?"

Secret Ingredient popped out again, his greenish-yellow eyes rolling, his voice unpleasant. "Never, ever, ever shake Secret Ingredient."

"So very sorry. It won't happen again," said Kar, glaring at Jack. "We know we're lost, but how do we get to the mountain?"

"Must take the secret water path."

"If you go back in again," cried Jack, "I'll shake you silly. I swear. We need more information. Where is this secret water path?"

Secret Ingredient turned his head and glowered at Jack. "Turn five degrees east. Go five knots and make a sharp right turn. Now I'm going to sleep, so don't bother me. My head is spinning!"

The trio whipped out the compass and struggled to determine how to go five degrees east. Kar and Jack took the oars as Haylen sat at the stern, compass in hand, trying to ease the raft towards the intended direction. But they had no idea how far five knots were or even how long it took to get to one knot. Jack decided that they should take sharp right turns every now and then to see if they could find the secret water path. But as the day wore on, they got dizzier and dizzier taking a sharp right every time Jack screamed "Now!" It was making Haylen feel even worse.

In the end, Jack lost his temper with the futility of the plan and, struggling against Kar, pulled the bottle out of Haylen's coat pocket. He shook it vigorously and pulled the stopper out. "Come out, oh, Great One—before I smash this bottle to pieces!"

Secret Ingredient once more poked his head out, none too pleased at Jack's threat, but at least recognizing it as a real possibility. But Jack gave him no time to reply. He grabbed Secret Ingredient by the head and pulled. He kept pulling and pulling until his head stretched and his tiny shoulders popped out. Soon the arms shot out and the rest of him followed. A little green man, the color of lime and three times the size of the bottle, lay panting and very irate on the raft floor. He stood up and flecked drops of green water off his body.

"You could have waited until I was dressed properly," he said. He was wearing a pair of shorts splattered with red hearts and a shirt with short sleeves that had three words embroidered on it: OH GREAT ONE.

"Now, you listen here," said Jack, waving a finger at him. "Where is this sharp right turn? Answer me now before I throw you in the lake!"

"No need to get nasty," hissed the little man. "It would behoove you to make the turn right about now."

Jack and Kar flung themselves at the oars as Haylen steered. The little green man held on to a piece of twine that was sticking out from the floor while clasping his bottle to his chest. He looked even sicker than Haylen. Just as they made the turn, the blanket bellowed up once again and, without assistance from any of them, took off at a tremendous speed. The little raft sped over the waves. Haylen, joined by Secret Ingredient, crawled to the edge of the raft and hung her head over the side. Another giant wave lifted the raft high up in the air and with another burst of speed carried them to shore. They landed in the middle of a beach, battered and hardly able to move.

Teapot Mountain, bigger than ever now that they could touch it, was sleek and shiny. It looked impossible to climb. Trails of smoke bellowed from the top of the mountain. Meanwhile, the little green man tried to get back into his bottle, but he was having a lot of trouble accomplishing the task. He stomped around the shoreline, clearly upset about his inability to get home again, shouting things they couldn't understand. His head was the only thing that he could fit back into the bottle. It got stuck. His shrieks of indignation were muffled and far away. Haylen giggled. Soon they were all rolling on the grounded raft, holding their sides. Their laughter came to a halt only when a wave broke over the side of the raft and soaked them. Chortling and thoroughly drenched, they grabbed the bags that were still tied to the mast and hauled them off the raft. Secret Ingredient followed with the bottle still stuck over his head. He had no intention of removing it. He was halfway home.

They dried their wet clothes on large, flat rocks scattered about on the pebbly beach and soon they were baked hot from the sun. The boys found some kindling to light a fire and they all huddled around it, steam rising from their long underwear. Haylen was eternally grateful to be on solid ground again. She suddenly felt extraordinarily hungry.

Even though the mountain looked like a large, ominous teapot, its walls were steep and no plant life grew on it. They needed to rest and dry off and then they would need to find some food.

Secret Ingredient wouldn't talk to them and sat crouched near the fire holding his bottled head. Jack complained constantly of his rumbling stomach until Kar got up and walked off. He had noticed a small waterfall in the distance. After a few minutes, he returned carrying a fat fish in his arms.

"It was easy," he said, dumping the fish on Jack's lap and answering his friends' surprised faces. "They were swimming around and around with nowhere to go. I just plucked one out of the stream."

"How do we cook fish?" asked Haylen, making a face.

"Leave it to me," said Jack eagerly. "My dad taught me."

Triumphantly he pulled out the large frying pan from Kar's backpack and waved it in Haylen's face. "What are we going to do with this?" he mimicked her girlish voice.

Haylen stuck her tongue out at him but could not help smiling.

Pulling out a small jackknife, Jack cleaned and scraped the scales off the fish on one of the flat rocks. Haylen looked on in disgust. She hated touching raw food.

The smell of baking fish was soon wafting through the air. Secret Ingredient pulled the bottle off his head and laid it carefully beside him. He sniffed loudly, his yellow eyes appearing to be normal again. "Smelly fish," he said. He stuck his hand into the bottle and pulled out a leg of fried chicken, the size of a thumb, and set to munching on it.

"Hey," Jack yelled. "Could you make it a bigger size and give us some? You can see we're all starving to death here. That's not enough to feed a bird."

"I'm a Secret Ingredient," he retorted, before taking another tiny bite, "not a magician." He plunged his hand into the bottle again and pulled out a silver goblet filled with a red liquid that spilled over and down his chest. He smacked his lips.

"Should've thrown him in the sea when I had the chance," fumed Jack, eyeing the tiny morsel of food hungrily. But in no time at all their bellies were full of perfectly cooked fish and they lay content on the beach, arms cradling heads.

"Ah," said Jack with a huge sigh. "Camp life is the life for me."

Haylen was too full and sleepy to reply. But if she'd had the energy, she would have vehemently disagreed. She frowned instead.

Kar stretched his body out and stared up at the mountain. He could hardly see its shape in the darkness. Everybody was too tired to swap ideas of how to climb it and soon the soft sounds of sleeping children filled the night air.

Secret Ingredient pulled a bed, a pillow, and a flannel blanket from the bottle. He had changed into a pink nightgown. He snuggled under the covers, his thin mouth curving into a tiny smile and his bottle snug against his chest.

The tide was slowly retreating when they finally awoke. Its soft lapping sounds were soothing. They hardly spoke a word as they dressed. Kar returned with another fish and handed it to Jack, who cleaned it and placed it neatly over the dying fire. They crouched in silence, waiting for breakfast to cook and wondering what their next step should be.

Secret Ingredient wouldn't talk to them—even when they bowed before him and called him the greatest one in the whole wide world. He had reinserted his head into the bottle, deciding it was safer that way then trying to carry it under his armpit. Haylen sympathized with his predicament, but Jack threatened to throw him into the fire if he did not offer them the help they needed. Secret Ingredient dared him with raised fists while the bottle mashed up against his button nose, making him look even stranger than he already was. Kar suggested they calm down a bit and walk along the side of the mountain and see if they could see some kind of path that could lead them up. Jack and Haylen reluctantly agreed, and they broke camp, cleaning up what remained of breakfast.

Before they set off, they decided that it was best to hide the raft behind some bushes that grew abundantly along the small waterfall. They had no plan for their return and figured it was safer to be able to access the raft if they needed it. Plus, Haylen added, it might be a good idea to hide the raft in case anyone was following them. As the raft inched its way along the beach, it vibrated in their hands. The three of them let go of the raft and stepped back. Secret Ingredient, who was still standing in the middle of it, pulled the bottle off his head and looked down to try to determine the source of the shaking. His lime-green toes poked out from under red robes. He had a blue towel wrapped tightly around his head.

"I think the raft is moving on its own," said Kar.

"Of course it's moving," said Jack. "We're pulling it."

"I mean up!" Kar motioned to the sky.

Haylen stepped back and leaned down to look at the bottom of the raft, tilting her head to one side. She was shocked by what she saw. The raft was hanging a few inches above the ground. She pulled at Jack's sleeve.

"It's hovering above the sand," she yelled. "Look!"

Jack and Kar bent down to take a look. Indeed the raft was vibrating and hanging a few inches over the ground. Kar gingerly stepped on the raft. Even though it swayed, it still held his weight and floated just a few inches above the ground. Beginning to understand their marvelous luck, Kar steadied himself. "How do you think we work this thing?"

"Let me try," said Jack. He jumped on the raft and it tilted suddenly, throwing Secret Ingredient into the air, over a rock, and into a pool of water while Kar fell onto the pebbled beach. Nobody heard Secret Ingredient's muffled screams as they helped Kar to his feet. They were too fixated on the possibility of a flying raft to remember about Secret Ingredient. Finally, after poking and probing the raft, they sat down, exhausted.

"It's no use," said Haylen, wringing her hands. "It would have been perfect, though."

In the sudden quiet that followed her words, they could hear feeble cries of help. They looked around. Secret Ingredient was sitting on a rock. The towel had unfurled and lay hanging over his shoulders, dripping wet. Tears flowed freely down his flat, green face and he wiped his yellow mournful eyes with the soggy towel, finally blowing loudly into it.

The three stared at him for a while.

"Why are you wet?" asked Jack.

Secret Ingredient glared at him and stomped his tiny feet.

Haylen punched Jack in the arm. "Can't you see he's troubled? You have no heart."

"Me?" Jack cried, shaking his head. "He's the one with no heart. He won't help us anymore."

"Well, to be fair, you did yank him out of his bottle," Haylen yelled back. "He's no longer a Secret Ingredient. He's a … he's now a … well, a known ingredient."

"Yeah, and what do you call this 'known ingredient'?" Jack's lips curled into a sneer. "Lousy helper?"

Secret Ingredient opened his mouth until it looked like a huge round disk and let out a piercing wail of pain and anger.

Kar dropped down to his side and gently patted him on his head. It felt strangely warm to the touch. "Don't pay any attention to him. He gets like that when he doesn't have enough to eat. What's wrong?"

"I lost my house," cried Secret Ingredient, pounding on his chest.

"Where did you lose it?"

"There," he said, pointing behind him, "there, in the water. I lost it when he knocked me off the raft. It's his fault," he said, pointing his thick green finger in accusation at Jack. Kar noticed incredulously that his fingers were nail-less.

"Me? Why me? I didn't throw you in the water," said Jack, offended.

"Yes! Yes, you did."

Kar stretched his hand out and pulled the bottle from where it was stuck in the weeds.

"Here," said Kar, handing him the miniature bottle. "Are you okay now?"

Secret Ingredient nodded his head and blew his nose again. "Thank you," he squeaked. He beckoned for Kar to come closer and whispered something in his ear.

"Oh, I see," said Kar, nodding vigorously. "I see, now. Thanks!"

"See what?" asked Jack, irritated by the secret exchange.

Kar ignored him, picked up Secret Ingredient (who now held the bottle closely under his arm), and settled him in the middle of the raft. He continued in silence as the other two watched him pick up what bags they had and dump them one by one near Secret Ingredient. He sat down at the oar that was still stuck to the side of the raft and motioned for Jack to do the same. He pointed to Haylen to take her place at the stern. Secret Ingredient walked up to the broom that was a part of the sail. He pushed a little dent in the side of the broom. The raft shook slightly and lifted straight up in the air.

"We have to guide it just like we did in the water," yelled Kar over the rush of the wind.

The ride was exhilarating, to say the least. The wind roared like a beast past their ears, covering their screams of excitement and fear as they sailed over the mountain. Cresting the summit, they looked down and saw nothing but miles and miles of desert stretched before them on the other side. They struggled to control the wild raft as it buckled and leaped under the cloudless sky, but eventually Jack, exhausted from rowing into the wind, stopped rowing and yelled loudly at Kar to do the same. Within seconds, the raft's pace shifted and it hovered above Teapot Mountain.

The boys turned to look at Haylen and choked back the laugh that was ready to spring from their mouths. Haylen's hair was standing on end. She looked like a ferocious, furry white kitten ready to attack. She smiled sweetly back at them, her face flushed and her eyes brimming with tears from the force of the wind.

"I thought I was going to die!" she screamed in delight. "I've never had so much fun in my life!"

The boys' pent up laughter burst forth in snorts and gasps.

Haylen, thinking they were agreeing with her, flung her mangy head of hair back and joined them loudly.

After much sniffing and wiping of tears, the raft slowly descended until they returned to the pebbled beach from where they had launched.

Secret Ingredient had changed his wet clothes during the trip. He now sported a checkered red pair of shorts and a white shirt. A tassel hung down from the middle of a red beret, swinging freely at the back of his head. He was drinking from a silver goblet. "I assume you got the hang of it while I was changing," he said. They took one look at him and burst into laughter again.

Happily they took off once more, maneuvering the flying raft around the mountain and trying to find a way in. But the mountain seemed impenetrable. They flew up to where they had seen smoke spewing. It looked as if a chimney had sprung out of the mountain. It also smelled like something delicious was cooking. Jack sniffed the air like a hungry dog.

"Do you see anything?" asked Haylen, squinting from the sun.

"No, nothing," replied Kar, shading his eyes with the palm of his hand. He let go of the steering broom and rubbed his aching arm. The raft lay calm in the wind. He glanced at Secret Ingredient, who was sipping a drink and enjoying himself.

"I'm hungry," Jack whined, sniffing the air. "Let's go back down and cook some fish."

The scent of food was making all of them hungry, so they quickly turned the raft back to shore. In no time at all they were sitting cross-legged around the fire, staring at the fish cooking slowly in the frying pan.

"Someone is in the mountain. We know that at least," said Kar, sniffing the air.

"You know something? This is all his fault," said Jack, pointing to Secret Ingredient, who was sitting on miniature table eating soup.

"How so?" asked the little man between slurps.

"You're the one who gave us these directions, and now that we're here, it's all a dead end. And furthermore, how are we going to get back to SouthWyck? You won't help us anymore."

"That's because you're still being mean to me, and I did help you. I told Kar how to fly the raft," said Secret Ingredient, cutting into a miniature leg of lamb.

"Me! I'm not being mean to you."

"Say you're sorry." Haylen placed a hand on Jack's shoulder and squeezed it.

Jack sputtered. "Never!"

Kar turned the fish over and sat back. "With all that's been going on lately," said Kar, "I had almost forgotten why we're here. Sometimes I even forget about home for a little while."

Jack looked embarrassed. "All my life I have been pounded on by the Nasty Boys, and here I am acting no differently. Just because Secret Ingredient doesn't look like us, I assumed he had no feelings." He turned to Secret Ingredient, who was wiping his mouth with a tiny white handkerchief. "Sorry, buddy."

Tears poured down Secret Ingredient's face and into his empty bowl of soup. "No one has ever called me 'buddy' before." He began to wail. His mouth was open so wide that they could almost see the back of his throat.

"Well, get used to it. Now you're my bud," said Jack, tapping the little man's tiny head with a finger.

Secret Ingredient pulled out a bowl of soup from his bottle and handed it to Jack. The bowl barely covered the tip of his thumb.

"I wish you could make that a bit bigger," said Jack. It felt like a drop of water on his tongue.

"Me, too," Secret Ingredient sniffled.

"That's all right," said Jack. "Fish will do for now."

Suddenly Kar jumped up and bowed before Secret Ingredient. "Oh, Great One," he asked. "Which way to the opening in the mountain?"

"Right through there," said Secret Ingredient. His tiny, plump, nail-less finger pointed straight ahead.

"I don't see anything," said Haylen, peering into the semi-darkness.

"Don't worry. You will be able to see it in the morning," replied Secret Ingredient, pushing his stubby fingers into his bottle and pulling out a bed. It had been an emotionally exhausting day and he was very tired.

PATHOS

WHEN THE drizzling rain finally woke the damp campers on the beach, they saw that they had slept most of the morning away. Secret Ingredient, when asked again with the utmost courtesy and much bowing, where the entrance was located, pointed to a black boulder on the side of the mountain. Behind it, they discovered an opening to a cave. Inside the cave, they found a wooden platform that swayed a few inches above the ground. Testing it carefully first with their toes, and seeing it held their weight, they all clambered onto it. Each corner of the platform was knotted to a thick rope that reached down from the blackness of the mountain's interior. Two round metal cans tied to the ends of strings and a large bronze bell also hung down from above. Kar spotted a gray piece of parchment that had been nailed to a wooden pole on the platform. It had writing on it.

Kar read loudly: "Visitors, please ring BELL. Place opening of can marked '*EAR*' over right ear. Press opening of other can marked '*MOUTH*' over your own. *Make sure strings are taut.*"

Kar rang the bell too vigorously and the ensuing noise almost deafened them as it echoed up and down the shaft. They covered their ears in agony while Jack swore soundlessly at Kar. When the last note died down, Kar heard a voice, as if from a mile away, seeping through the can that he was still holding tightly against his ear:

"Who's there?"

"This is Kar." Kar found it very difficult to speak with his mouth jammed into the opening of the can.

"Who's Tar?" he barely heard back.

"Kar, sir, Kar! With a *k*!"

"Car, ter, car?"

Before Kar could scream his reply back into the can, the platform groaned and creaked beneath them and with a sudden jerk slowly rose up. Haylen picked up Secret Ingredient and tucked him safely in her pocket. The platform moved upwards through complete darkness. They clung together, fearing that one false move or shift of their weight would break the wobbly platform and plunge them to certain death. Still quaking in fear, they were surprised to find light exploding over their heads. It took their eyes awhile to adjust. The platform jolted to a halt and they found themselves looking into a room lit by a chandelier. A cozy fire added more light to the room.

The mountain hideout was by no means bare. Shelves stocked with tomes lined the walls. More tomes were tossed here and there, as if someone had been looking for something in particular and had discarded them, opened. A sofa and armchair faced the fire and a small oval table stood between them. The table held an equal share of books and glasses of water; some empty, some half full. Even the soft carpets seemed to be thrown helter-skelter, just covering the rocky floor beneath them.

The finest looking man Kar had ever seen stood facing them. His soft eyes, like two almonds, were the same color as the light brown tunic he wore, which barely covered his knees. His black hair hung thick and silky, straight to his shoulders. He stood barefoot on a square burgundy carpet. A large tome was pressed against his chest. His eyebrows lifted in shock as Haylen came into view. She had tried her best to fix the messy tangles, but some parts of her hair still stuck out like straw.

"What brings children to my humble abode?" he asked, staring in wonder at Kar. In defiance of his youthful appearance, his voice sounded weak.

Kar cleared his throat and stepped forward.

"My name is Kar." He wondered if he should shake the man's hand, but the handsome man made no move to offer his. As Kar waited for the man to reply, his eyes wandered a bit more, and he spied a large tapestry hanging on the left wall. It depicted a bearded man in flowing white robes with hands stretched out before him. Two globes lay on the palm of each hand. Not waiting for a reply, Kar pointed excitedly to the tapestry.

"Do you see that, Haylen?"

The man turned to see what Kar was pointing at. "Do you recognize it?" he asked, clearly surprised by Kar's interest.

Kar rifled through his bag and pulled out what remained of the book he had found in the councilman's cave. He offered it to the stranger.

"Where did you find this? It's been missing for many years." He took the book gently from Kar and lifted the cover. "There's nothing here. What happened to the pages? You've ruined it." He waved the empty book furiously in Kar's face.

"We found it like that, sir," said Kar, stepping back and instinctively throwing his hand up to protect himself in case the man was about to throw the tattered book at him. There was a stony silence while the man stood fuming, the torn book still clutched in his hand.

Before he could say another word, a matronly woman in a long black dress walked through a side door. She stopped when she saw the children. "Ah, why didn't you tell me we had company?" she asked, clapping her hands, clearly delighted. "Let me set more bowls for lunch."

"It is not necessary, Mistress Rewain," he said, his eyes still on the children. "The children will be leaving."

Jack's face fell. The mere mention of soup had made his stomach growl.

Haylen's eyes moistened with tears.

Kar felt his friends' disappointment and wasn't ready to give up just yet. "We just came to ask you about the Marcel family."

"Why do you want to know about this family?" asked the man, tossing the torn book with the others on the floor.

"I just need to know." Kar looked up beseechingly. He could not bear it if the man turned them away. Where would they go next? Who could help them? He was desperate for information.

"Speak up, boy. I might look young, but I am two hundred years old, and I have the frailties of the aged."

Jack suddenly blurted out. "He'll tell you everything over a hot meal!"

"Jack!" Haylen's eyebrows shot up and her tanned cheeks turned a dark crimson.

The man scowled at Jack, who stood his ground and stared back at him, hoping his plan for a free meal did not backfire.

Kar figured that the heavenly aromas of food wafting through the room must have given Jack the nerve to speak up like he did.

After an intense moment of silence, the handsome man lifted his chin and chortled. "You are a bold one, aren't you?" His smile made him look even handsomer.

"They don't call me Jack Bold for nothing," said Jack, grinning back at him.

It was a simple meal but it was delicious. Jack had several helpings of duck soup. Still remembering their last true meal at the restaurant, Kar half expected the bowl to quack, but he wouldn't have cared if it did.

Mistress Rowain was pleased at the way the children ate the meal with gusto and kept filling the large silver tureen with more soup. She kept patting Haylen's stringy mass of hair and admiring the way it seemed to give extra light to the small dining room. Neither the handsome man nor Mistress Rowain seemed surprised when Haylen brought out Secret Ingredient from her pocket. He sat behind his own table next to Haylen's bowl, also enjoying the drop of soup Mistress Rowain spooned carefully into his tiny bowl. After the meal they returned to the sitting room, feeling immensely satisfied and in better moods.

"My name is Pathos," said the handsome man, picking up a carved wooden box from the side table. "These are rock candies Mistress Rowain seems to enjoy making for me," he said, handing them each a treat. "It keeps my throat from drying up."

"And cracking," whispered Jack in Kar's ear. Kar turned his head away so as not to be seen grinning.

For a while everyone contented themselves with noisily sucking on the candies. Pathos also broke a small piece of rock candy from the pile in the box and handed it to Secret Ingredient, who accepted it with a graceful nod. He was sitting in a tiny armchair. It was just part of the never-ending supply of luxury items that he could pull from his bottle.

"You say you are Kar of the Homelys?" inquired Pathos.

"I am Kar," said Kar, "but recently I've come to doubt that I am of the Homelys. I have come all this way with my friends to find out about my real parents."

"Tell me your story," said Pathos, "and maybe then I will be able to answer your questions."

With help from Haylen and Jack, Kar repeated the events that brought him to Teapot Mountain and, sparing no detail, even explained how Secret Ingredient had come to join their quest and why he was not in his bottle. Pathos couldn't help laughing again, which caused the rock candy to lodge in the back of his throat. He began to choke and managed to eventually dislodge the slippery candy, but it took him a few moments to get his breath back to normal. Secret Ingredient pouted childishly at them from behind the bottle, which was now back on his head.

At the end of Kar's story, Pathos sat quietly for a moment in reflection. He looked over at Kar; his eyes brimming with unshed tears. "I never thought I would see this day."

Kar squirmed in his seat, sensing that something big was coming. Although he was on a quest for answers, he was still uncomfortable about what those potential answers would mean for him.

"I knew who you were from the moment you entered, Kar. You look so much like your mother. Your father was my best friend and my cousin." He paused for a while, staring down at the torn carpet under his feet. Kar kept his eyes on Pathos, ignoring the excited glances of his friends. He was not in the mood for their sympathy. "We were all told to leave things as they were. The councilmen held magic that we had no idea how to thwart. So, afraid of making things worse, we left you in SouthWyck, hoping that you would be happy with your family there. But now this …" He sighed heavily. Randomly picking up a glass from the cluttered table, he gulped down the remaining bit of water and sat back in the tattered armchair, his face ashen.

"Your story has already been written." His voice was still brittle to the ear. "She of hair as white as snow." He smiled at Haylen, who shyly dropped her head, cascading her freshly combed hair over her blushing cheeks. "Now let me tell you a story." He picked up another glass of water from the side table and sipped it. "Many years ago, long before people had last names and back when everyone was called the son of this man or the other, there lived some very wise men. They were born wise. Nobody knew why or how. That was how it was meant to be. All these wise men lived in one village that no longer exists now. They had many names, but mostly they were known as the Keepers of History. They did not indulge themselves in war but sought only peace and tranquility, writing history as it should be written and not as versions of truth that each conqueror wanted their people to know or the versions of truth put forth by failures wanting only to blame their defeat on others. They wrote history as it unfolded. The whole truth and nothing but the truth." Pathos paused and looked at their intense faces staring at him.

"Then one day, there was born among them another wise man. His name was Artimus. He was something of a black sheep of the village. Most of his young life was taken up in reading all that took place before his birth. He had this theory that history seemed to repeat itself over and over again. They all scoffed at him, and soon afterwards, he left the village very upset and came to live here, in Teapot Mountain." He picked up another rock candy and dropped it into his dry mouth.

"In the beginning the wise men would visit, hoping to get him to change his mind, and he would constantly warn them of tragedies and wars to come. But his warnings were always set in verse and they could not understand him. He kept saying he was the Keeper of History to Come and soon their visits became few and far between. The other wise men thought this Keeper had gone mad. They asked him how he knew all this and he would always reply that all you had to do was read what was already written."

"One day, so the story goes, he came to the village to warn them of dire events. They welcomed him warmly, but still considered him a madman. He told them, 'Beware the hungry ground that will consume you. You must leave the village immediately.'"

"They pretended to heed him but were relieved when he returned to his mountain. The following week, the ground shook for hours and opened up, swallowing the village whole and leaving only a cherished few. Those who were left hastened to the mountain; for they, at last, understood Artimus' warnings. But he had died in his sleep the very same night the village disappeared into the hungry jaws of the earth."

At that point, Pathos paused and sipped more water. "I hope I am not boring you."

The children's eyes seemed to have grown bigger as they sat still in their chairs. Kar shook his head and could barely mutter "Go on. Please."

Secret Ingredient was fast asleep on Haylen's knee now, snoring softly. He was along for the ride, but their quest did not really interest him.

"Artimus' works became a treasured heritage. The remaining wise men moved from their wasted village and set up their new home in Teapot Mountain. They lived their lives trying to decipher what Artimus had written in the many tomes he left behind. Soon understanding dawned on them and they foolishly boasted that they could alter the future with their findings. They set forth to the villages in pairs, trying to warn them of what was to come. But they were met with hostility, grief, and sometimes death. Another wise man claimed that the histories of the past and the predictions of the future were both carved in stone and could not be changed without causing grave damage. Those who finally understand this truth returned to Teapot Mountain to continue their work. However, they recognized that one urgent matter still remained. Someone had to be the Keeper of History to Come and guard the books from young undeveloped minds that might be foolish enough to want to change the world again."

He bowed deeply. "I have been the Keeper for the past twelve years. My duty is to protect the books of Artimus and keep them safe from those who want to change the future. For there are those who might take advantage of such knowledge and some are not of us, nor even in our image."

Mistress Rowain interrupted them. "My goodness, Pathos, look at the children. They look bushed!"

Kar blinked and slowly came out of the trance that had fallen on him. Haylen wanted to hear more, but Mistress Rowain said she had made tea for them. She had been baking cakes and cookies all afternoon. They had no idea that so much time had passed. Naturally, Jack was the first to follow her eagerly to the table. Kar was glad, too, as his stomach was rumbling so much he was afraid it would interrupt Pathos' story.

After tea, Pathos gave them a tour of the rest of the rooms. The mountain contained chambers filled with what they could salvage from the old village after the quake. There were so many corridors and rooms that signs were hung at the corners to catalogue where the different areas were situated. He introduced them to the remaining wise men gathered in one of the larger chambers. At the moment, they were seated at long tables filled with tomes and parchments, where, Pathos explained, all the records were kept. Men and women filled the recording chambers. They wore ankle-length versions of Pathos' tunic. Their brown leather sandals made no sound on the thick carpets as they walked around rearranging the huge volumes of books on the shelves and adding more to them.

A few misty glass globes, the size of large melons, were scattered randomly on the table. Some Keepers were staring into their depths and others were eagerly scribbling with fancy quills on parchment paper. A few others were drawing sketches. At the end of each table, men and women were carefully sewing the manuscripts together between thick leather covers.

Kar walked over to one of the globes. In its murky depths, he could make out an army of soldiers clashing with people dressed like peasants on a hillside who carried tools for weapons. Behind the peasants, a village burned.

"What's going on?" Kar asked the woman sitting in front of one of the orbs.

"The Torallies are up in arms against the Barons," said the woman peering closely into the globe. She was writing the events as they unfolded in front of her on a clean yellow parchment.

"Why?"

"They are overtaxed and hungry and the Barons have not eased up on them, so they chose to fight."

"Why?"

"Because they are overtaxed and hungry ..." Kar could feel her teeth grinding in irritation. She looked up at him and her face eased. "This happens when certain heads of state are greedy for money and push the local people beyond their income limits. They end up fighting to change the laws."

"Who's winning?"

"We can't be sure. The Torallies are weak from hunger, though."

Kar looked sympathetically at the war going on inside the globe. He left when it seemed to get bloodier, and he peered into another one. In this one, a man and a woman were being pulled out from their home by an angry mob. The figures looked familiar to Kar. The globe cleared and he recognized them immediately. "Haylen! Jack! Over here!"

They ran over to the table and looked into the globe on the table next to Kar. An angry crowd was gathered outside of what seemed to be Kar's own house. Mrs. Beadlepoof was leading the protestors. She was pointing at Mr. and Mrs. Homely. The children watched in horror as Mrs. Beadlepoof pushed the Homelys out into the street. Their hands were tied in front of them.

"What is she doing?" Kar cried in a panic. "Where are they taking them?"

"They have been declared traitors." The elderly man in charge of the globe spoke as if the event was an everyday occurrence to him. He was calmly recording everything that was going on within the confines of the globe.

"Why?" Kar shouted, wanting to shake him.

"Lucas has decreed that if the boy, Kar, does not show up in ten days, they are to be executed, hung, or burned at the stake. I can't tell which will happen yet."

Kar suddenly felt weak in the knees and leaned on the table. "They are my parents. I must go back."

Pathos arrived at the table and put his hand on Kar's shoulder. "Let us not be too hasty. Bad things happen when one does not fully think things through."

"I don't care," cried Kar. "I have to go home. It's me they want!"

SOLARIS MARCEL

THE EVENING wore on and dinner was a tense and awkward affair for the three young travelers. This time they ate with the rest of the inhabitants of Teapot Mountain, who were thrilled to meet them and kept them occupied with questions about the outside world. Kar's patience with their eager questions was dwindling as fast as his appetite. Mistress Rowain clicked her tongue in displeasure when she cleared the table for dessert and found Kar's food hardly touched and his face masked in sadness. She smoothed the top of his silky head and said nothing.

After dinner, Mistress Rowain took Haylen under her care while Pathos showed the boys where they would sleep for the night.

"Tomorrow, I will relate to you one more story," he told the subdued boys before they undressed. "Maybe it will answer all the questions you have not yet asked, Kar. It might help you make a decision."

Jack had hardly whispered goodnight before his leaden eyelids shut down for the night. As for Kar, he struggled to fall asleep even though the bed was firm and the covers were as soft as silk. The image of his parents being treated viciously by the other Wyckians tore at his heart. He had never heard of anyone ever being executed. Hate for Lucas and the councilmen, alive or dead, surged through him. Maybe he could escape and return on his own. He didn't know if he could afford to wait for tomorrow. But how would he get back alone; and if he could manage it, then how would Haylen and Jack get home without him? He flipped on his back and stared up into the darkness, his eyes unblinking and burning with unshed tears for his family. How had everything in his life changed so much?

At breakfast the next morning, Haylen dared to ask Pathos the one question that was bothering her: "How can you be two hundred years old?"

Pathos gave her a big smile, acknowledging the compliment on his youthful looks. She blushed feverishly all over again. "The

159

wise men may be wise, but they also can be just plain foolish. In my youth I wanted to travel and see what lay beyond this mountain hideaway. I took the secret path across the water and visited many villages. One of them was Yongtown."

Jack nodded, his mouth full of bread. "That's where we got Secret Ingredient."

"I know," said Pathos. "It was about this time of year when I was there. Like a fool, I celebrated their New Year's Eve with them and even danced the night away. Since then, I never grow old—from the outside, that is. The rest of me is getting weary." He rubbed his face.

"Oh, no," lamented Haylen. "We were there at the New Year's Eve celebration as well and we danced, too. Oh, no, I'm never going to grow up. I'll look like a thirteen year old my whole life! I can never go home again."

"Don't fret, Haylen," said Pathos, patting her hand. "The New Year is different for everyone. You have to be at least thirty years old for the spell to have any effect on you. Secondly, if you are a man, you will stay young forever. All women who take it upon themselves to visit Yongtown during the festival will have youth bestowed on them for ten years. On the day before the tenth year the women's true age shows, but the men leave the village and return on the first day of the New Year. They have no interest in looking young while their insides grow old and feeble. Not even the younger ones take that chance anymore. They like everything to age at the same time. Wish I had known about that before I got myself into this mess," he grumbled.

"Oh," said Haylen, "that's a relief. But will you really live forever?"

"No, alas," said Pathos, "the rest of my body ages eventually. The mind. The heart. These are things that do age. But they just take a longer time to waste away."

Jack wiped off the beads of sweat that had sprung on his forehead.

"They must hate that," said Haylen softly. "Why don't the women leave the village, too? Why don't they accept growing old?"

"Because they take the magic with them wherever they go; they do not want to burden others with it," answered Pathos. "Well, if everybody has finished, let's go back to my sitting room. I promised Kar another story last night."

"Do they ever die?"

"Oh, yes, eventually," replied Pathos. "In their sleep, I'm told. Not a bad way to go."

Back in his study, they settled down on the worn-out couch near the fire for the rest of Pathos' tale. He passed around the box of hard candy. A stale smell of mold from the sofa wafted through their nostrils as the three of them gathered together to hear it. Haylen wrinkled her nose in distaste and sneezed loudly. Even though the weather on the outside was balmy and pleasant, the rocky walls glistened with condensation. A fire roared pleasantly to offset the chill in the air, but it could not diminish the mountain's musky smell.

Pathos' tumbler was filled with fresh water, and he took a small sip and cleared his throat. "I used to sit here for hours staring into the depths of the fire and looking for answers, hoping that I, too, could see a clearer future for us all."

They snuggled deeper into the couch. Secret Ingredient, showing more interest this time, sat patiently on Haylen's knee playing with dark-green worry beads.

Pathos continued, coughing slightly, bringing his voice to life again. "As I said, the wise men set out in pairs to warn people of events that could be detrimental to their future. Most of them returned as failures and others were never heard from again. So the High Council of the Wise ordered that the books be closed and that we were to let the future take its natural course. It was Solaris Marcel's turn to be the Keeper of History to Come. For years, he sat reading the ancient books, trying to decipher their meanings on his own. Then he came upon a verse that he believed would happen in his lifetime. He even thought he knew its exact date, so he set off with his beloved wife, Lunata, to the villages of Wyck, for he thought that was where the tragedy would occur. We pleaded for him not to cross Mount Footsteps. It was a treacherous climb even for the most experienced, but he left anyway. We were sorry to see him go. He was loved by all."

"When was this?" Haylen asked. Kar was sure she was reading his mind. He was too numb to ask anything.

"Thirteen years ago," said Pathos, still gazing into the flames. "Thirteen years ago."

Kar felt as if Pathos had poured a bucket of icy water into his veins.

"Solaris tried to make the people of Wyck understand what lay ahead, but the ten councilmen berated the villagers for being fools and for listening to a fool. Like a preacher with new insight, Solaris journeyed through the villages predicting catastrophe for all. The councilmen banned prophesying not long afterwards, but Solaris would not stop. He held secret meetings to try and make the villagers understand." At that point, Pathos paused and looked at Kar. "He was betrayed."

The children squeezed themselves further down into the folds of the couch. Secret Ingredient's yellow eyes were rounder than ever. He had dropped the worry beads back into his bottle, pulled out a rocking chair, and perched it on Haylen's knee. He rocked vigorously.

"Lunata was with child during that time." He threw a couple of logs in the dying embers of the fireplace and sat back as they caught fire. The smell of roses exploded into the air and Kar found he was holding his breath. "The councilmen decreed that Solaris and Lunata be punished and sought them out. That night Lunata was able to persuade Solaris to leave the EastWyck village and return home. He finally agreed. A year had passed since he had left Teapot Mountain. The night was cold and snow fell earlier than usual. They were nearing SouthWyck when Lunata could not travel any longer."

"Her twin boys were born in a barn among the cows and pigs in SouthWyck. One was small and weak, the other large and powerful looking, as if he was already a month old. The councilmen were almost upon the small family. They had ways of seeking them out. The boys were wrapped in bits and pieces of dirty cloth Lunata had probably found in the barn, and knowing that they were too late to cross the mountain, she placed each baby on a different doorstep."

"Why on different doorsteps?" inquired Haylen.

"Good question. I guess their parents thought that by giving one baby to each family, it would be more difficult for the councilmen to find the children. Even if they found one of them, the other child might be saved."

"Oh," said Haylen, "that makes sense."

"With each baby, they placed a note with only their first names on them. They stole a broomster to get away. When they were halfway up the mountain, they were caught. They fought long and hard but could not beat death because the councilmen are nothing but the skeletal remains of sorcerers."

This time it was Jack's turn to interrupt. "Why are they skeletons? They really are ugly." Kar and Haylen nodded in agreement.

Pathos snorted. "That is really a funny story."

"Tell us!" Haylen cried.

"Well, from what we could gather through the eyes of the globe, they were trying to put together a spell that would give them a very long and healthy life of immortality. When they thought they had all the ingredients together, they gathered all the councilmen in one room and threw everything for the spell into a large black cauldron. They waited until vapors rose before they poured in the last of the ingredients. We were not able to find out what the ingredients were. Anyway, one of the councilman's long fingernails broke off and fell in without anybody noticing. After it had all cooled down, they dipped their cups in, toasted each other, swallowed the contents in one gulp—and poof!" Pathos snapped his fingers. "They immediately turned into these skinny white skeletons and began screaming and running around like madmen. It was so funny! Honestly, we laughed for days about it."

It took a while for Jack to calm down, he was laughing so hard. "They deserved it!"

"As I was saying," said Pathos, fishing around for another glass of water. He found two near his feet and poured one into the other. He drank thirstily. "Where was I?"

"They were fighting the skeletons," said Haylen.

Kar had not joined in the laughter, nor was he in the mood to ask questions. He could imagine Solaris riding the stolen broomster and desperately trying to save his family's life. If only he was half as brave.

"Oh, yes," continued Pathos. "Solaris had ahold of one of the skeleton's necks, but he was able to free himself and they struggled, each trying to throw the other off their broomsters. Eventually they crashed against the mountain. The next day, the villagers spied bits and pieces of the councilman's bones scattered at the bottom of Mount Footsteps. Solaris was buried by a friend in one of the caves."

At that moment, Secret Ingredient swayed forward too far and toppled off Haylen's knee. Nervous giggles broke the somber mood. Secret Ingredient tried to stand up, but his long red robes kept getting in the way. Finally he gathered them up around his waist, picked up the matching hat, and slid under the couch to sulk, pulling his precious bottle after him.

"What happened to Lunata?" asked Jack. The smiles on their faces slowly disappeared.

"Lunata was able to escape, but she did not live long afterwards. The pain of losing her husband and children was just too much for her. She could not even remember on which doorsteps she had placed them, and we were banned from entering the Wyck villages. We had to keep silent about the children, afraid the councilmen would find them."

"So, you see, children. You cannot change fate. In trying to change the future, Solaris confirmed it. 'For unto them two sons were born.' That is why they never believed it was their own fate they were unfolding. They never expected to have children. Why, I don't know."

Kar had one question on his mind as he waited for Pathos to continue, but it seemed like Pathos had forgotten about them as he stared into the dying embers. Mistress Rowain interrupted the silence and gathered them into the dining room for lunch. The other inhabitants of Teapot Mountain were already seated, and soon the children were eating and answering more questions about what lay beyond the Mountain.

Still one question burned on the tip of Kar's tongue. It wasn't until late in the afternoon while they were drinking tea that Kar plucked up the courage to ask Pathos. Even Jack, surrounded with all the goodies that Mistress Rowain had baked for them, seemed to be finally (if only briefly) sated.

"Sir," said Kar, loudly sucking in air as if it would bolster his courage. "I have a question to ask."

Pathos placed the cup of tea he was drinking carefully on the saucer and looked up at Kar warmly. "Yes, Kar?"

"What were the children's names?"

"I guess it is your right to know," said Pathos. His deep, brown eyes shimmered. "I, too, hoped to avoid the future, but it is inevitable." He reached out for Kar's hand and took it lovingly into his own. "One was, of course, you, as you might have guessed by now, and the other child," he paused a bit, pressing his lips together, " was Lucas."

Haylen dropped her teacup, barely missing Secret Ingredient's head, and, pushing her chair away from the table, ran out of the room. Jack's teacup froze on his lips and he looked quickly at Kar, whose face was wiped of all color. Like Haylen, Kar pulled himself away from the table and left the room. Unlike Haylen, his steps were unhurried. He walked like a dying man.

But the moment he passed the doorway, he took off at a run, passing through the narrow, sweaty corridors, turning sharp corners, and slipping in his haste to distance himself from it all. He fell, panting, in a dark corner of a corridor where he banged his head on the stone wall. Lucas! It couldn't be! The name seemed to ring like the heavy toll of a million bells. No, it couldn't be. Not that nasty boy who had hated and taunted him all his young life. Why couldn't it be anybody else? He could not handle the thoughts that seemed to flow in his mind like a river that suddenly found an outlet. He slipped into a deep sleep, curled up on the cold stone floor, relieved from his tormented thoughts for the time being.

He woke up and found himself tucked in bed. Jack was breathing softly in the one next to him. He had no idea what time it was or how long he had slept. A single name leapt into his mind and he felt as if his heart had been gripped by a vice. Lucas. He slipped out of bed and went in search of the kitchen. He needed a glass of water.

A small candle illuminated a corner of the dark kitchen. He could make out a soft glow, and as he came nearer, he recognized it was reflecting from Haylen's hair. She was seated at the end of the kitchen table.

"Hello," he said.

Haylen jumped. "You scared me." She was wearing a long white nightgown embroidered with blue flowers around the collar. It hung loosely across her shoulders. Secret Ingredient was sitting on the side of his bed, on the table, holding his bottle and looking worried.

"I wanted a drink of water," said Kar, dipping a tumbler into a giant clay vase standing in one corner of the room. He sat next to Haylen on the table. "I guess now I know who my real parents are, thanks to Secret Ingredient, here."

Secret Ingredient whimpered and threw the bottle over his head.

"I guess you do," said Haylen. "Now what?"

"My head hurts from thinking about it, but my home is where my parents are, real or not, and I'm lucky to have them. They need me right now."

"Well," said Haylen, "look on the bright side. You could have been placed on the Nosty's doorstep."

Kar smiled for the first time that day.

166

"What about Lucas?" Haylen asked.

"What about him?" Kar looked away. He didn't want her to know how deeply that name affected him now.

"He's the reason we're here in the first place, Kar. We can't hide that fact. And if you return, the councilman will hunt you down—if the villagers don't get to you first."

Kar jumped up. "I don't care," he shouted, not caring who he woke. "My real parents started this. If they had minded their own business, this mess would never have happened!" Kar pounded his fist on the table, ejecting Secret Ingredient from his bed and into the tumbler of water.

Haylen fished him out. "Well, I do. I care." She grabbed a kitchen towel and gave Secret Ingredient a brisk drying before depositing him clumsily on his bed. He remained silent during the humiliating encounter. "We have come a long way, Kar, and we only have half the answers we need."

"What more can we find?" cried Kar. "Lucas Nosty is my brother, my twin!" He threw his hands up into the air. "I just can't believe it!"

"Yes, he's your brother, but the Wyck villages are burning because of him, and we have to find him and put a stop to it!" This time she pounded the table.

Secret Ingredient angrily pulled himself out of the tumbler again and hung over the rim, sputtering.

Haylen and Kar stood facing each other, eyes locked in anger and sympathy, until Kar leaned forward and put his head on the table.

"I guess you're right, Haylen. But what else can we do? We are kids with no power, especially me. In fact, I actually un-magic things. I have nothing to fight with," he sighed. "We have lost the fight with Lucas before it even started."

Haylen gently patted him on the head. "We will try and find out more from Pathos in the morning."

OVER TEAPOT MOUNTAIN

THAT NIGHT, Kar, Haylen, and Jack met in the kitchen after everyone had gone to bed. They had been secretly preparing to leave. Kar knew that if they told Pathos what they were going to do, he would not allow them to leave the mountain. He was determined to protect the children. Pathos thought they were content to keep searching for information. Jack, however, was eager to leave the mountain's clammy rooms, which were getting on his nerves. He missed the sunshine. He was also afraid the musky smell would never leave his body.

As they gathered together quietly in the kitchen, Jack showed Kar a sword he had found in one of the chambers. It was rusty and could not even cut through butter. The tip was missing and the handle was worn, but Jack was adamant about taking it. Scrawled in poor handwriting on the side of the beaten metal handle, with a few letters missing, were the words *ragon kille.*

"I'm sure it means *dragon killer,*" said Jack, excitedly. "I've just got to take it!"

Kar was furious and demanded that Jack return it. Jack refused and said he was going to clean and sharpen it himself. He wasn't going unarmed into hostile territory, and what if they met a dragon there? The book *How To Kill a Dragon in Ten Easy Steps* mentioned that a sword was a necessary piece of equipment. Kar wrote a short note of apology and left it in the room from where he had taken the sword. The note explained that they would return the sword when they returned to the mountain. Hopefully, thought Kar. Hopefully.

Just before dawn they said their farewells to Secret Ingredient, who could hardly speak between his sobs and his heartfelt sorrow and shame for not having the courage to go with them. He had grown fond of his traveling companions and was worried he'd never see them again. Jack called him a crybaby and a Wyckian chicken.

Before they sneaked away, Jack had found a room that held an amazing assortment of weapons as well as a file that he used to clean and sharpen the sword. He polished the rusty parts as well as he could.

While rummaging through the artillery, he found a sword belt that fit around his waist. The sword just barely touched the floor. Any longer, and it would have scraped along the stone floor, emitting sparks.

"Don't you think that sword is a bit too long for you?" asked Haylen sweetly. "You might trip on it."

Jack shook his head. "Uh-uh. It's just the right size."

They gave up trying to persuade him to leave it behind. After packing a few supplies from the kitchen and assembling their bags, they tiptoed to Pathos' sitting room right before dawn. Standing on the wooden platform, they pushed the heavy lever on the cave wall and slowly dropped into the darkness.

Upon exiting the mountain, the morning sun shot into their path and sent whoops of delight through Jack, who dropped his load and cartwheeled his way to where they had left the raft. The sword hit him on the head, but despite the large bruise forming on his forehead, he remained exuberant. It seemed nothing was out of place, and soon they were soaring over the mountain on their makeshift raft made of broken broomsticks, into the desert beyond.

Haylen pulled out the parchment on which she had written Secret Ingredient's directions. "'Pass the mountain going straight east. Never waver. Cross half the ocean of sand and drop straight down. You will know it when you see it.' He wouldn't tell me what 'it' was. He said he didn't know. And Jack's not the only one who took something from the mountain. I took this, too," she said meekly, not looking at Kar's face, as she pulled out another piece of rolled-up parchment from her bag.

"What is it?" Kar was almost afraid to ask. The worry lines in his forehead deepened. The stolen sword was still grating on his nerves. He did not want the people in the mountain, his ancestors, to consider them thieves.

Haylen answered: "It's a map."

"Let me see," said Jack. "Hey, this shows a lot more than the one you took from the school library. It shows the world, practically," he cried. "Wow, can you believe it? The villages of Wyck are just specks."

Kar's curiosity won him over, and he took a look at the map. "It even shows you what lies past the desert. And look here! There is a small dot - right here, see? - in the middle of the desert." They looked over his shoulder. "Maybe that's the place Secret Ingredient was talking about."

"Well, I'm glad you took it," said Jack, pulling out his shiny sword and waving it about. "We don't need that crybaby, Secret Ingredient, anymore."

"Too bad," said Secret Ingredient popping out of Jack's backpack. "I'm coming anyway!"

"What?" they cried in unison.

"I thought you were too chicken to come," mocked Jack.

"Yeah, well; I remembered how boring it was there, and hopped a ride."

"Good," said Haylen. "We might need you. Thanks for changing your mind."

"Yeah, thanks," added Kar. "It's good to have the gang together."

Secret Ingredient's eyes watered up a bit, but he brushed the tears aside and smiled widely.

"Hey! Watch it!" cried Haylen, ducking her head as Jack continued to wave the sword about. "You almost decapitated me with that rusty thing! Have you ever used a sword before, anyway?"

"I've honed the blade to perfection." Jack waved the sword above his head.

"Please," said Kar, putting his hand on Jack's shoulder, "put it away before you hurt someone."

"All right." Jack pouted and sheathed the sword.

At that moment Kar and Haylen screamed in horror. A giant black bird with three legs and three beaks swooped suddenly over their heads. It easily picked up Jack by his backpack with its curved talons and flew back towards Teapot Mountain. They could hear Jack's screams fading away.

Haylen jumped up and down, pulling at her hair and screeching at the top of her lungs. "Jack. Jack!" she cried. Then she slumped to the floor, weeping.

Kar gathered her in his arms. "It's all my fault. I'm to blame. I'm so sorry, Haylen. I should not have brought us here. We'll go back for him. We'll get him back!"

Haylen continued to sob. "Oh, Jack! What would that horrible big black bird want with him?"

Kar turned the raft around and headed back. Haylen was crying softly. After a few minutes, he pointed to something in the sky.

"Is it another one?" asked Haylen, frightened.

As it grew closer, it seemed much smaller than the black bird with the three beaks. Kar looked for something to defend themselves with. But they hadn't really brought anything that could be used as a weapon. He should have listened to Jack and brought his own sword. He grabbed Haylen's leather bag, preparing to swing it against the enemy. An eagle with a bloody sword in its beak, carrying a backpack, landed on the edge of the raft. Kar swung Haylen's bag at it to throw it off balance, but before the bag could hit the bird, Jack appeared, disheveled, slightly bloody, and grinning broadly.

"Hey, watch it," he said, ducking his head. "I told you the sword would come in handy."

"Oh, Jack!" cried Haylen, throwing herself into his arms.

Kar's knees felt wobbly with relief. "What happened?"

Jack recounted his adventure. The ugly bird had flown him back to Teapot Mountain and dropped him into a huge nest of baby birds, their many beaks wide open and eager to swallow him whole. As soon as she dropped him, he had whipped out his sword and hacked away at the mother's legs before swiftly turning into an eagle, grabbing his sword and backpack. He left the mother nursing her three injured talons.

"I'm so glad you are able to shape-shift into an eagle," said Haylen, hugging him again.

"Yeah," said Jack. "Can you imagine if I could only turn into a mouse?"

They all shuddered visibly at the thought.

Suddenly they remembered Secret Ingredient and desperately searched for him in the backpack. They found him curled up at the bottom, still shaking. "Should've stayed in the mountain!"

Relieved that Secret Ingredient was safe, Kar advised that they keep their eyes on each other from then on. He realized how differently the story would have ended if either he or Haylen had been taken by the bird (except maybe for Haylen, who might have moved all of Teapot Mountain to another place). Still, it would not have bode well for any of them.

The day came to a close and still the only thing they could see were miles and miles of sand dunes on all sides. Teapot Mountain had already disappeared from sight.

They stopped the raft in midair and took turns guarding each other through the night. Kar was the last to take over and he stood at attention scanning the night sky, his hand on Jack's sword, ready for what may come. It came sooner than he expected.

As dawn approached, Kar felt a slight shift in the air, as if the breeze was changing direction. Without warning a gust of wind hit him full force in the face, almost knocking him down. The raft started to buck like a wild horse, as if being ridden for the first time. Sand blew in a circle around them. Suddenly the raft began to rotate. Faster and faster it turned until they were yanked into the swirling vortex. For a while they spun madly in the eye of the giant whirlwind, unable to open their mouths for fear grains of sand would fill their lungs and choke them to death. Just as quickly as it began, it stopped. They plummeted down. An eagle broke free of the sandstorm and watched as Kar and Haylen fell, shrieking, until they were swallowed up in the dunes below.

Kar was the first to try to open his eyes, but couldn't. He groaned and tried to move. He couldn't. He felt a huge weight bearing down on him. His mouth was filling with sand. He struggled for a while: one hand felt free while the other seemed to be lodged underneath him. He felt someone grab at his hand and yank hard. He felt sand loosen around his body. Jack stood overhead, his face streaked with specks of sand and sweat. Jack wiped Kar's face.

"Kar! Kar!" cried Jack. "Are you all right?"

"I think so." He spat sand out of his mouth. He could hardly see. "Where's Haylen?"

"I don't know," Jack said, looking around in panic. "I can't find her!"

"What?" Kar clumsily tried to steady himself while rubbing the gritty brown sand out of his eyes. "What do you mean you can't find her? She has to be here." His eyes hurt badly.

"I saw your hand," said Jack. "But I can't see Haylen anywhere." He began pacing around the site again, scanning for any sign of movement or limbs.

"Go up again," cried Kar. "Maybe you can see her better from the sky. I'll keep looking from here."

The eagle flew off and returned after a few minutes. "I can't see her anywhere," sobbed Jack. "I really, really looked."

"She'll suffocate under the sand! We have to find her soon! Go again!"

The eagle screeched and soared upwards again. Kar watched in a daze as the eagle circled the area, shrieked again, and dove out of sight behind a sand dune. He could barely walk on the soft grains of sand, but he pulled himself over a small dune and slid down to find his friend. Jack was furiously digging in the ground. Kar ran over and joined him on his hands and knees. They pulled Haylen out, sputtering sand all over their faces. She coughed slightly and moaned.

"It's okay," said Kar, "you're fine now. Jack found you."

Haylen sat up and looked around. "You know, I think I saw my life flash by." Her voice sounded hoarse. "It was a very short flash."

They laughed; more out of relief than at Haylen's attempt to lighten things up. They knew they had come very close to losing her.

"We'd better sit down for a while and assess our situation," said Kar.

"I can summon it up in the words of Secret Ingredient," said Jack, mimicking the tiny, green imp's voice and widening his eyes: "Lost. You are lost."

Kar didn't think it was funny at all and the look on Haylen's face stopped Jack cold.

"Secret Ingredient," cried Haylen. "Where is he?"

After two hours they gave up. Secret Ingredient was nowhere to be found. Haylen cried while the boys felt so bad they could barely look at each other. What Secret Ingredient dreaded the most, had happened.

Jack left them to search for anything that might have been thrown from the raft. It took him time to find the few things that had not been buried deeply by the sudden desert tornado. He dropped each load next to Haylen. Most of their clothes were gone. He found a few loaves of bread and some cheese, as well as two out of the three leather pouches of water they had brought with them. Jack came back to tell them the raft had busted and broomsticks were lying everywhere. Most of them were broken to bits. He could find only one that seemed to have weathered the desert storm.

"It's better than nothing," said Haylen, testing it. "I wonder if the tornado took us off course? We will see better when we get up in the air."

"I wish there was a better way," she said, getting to her feet again. "I'm really beginning to hate heights. I miss Secret." She began to cry again.

"You know Secret, Haylen. He'll pop up somewhere."

"But he's out of his bottle, and he can't live without it!"

They stood silently, absorbing the new revelation.

"We'd better get up in the air. Maybe the wind threw him way off course. He is lighter than us, you know. I am sure he'll make it," said Kar.

"It beats walking, though," said Jack. "This sand is just too hot! Any more of this and my shoes might melt."

Haylen and Kar rode the broomstick while trying to balance the weight of the remaining bags on the handle. Jack flew next to them, carrying his sword in his beak. They flew for a while until Haylen complained of a backache. She had been searching for a glimpse of the green imp. But there was nothing but sand as far as she could see.

After resting a bit, Kar remarked that they should be taking off again before it got too dark to gain more ground before nightfall. It would probably be cooler at night, but it would be a lot harder to see anything. They had to find a balance between enduring the desert heat and keeping an eye out for Secret Ingredient. The early morning hours would be the best time to fly.

It was towards dawn when they saw it. For a moment, Kar thought it was only a mirage. Something dark shimmered in the sand below them. They almost passed it when Jack suddenly swerved and dropped below them. He came back up again, flapping his wings and playfully spraying them with water from his beak.

HOW TO KILL A DRAGON

IT WAS an actual swimming pool in the middle of the desert; surrounded on one side by swaying palm trees ripe with fruit and on the other, by broken pillars and statues that were once upright but now lay in pieces, half buried in the sand. In the middle of the pool, Secret Ingredient was doing the back paddle.

Haylen was so happy to see him that she dived in and, upon reaching him, smacked the top of his tiny head with kisses. Secret Ingredient giggled and laughed delightedly. Kar and Jack had followed Haylen into the pool and were equally excited at finding him.

"What happened to you?" asked Jack, relieved. "We thought you were a goner."

Kar spoke out: "Finding Secret is one thing. But what in the world is a swimming pool doing in the middle of the desert?"

"Magical mishaps?" answered Haylen. "No?"

"I guess," said Kar floating on his back. "A swimming pool. With water, no less, in a desert. I think I'm dreaming."

It was fun playing in the pool. They couldn't remember the last time they had laughed so much or had a good time, even with the thought of doom hovering over their heads. Beside the pool, a giant statue of a warrior lay armless, staring lifelessly into the sky.

Bits and pieces of twigs made up a campfire. They passed the bread and cheese around and drank from the remaining water. Jack mentioned once again how camp life was good enough for him. This time, Haylen got up and dumped a bowl of sand on his head.

Secret Ingredient pulled out a cold drink from his bottle. He had explained to his fellow buddies that his bottle had an invisible string that would always be tied to him.

"That's a relief," said Haylen. "Anyway, if we ever get out of this, I never want to see the outside of my house."

By the time they were ready for bed it had grown very cold.

"Brrr," said Haylen, rubbing her arms, "it's chilly in the desert."

Kar threw as many pieces of broken branches as he could find on the campfire until it was roaring again. "Hope this stays through the night," he said.

Haylen and Kar huddled together for warmth as Jack took up the first shift of the night. A desert scorpion came out from underneath a rock and approached the campsite, but Jack was ready with his mighty sword and it scuttled out of sight. Other small creatures met the same fate.

Haylen took the last shift and they woke up to her screams as she stood, swinging Jack's sword at a large dragonfly, its head almost as big as her hand. "Will you do something?" she yelled at them. "It's attacking me!"

Jack swatted it with his hand and it flew out of sight. "I told you we'd meet up with dragons. You just have to know how to defeat them." He grinned.

They breakfasted and cleaned up. Kar squatted next to a small pool of clear water bubbling under the palm trees to fill their leather drinking pouches. From where he sat, the swimming pool looked like blue glass. Not even a ripple marred its glossy surface. He walked over and looked straight to the bottom. He gasped. "Come!" he yelled. "Come see this!"

The bottom of the pool had been laid with white marble tile. In the middle, steps led down into a watery hole. The pool was deeper than any other pool they'd ever swum in and so none of them had bothered to check out the bottom.

Haylen was delighted. "We almost missed it."

"Yeah," said Jack. "Imagine: by tomorrow we'd have been on the other side of the desert. And you'd never know what's out there. Dragons?"

"Oh, you and your dragons," said Haylen, shoving him in exasperation. "I just wish we'd see one just to shut you up. Well, Kar, how do we get down there without drowning? Any ideas?"

"There must be a way to drain the pool," said Jack. "They wouldn't have built the stairs like that just for fun."

"Let's all spread out and look around," said Kar.

They walked all around the oasis, checking around the rocks and bushes, but found nothing that looked like a lever that would do the trick.

"Maybe it's not a lever," said Jack when they reassembled. "Maybe we have to push something."

Once again they walked around, pushing at the boulders and stomping on the ground. Finally, tired and hungry, they sat around the small fire. Haylen doled out the remaining cheese and bread.

"Maybe it's not this place," said Kar. "We don't know exactly. Probably the dot on the map was just the oasis."

"Well, we better find it quickly," said Haylen. "This is the last of the food, and unless we want to starve to death, we have to either return quickly or start eating desert scorpions."

Kar made a face. "We have to save my parents with or without this globe."

Jack licked the remaining crumbs from the palms of his hand. "There are plenty of dates to eat."

They glowered at him.

"What?" He grinned.

"Wait! I've got an idea," exclaimed Kar. He took off his clothes and jumped into the pool. He returned, grinning up at them. "Found it!"

"What? What did you find?" asked Haylen, running up to him.

"There is something on the side of the pool wall. I remembered it from our swim yesterday. I noticed it and thought was kind of out of place. It's not a lever. It looks like a huge bolt screwed into the side. I need something to unscrew it. Hand me the sword."

Haylen handed him the sword and he dived back in. After what seemed a very long time to Jack and Haylen, he returned, gasping and spitting water. "After a bit of a struggle, I was able to turn it. Anything happened yet?"

They looked down at the pool, but water seemed not to have lessened at all. In fact, it seemed to be slowly rising.

"No," said Jack. "It's not going down at all. In fact, it looks like it's about to overflow."

Kar dived back in again. "Turned it the other way this time," he said, returning a few seconds later. "Now what's happening?"

"It has stopped overflowing," said Haylen. "Nothing else."

"Fancy meeting you here." A voice rang out in the desert above them.

Three heads shot up to look at the man in purple robes riding a black broomster. They recognized the face immediately. It was the same man they had met at the parking lot. His beady charcoal eyes glinted in the harsh sun.

They were too shocked to answer. Jack slowly got up from where he was kneeling next to the pool.

"Surprised to see me, I bet," he said. "I should say the same of you. I would never have thought of meeting children in this forsaken place." He looked around. "What are you doing here?"

"What are you doing here?" retorted Kar, pulling himself out of the pool. "Are you following us?"

"This is a free desert," the stranger answered. He lowered the broomster to the ground and got off. "Ah, it is good to stretch the legs. Real legs, I might add."

"We were just leaving," said Kar, pushing Haylen in front of him. "Jack, get your stuff. We should go now."

"I hope it is not my fault you are leaving," said the stranger. He laughed as if what he said was funny.

A look of shock and surprise spread across their faces as they recognized the councilman's hideous laugh. They looked at each other in bewilderment.

But before they could react, a musical sound filled the air. Haylen grabbed Kar's arm and whispered, "Can you hear that?"

Kar nodded.

"It sounds like a harp," said Jack.

"Oh, Kar, I don't have a good feeling about this," whimpered Haylen.

It seemed that the councilman had the same feelings. He flung himself on the broomster; but to his dismay, it sputtered and died.

Angrily he kicked it with his feet. It turned over on the sand as if defying him. Without a word, he raced to hide behind the giant statue. He squeezed himself beneath its giant armpit. The three of them watched, amused by his frantic dash to hide.

"What's with him?" asked Kar, pulling on his trousers over his long, wet underwear. "Why doesn't he just wave his hand and disappear? Why is he running around like a madman?"

"Look up there!" cried Haylen, pointing towards the sky.

Something was blocking out the sun.

"I guess you got your wish, Jack!" screamed Kar. "It's a dragon! Hide!"

A scaly emerald beast, glinting like a jewel in the sky, its wings spanning far and wide, noisily flapped over their heads. Black smoke leaked out the corners of its mouth and spurts of fire spewed from its round black nostrils.

Jack grabbed his bag and sword and ran after them. They also squeezed themselves between the other armpit of the fallen statue. Shaking, they peered up at the dragon. Giant claws, yellowed with age, dug into the sand as it landed next to the pool. It snorted and pranced.

"We should have listened to Pathos," said Haylen. Kar could feel her trembling. "No wonder nobody has ever returned from here. That's a real monster!"

Secret Ingredient flung himself into Kar's pocket. He could feel his little body trembling. The dragon tilted its head to one side. Trails of fire streamed from its flaying nostrils and over their heads.

"Did it see us?" Jack gulped the final word, almost choking on it. Haylen's throat had frozen in terror, unable to answer.

Kar poked his head out from the side of the stone arm. He could see the councilman's purple cape as he tried to dig himself deeper into the other stone's armpit.

The dragon turned its attention to the pool, and dipping his head, drank long and hard until he emptied it.

"So," mused Kar, sarcastically, "that's how you drain the water. You call the dragon. We should have known that." He smacked his forehead quietly. "Now, Jack, why don't you just go ahead and read your dragon bock and use your mighty *ragon kille* sword on it."

"The book says you have to stare him in the eyes first," Jack whispered fiercely in reply.

"I'm not staring him in any eye," cried Haylen, anger suddenly breaking the fear that had taken ahold of her. "Look at those eyes. Each one is as big as the pool of water he just swallowed. You go stare him in the eyes. Whack him with the sword. Do something!"

Kar swallowed and nodded in agreement. "Do something, Jack. You're the only one who is ready for this."

"Then we're doomed," cried Jack.

"Well, sorry, guys," said Kar. "Sorry I got you into this. At least my death will be the end of Lucas' power, too. Something good will come of it."

"Yeah, well, mine will just be the end of me," wept Jack.

"Listen, I will try to get his attention and you, Haylen, grab the broom and take off," said Kar. "Jack, make like an eagle and get out of here." The dragon coughed up a few more spurting flames, but the water had taken the fire out of him.

"Oh, stop that," whispered Haylen, her voice stronger now. "You got your wish, Jack. Do something. Hit him with your sword."

The dragon snorted and shifted his immense body towards them. Weak flames shot out from his nostrils.

"Shush; it can hear very well," whispered Jack while trying to squeeze himself more between them. He pulled a book out from his backpack that he had flung on his back at the last second.

"Give me that book," said Haylen. She grabbed the book from Jack's trembling fingers and put her finger on her mouth to silence his whimpers. The book was very thin. Each step was written on one page. A drawing of a dragon was on the first page. She turned to the second page. Jack looked over her shoulder at the book while Kar kept his eyes glued on the dragon. He knew all the steps by heart.

First step: Do not take your eyes off the dragon. Dragons feel compelled to stare back. This gives your partner an advantage. If you have a partner. Otherwise, bid yourself farewell.

(A word of advice. An older dragon's vision is blurry: therefore, locking eyes on a partially blind dragon does nothing to further your career in dragon slaying. The nearer you are, the blurrier its vision becomes. Younger ones see everything in perfect detail. You should hope for a young one, as it is easier to lock eyes with it as you draw near).

"How old do you think it is?" asked Haylen.

"How can I tell? It doesn't exactly have rings that tell its age," answered Kar nervously. "Shall I ask it?"

Haylen shot him a glance. She turned back to the page.

Second step: Dragons have excellent hearing. Any undue noise from your partner will cause dragon to break its stare. Otherwise, forget about the whole thing. Keep the attention of the dragon towards the front as your partner heads to the tail of the dragon. If you are able to lock eyes with the dragon and keep deathly silent, you are ahead, for the time being.

Third step. As you keep the dragon mesmerized, your partner should fill a sack of sand.

Fourth step. Carrying the sack full of sand, jump on dragon's tail from the lowest point and follow the yellow line that runs all the way up to the top of its head. At the end of the line is a deep round hole on top of its head.

Fifth step. Fill this hole with sand. This will render the dragon motionless and unable to move for at least an hour.

Sixth step. Now that you have come this far (which would be considered a miracle and nothing magical about it), take your sword and hack the dragon's head off. Sword must be exceptionally sharp. Be quick about it. It would be advisable to own a dragon-killing sword; but not compulsory.

"See," said Jack. "I was right. Without this sword we'd be goners for sure."

Kar and Haylen turned to glare at Jack for a moment and turned back to the dragon that was sniffing the robe of the councilman. They could hear muffled screams of terror.

Seventh step. If you like, drinking dragon's blood will give you its strength. Very unpleasant taste, but worth it when the other dragons arrive. My advice: drink it.

"We're goners." Jack slapped his forehead.

Haylen said nothing and continued reading.

Eighth step. If you have enough time before another dragon arrives to the sound of the dying screams of the first dragon, you can pull off a few scales. Great for shields and the making of magical urns. Zero percent survival rate.

Ninth step. This is very important. You must bury the dragon's head in the sand, otherwise it will be very upset upon waking up and finding its body gone. If other dragons arrive first, bury yourselves along with it.

Haylen and Kar's eyebrows shot up. Jack swallowed hard.

Tenth step. There is no tenth step. Good Luck. The above has not been officially confirmed. All those who have gone to test this theory have not yet returned. If any of you succeed, please pass this information back to me. That is, if I am still alive by then.

Griff Tudalor

"What a bunch of nonsense," cried Haylen, slamming the book shut and regretting it.

The dragon roared. They felt their hair catch on fire. They frantically pounded on each others' heads to put it out.

Finally, upon pain of his own death, Haylen persuaded Jack to fill his water pouch with sand. "You just change into an eagle, pick up the pouch, land on his head, and pour the sand into that hole of his," explained Haylen simply to a very pale version of Jack. "We'll grab his attention and freeze him with our deadly stares."

"Just like that," he said, trying to snap his fingers. The attempt at sarcasm was lost on them.

Without answering, Kar and Haylen took a deep breath and jumped out from behind the boulders, waving their hands. The dragon shifted its heavy body towards them and lowered its head to get a better view. It blinked and turned away.

"Oh, no," cried Haylen, "it's an old dragon!"

Locking eyes was out of the question. Kar could see the dragon's eyes were as blurry as the water it just sucked up.

"What're we going to do now?" she asked uneasily.

"Let's back up a bit," said Kar. "My dad can't see so well and when he tries to read, he moves the book back and forth in front of his eyes to find the right focus."

Slowly they backed away from the dragon and away from the safety of the boulders. Holding hands, they took a few steps forward and then a few steps backwards. The dragon tilted its head and looked perplexed at the figures dancing in front of him.

Kar wondered where Jack was now. He could not see him anywhere.

"Let's each take one eye," said Kar. "Maybe that will confuse it a bit."

They separated, trying to keep the dragon's giant round eyes in view. The dragon snorted loudly, but only black smoke filled the air around its head. They could not see its eyes anymore. Suddenly it lifted one giant leg and pounded the ground. Kar and Haylen lost their balance and fell on their backs. It lumbered towards the bodies curled up in terror and then stopped, suddenly lowering its head, each blazing red eye transfixed on a face.

BACK TO LILLIAN

LILLIAN STOOD in the center of the field near the SouthWyck village watching the villagers try to clear away the damaged stage where *What's My Magic?* Day had taken place when a sandstorm appeared. A number of villagers, who were struggling to push poles back into the ground, were now practically knee deep in fine sand. An empty swimming pool surrounded by tall, swaying palm trees laden with ripe dates also appeared to be a part of the new landscape. Lillian recovered quickly from the shock.

Holding Haylen in a tight grip and standing on top of an armless statue was a stranger who seemed to be as shocked as all the others at the unexpected twist in scenery. Lillian trudged her way through the sand and climbed up onto the statue.

"Why, Haylen," she cried, "we were so worried about you! Welcome home! Why is that man holding you like that?"

The man let go of Haylen and stepped back. "You think you're real smart," Lillian heard him hiss at Haylen, "using your magic like that. It will be for the last time, I assure you. Kar will be coming back this way to save his foolish parents for sure, and then I'll take care of the lot of you. All of you stupid Wyckians."

Lillian strode quickly towards the pair. "You just leave her alone!"

Haylen turned to face him, but he had already jumped off the statue. He looked up at her with contempt. "This does not end here." He turned and stomped angrily away, kicking at the sand, tripping, getting up again, and kicking the sand once more in frustration until he disappeared into the crowd that had gathered to check out the pool.

Lillian ran over to Haylen and helped her off the statue. "Are you all right?" she asked.

"Yes, I'm fine," said Haylen, a bit bewildered. "Just fine." She pushed past Lillian, pulling Jack with her, and ran up to the group of people who were sifting sand through their fingers.

"Fine sand," one said.

"Wonder where it came from?" said another.

"Great swimming pool, too," said a young woman. "Just the right size for the school. I wonder why there are stairs running down the middle of it?"

"What are you doing?" asked Haylen angrily to the men driving a pole in the sand.

"Haylen, Jack - we had put out missing children cloud ads all over the place. Where were you?" said one of the men, approaching them. "And where is Kar?"

"Trying to save your b ..." Jack poked Haylen hard in the back. "What?" She turned to glare at Jack for a second. "What are you doing here?" she demanded again.

The man's face changed to an ugly frown. "This is the way we deal with traitors."

"By burying them in the sand?" she retorted, kicking at the sand and spraying them.

"You had better leave." He spat out granules of sand. "Children should not be around to witness this." He turned his back. "Everybody," he yelled to the crowd. "We should push everything out to a new location. There is too much sand here."

"We've never had a swimming pool before," said a woman, following the man. "Or, I guess, more accurately, an oasis. Look at all those lovely palm trees. That fallen statue adds a nice touch too!"

"Yes; but did you notice," said her companion, "that the pool has stairs at the bottom? I wonder why?"

Lillian watched as the town folks pulled their legs out from the sand and began treading carefully across. She turned to the pair of lost travelers. "Where have you been? And where is Kar?"

Haylen turned to Lillian. "He's gone! And no one can find him," she cried.

Lillian took Haylen's hand. "Wait! I know everything, and I hope that Kar is safe. We were so worried about you."

Tears welled up in Haylen's eyes and spilled down her cheeks, leaving sandy streaks. "I left him in the desert with a stiff dragon."

"Huh?"

"What are we going to do now?" asked Jack interrupting them.

"I know," said Haylen. "If Kar is smart enough, he'll try to get the broomster fixed that the councilman dumped behind."

Lillian bumped into the handle of a black broomster poking out from the sand. "Whose is this?"

"Oh, no!" Haylen and Kar looked at each other in horror. "It's the broomster!"

There was nothing but desert as far as the eye could see. Beams of colored light spewed from the globe in his hand. Kar stood under the giant leg of the dragon, which was still motionless in the air. He quickly stepped away, afraid it might come crashing down on him any moment.

There was nothing he could defend himself with. He remembered what the book said. *Bury yourself.* Maybe if he dug himself into a hole and waited until the hour was up, the dragon might just fly away.

His trouser pocket being too small for the globe, Kar took off his shirt and wrapped it carefully. He tied the arms of his shirt around his waist so the globe hung in front of him. The sagging pouch reminded him of his dad's belly. He suddenly remembered the urgency of his plight.

He tried to dig a hole where he was standing, but the sand just collapsed in on itself. "It's no use," he said aloud, wiping the sweat off of his brow. "I guess I will just die here. At least my death will be worth it."

He looked up at the dragon. Its eyes were also covered in sand and it looked as though it was in a lot of discomfort. Kar thought that having sand in ones eyes would certainly be very uncomfortable. He walked around to the end of the tail and pulled himself up on the first scale. The book was right. Its scales were layered on top of each other like a giant staircase. It took time to reach the top of the dragon's head. He knew he had just a few minutes left before the dragon would be able to move again. He lowered himself flat on the dragon's head and crawled over to where he could see the dragon's eyes; his own eyes changing color from sky-blue to emerald green, in recognition of the dragon's proximity. He untied one sleeve and brushed the sand from one eyelid and then from the other.

"There," he said, patting the huge head. "That's probably a lot better."

"Quite commendable, my brother."

Startled, Kar jumped up. The globe slipped from the confines of his shirt and dropped to the ground. He watched as it rolled to the image of Lucas' face in the sand.

"Finally you show your face." Kar stood uneasily atop the dragon's head.

"Yes, we meet at last—as brothers. But it seems that you are in need of a bit of help," said Lucas.

"And let me guess. You want to help?" asked Kar sarcastically. "Fat chance. My life is your life. My death is your bad luck."

"Come, Kar. We can rule everything together. We can be the brothers we never were."

"And never will be," spat Kar.

"Let's not get touchy now," said Lucas. "I promise that your life will be long and fruitful."

"I'd rather live it short and sweet."

"If you give me the globe, I can make it so."

Suddenly the image of Lucas's face in the sand split in half and the councilman emerged from it. He picked up the globe.

"Leave that alone," cried Kar.

"Or what?" sneered the councilman. "Now, I have what *I want*. And when I finish sucking out your brother's powers, the both of you will have to duke it out as you always did in the playground. Did you take me for a fool?" He kicked at the image of Lucas.

"Only a fool would speak with a fool's tongue," said Lucas as the image of his face reappeared again in the sand. "And yes, I do believe I am looking at a fool."

"I have no time to chit chat," said the councilman. "It is time to meet your ma—"

The burnt ashes of the councilman floated to the ground.

Lucas' laughter rang hard. "Poof! That was just too easy. A fine ending for him, brother, don't you think? What is that saying? Never stand in front of a dragon unless you want to get cremated, or something to that effect?"

The dragon dropped his foot over Lucas' sandy features, rubbing them out. Then he bent to pick up the globe between his yellow teeth. "Doyouwanttheglobe?"

Kar had grabbed at a scale when he felt the dragon move and was swinging over its head staring into one very cloudy eye. He was focused on holding on for dear life and could hardly believe the dragon's question (or for that matter, that it spoke). "Huh? What?"

"Isaiddoyouwanttheglobe?" The dragon dropped the globe on the ground. "I said, 'Do you want the globe?'"

"Yes, yes, thank you. I do!" said Kar, still swinging.

"You're welcome." The dragon lowered his head to the ground.

Kar jumped off. "This is an unexpected twist."

"Kindness is always unexpected," said the dragon. "Usually they want to hack my head off and drink my blood. You chose to clear my eyes from the sand. It was bothering me so much. Thank you."

"Oh." Kar did not want to mention that he had nothing to hack the dragon's head off with anyway. They stared at each other for a while. Then he asked, "So, where do we go from here?"

"Could you step back a bit?" said the dragon. "You're very fuzzy close up and I'd really like to see you."

"Oh," said Kar, stepping backwards. "Is this better?"

"Stop, yes, stop right there. You were saying?" asked the dragon.

"Where do we go from here?"

"Anywhere you want. You have the globe. It is out of my hands, so to speak. I never liked that councilman. He wrote that book, *How to Kill A Dragon In Ten Easy Steps*. Never worked, though; until now, I guess."

Kar stood silent for a while, staring at the globe in his hands. "I need to get back to SouthWyck," he finally said.

"Just jump back on the top of my head," said the dragon, lowering his head to the ground again, "and I'll take you there."

"Can we stop by Teapot Mountain on the way?" asked Kar, putting his shirt back on. He picked up the globe and pulled himself up onto the dragon with the other hand.

"Of course," said the dragon as he lifted off the ground. "I have a bad reputation, but I'm really not that bad—for a dragon, anyway. Just hold on tight."

They landed on the beach near Teapot Mountain. Pathos was extremely surprised and relieved to see Kar and would not believe that a dragon had landed on the beach until he saw it for himself. The dragon flapped his immense wings as further proof, sending Pathos scuttling back into the cave.

Kar was in a hurry to return to SouthWyck. Nighttime was almost upon them by the time they reached the top of Mount Footsteps. Snow had already covered everything that Haylen had mistakenly transported from the councilman's cave and the mountaintop once again looked like a white linen tablecloth had been spread. From where they stood, they could see the villages still smoldering from the hooligans who had gleefully practiced dangerous magic on unsuspecting villagers. A long line of broomsters was seen heading towards SouthWyck.

"It seems they are all gathering in the field outside the village where *What's My Magic?* took place," said Kar, eyeing the view below. "I wonder where my parents are? I wonder what is happening?"

"Why don't we go down and see?" asked the dragon.

"No. Let's wait until they are all gathered together. They'll panic if they see you flying over their heads. They might hurt themselves in their rush to get away."

BURN THEM ALL

ALL OF Wyck had been cordially invited, on pain of death, to watch the burning-at-the-stake of Mr. and Mrs. Homely. The councilman had appeared previously around the village to make sure they had received their invitations on time. No one had been allowed to miss the event. Old folk, young folk, and dying folk— it did not matter. Everyone was to be in attendance. None of them had any idea that the councilman was no longer among the living; otherwise, they would have turned back and gone straight home to bed. But good news did not travel fast. All the townsfolk from the four villages had gathered in front of the makeshift platform where only a few weeks before, *What's My Magic?* Day had turned into a tragedy.

The moon had risen reluctantly over the crowd. Lucas, disguised as the dead councilman, made sure no one hid from sight. He wanted everyone there. By three in the morning, the reluctant people of Wyck stood in the field, chilled to the bone and almost hoping they would burn the Homelys soon just to add some warmth to the field.

Mrs. Beadlepoof was talking to an angry, shivering crowd from behind a makeshift podium thrown together at the last minute onto the remains of the broken stage. The Homelys stood in silence behind her. Lillian looked helplessly on.

"And so, fellow Wyckians, chaos will continue if Kar is not put to death." She wore her holiday best—a muddy yellow dress with a big black sash across the shoulders. A black hat adorned with yellow roses covered her head. "To get rid of Lucas, we must also get rid of Kar." She swept her gaze over the crowd to see their reaction to her speech of death. Having this much power in her grasp made her feel giddy.

"I don't see Kar anywhere," yelled Mr. Zerail from somewhere in the middle of the mob of people. "It seems he cares nothing for these fake parents of his."

"Yeah," cried another.

"Then why are we burning them at the stake?" cried Lillian. She pushed her way up to stand next to the podium. "We are not murderers. We are a peaceful, kind, and loving people."

"Why don't you tell that to Lucas the next time he comes for a visit?" cried Mrs. Beadlepoof. "Get out of the way, child." She waved her hand as if shooing at a fly.

"These people" (Mrs. Beadlepoof pointed at the Homelys) "kept the secret of this dangerous abandoned child from us all these years." The podium tilted. She grabbed it before it fell and straightened it. "They secretly adopted him and raised him amongst us."

"It's Lucas who's dangerous," cried Jack, "not Kar! Kar didn't do anything wrong!"

"Hear, hear," cried the crowd, muttering and murmuring.

Principal Larity walked towards Mrs. Beadlepoof. "I think that we should rethink this whole thing."

"The councilman has given me full, I say, *full* authority to deal with this matter."

"In return for what?" asked Miss Varnus, stepping out from amongst the crowd. "Has he offered you something in return for your help?" Her eyes drooped like a sad puppy beneath her layers of makeup. "Maybe a seat on the council?"

Mrs. Beadlepoof looked down at Miss Varnus. "You never know—so you had better be nice to me."

Miss Varnus, whose face was painted to reflect a person in mourning, stepped quickly back into the crowd.

"These people," she screamed, pointing at Mr. and Mrs. Homely again, "raised a dog in sheep's clothing and then let him wreak havoc on our beautiful town and just disappear. Is that what you want? Is that what is best for our village?" Her finger moved to point at the crowd.

"I thought it was Lucas in sheep's clothing," somebody cried out.

"I thought it was a cat in dog's clothing!" cried another spectator. Someone giggled.

"No, no, it was a wolf in dog's clothes," shouted another, laughing.

"Will you please be quiet down there?" shouted Mrs. Beadlepoof, banging her fist on the podium. It broke in two. She shoved the remains away from her and took a step forward. "It does not matter what clothes he wore!" More laughter erupted. "We must end the chaos that has ruined our villages. We are practically burned to the ground. Do you want them to finish us off completely?"

"NO! GET THE NOSTYS!"

"GET THE HOMELYS!"

"BURN THEM!"

"GET BEADLEPOOF!"

"BURN THEM ALL IF IT STOPS YOU FROM TALKING! WE WANT TO GO HOME NOW! IT'S FREEZING!"

"This is getting worse," said Lillian to Haylen, "and very silly."

Jack pulled at Haylen's coat. "What now?" she yelled, shoving his hand away.

"Don't say anything," whispered Jack. "Just glance up at what's on the roof of our school building in front of you. There's a big shadow that looks like it's breathing."

"Where?" asked Haylen, squinting her eyes towards the school. "I can't see anything."

Lillian stretched her neck out for a better look.

Jack spoke between his teeth. "Don't let anybody see you looking."

"Why?"

"'Cause I think it's the dragon!"

Haylen took a deep breath, shifted her gaze slightly upwards, and dropped it suddenly. "Yes, I think I saw it too. Do you think that Kar's…"

"No" said Jack. "Of course not."

"I don't know," said Haylen worriedly. "We haven't seen him or the councilman around lately. As long as Lucas is alive, we at least know Kar is as well."

193

A silence descended around them. Lucas had suddenly appeared beside Mrs. Beadlepoof.

"Mrs. Beadlepoof," said Lucas loudly, "I hear that you have done an excellent job in keeping the councilmen informed of the actions of the villagers for many years now."

Mrs. Beadlepoof stumbled backwards with her hands raised in front of her in horror.

"Why, Mrs. Beadlepoof," said Lucas. "I thought the councilman had put you in charge of everything? Are you relinquishing your control so soon?"

"Now, fellow Wyckians," he said turning to the crowd. "I do not want to impose myself on you, but we are gathered here for a purpose."

The crowd closed in, as if huddled in fear. A few stragglers at the back turned to flee.

"I do not think that would be wise," said Lucas, appearing in front of the frightened deserters. They turned and squeezed themselves back in again.

"Now, as I was saying," said Lucas, appearing on the battered stage again. "We have all gathered here to witness the punishment of those who have kept a secret hidden among us. Even if that secret was myself." He grinned in delight. "I must say it was as much of a surprise to me as it was to you. But all's well that ends well, eh? So, who would like to do the honors?"

Mouths were tightly pressed over clamped teeth while hands were shoved into pockets.

"I guess I must choose for you. Since Mrs. Beadlepoof has put herself in the position of authority, I think it is only appropriate she should light the fire."

Gasping loudly, Mrs. Beadlepoof turned, ran down the stage, and tripped over Lillian's foot.

"I'm so sorry," said Lillian, trying to help her up. It took three more men to place her back on her jittery feet.

"Now, now," said Lucas. "You wouldn't want me to wring your little wren's neck now, would you?" He smirked at the old woman. Mrs. Beadlepoof backed away, her beady eyes suddenly large and fearful.

"Don't even *attempt* to disappear, Mrs. Beadlepoof. I can get you back here with a snap of my fingers. Understand?" Her face turned a hideous shade of purple.

"Well, Mrs. Beadlepoof, go ahead," prodded Lucas. "You were so willing just a while ago."

Mrs. Beadlepoof moaned loudly in protest. She pushed Mr. and Mrs. Homely down the stage and over to the pyre. The burning-at-the-stake thing was new to the villagers.

"Please, get on it yourselves. Make this easy on me." Mrs. Beadlepoof pleaded to the Homelys. "Please?"

They refused to move another inch and glared at her. "How could you, Mrs. Beadlepoof?" asked Mrs. Homely quietly. "Is this how you save the Wyck villages?"

Lucas intervened. "Can I help?" Mrs. Beadlepoof looked gratefully up at him. Lucas wiggled his finger. The Homelys were gently lifted off the ground and onto the pyre. Lucas threw a box of matches at Mrs. Beadlepoof's feet. He smiled at her and gestured at the Homelys. "Since you do not have the magical ability to light fire, I guess you will be needing these."

Lillian tightly gripped Haylen's hand.

It took a lot of effort for Mrs. Beadlepoof to bend down and pick up the matches. Her hat fell off her head every time she bent over to pick them up. Then she stood to replace her hat and bent down again. The cycle repeated itself. Someone in the crowd eventually grabbed the matches off the cold ground and shoved them into her clumsy fingers. She struck the first match, but her hands were shaking so badly that it blew out immediately. By the third attempt she saw that no one was going to come to her rescue in this task. She shut her eyes and struck the match a fourth time. It flared. She took a few wobbly steps towards the pyre. Mrs. Homely looked at her and then at Lucas. She opened her mouth to scream. Her scream was cut short by a flame of fire that ripped through the sky, turning it a rosy hue.

The crowd sighed with pleasure as hot air enveloped them.

The dragon hovered over their heads, its wings spread so wide it almost covered the field. Large balls of soot blew out of its nostrils and spilled from the corners of its mouth. The crowd let out a round of applause accompanied by a few frightened screams.

Lillian gaped in amazement.

Lucas turned his gaze to the person sitting on the head of the dragon. "Kar! Brother, I knew you would eventually make it. If you do not come down on your own, I will do the honors myself."

Kar stood up on the head of the dragon, holding on to a scale with one hand. "Leave my parents alone, or I will let this dragon rid us of you as it did the councilman."

Gasps of joy echoed through the field. Somebody started to clap again, but the clap was quickly silenced. This was still not a time for celebration.

"If the dragon breathes one flame towards me," said Lucas, "your parents will go up in smoke as well; and probably half this village." He made a sweeping movement with his hand.

"Is that true?" whispered Kar to the dragon.

"I'm afraid so," said the dragon with a slight nod of his massive head. "My flames are deadly and I can't see well, so I'm not very accurate. I'm sorry."

Lucas struck a match and waved it. "If you do not give me the crystal globe that I can see tucked in your shirt, your parents will perish in moments. This wood is very dry." In the issuing silence, the alarming sound of a twig snapping under his boot jolted the crowd a few inches off their feet.

"I would do it with just a slight wiggle of my finger, but I just love the old method of burning at the stake, don't you?"

"Don't listen to him. Save yourself, son." Mrs. Homely pleaded

"Yes, my son," agreed Mr. Homely sadly. "Do as your mother says."

"Ah, such nice fake parents," said Lucas, bringing the match closer to the pyre.

"Stop," yelled Kar. "Here, take the stupid globe." Kar threw the globe to Lucas. "We have no need of all this stupid magic, anyway."

The globe soared in the air. Nobody dared try to catch it except for Mrs. Beadlepoof. She raised her dress and caught it in its folds. Meekly she handed it over to Lucas.

"What a stupid decision, my brother; but a decision I knew you would make." Lucas caressed the globe. "Ah, my destiny at last," he said softly. He walked slowly back to the stage and stood in front of a crowd that was already getting tired and listless. Mouths stretched wide in deep yawns and lips smacked in annoyance.

"Better get on with it," someone hissed from deep within the throng of people. "My feet are fallin' asleep."

"People of Wyck, please gather in front of me; for I am about to give you what you want the most." He paused and raised the globe above his head. "Freedom from magic." No one moved. "If you know what's good for you." The front of the crowd had no choice but to step forward, as they seemed to be forcefully pushed by those who opted to stay at the back. "Ah, good. That's much better. Now, everyone look at the globe." They stared at it until their eyes watered.

"I don't see anything," someone shouted.

"What do you think it is?" asked another.

"Don't know. Looks like a pretty bauble to me," said Miss Varnus.

Lucas shook the globe angrily. "Why doesn't this thing work?" He turned the globe around in his hands.

"Jack," whispered Haylen.

"What?"

"It will be dawn soon and then it will work," she said softly, just figuring it out.

"What will work?" asked Lillian.

They ignored her.

"Okay," said Jack. "What do you want me to do? Wrestle him for it?"

"Change into an eagle and grab it from him."

"If he doesn't wring my neck first," mumbled Jack. "Anyway, the globe is too round to pick up in my beak and too slippery to hold in my talons."

"What are we to do?" She stepped on Lillian's foot. "Oh, sorry, Lillian," she whispered. "I didn't mean to."

"That's all right," said Lillian, "it happens all the time."

Haylen's face lit up like somebody who had just thought up something. She pulled Lillian towards her and whispered something in her ear. Lillian shrugged and nodded. "What do we have to lose?"

Meanwhile, Lucas was shaking the globe angrily and knocking on the crystal. "I am not leaving here until this thing works."

THE DAY THE MORNING CAME PRETTY DARN SLOW

IT WILL be dawn in a few seconds, thought Kar, clinging to one of the dragon's scales on its head. He was surprised at the dragon's ability to hover silently in mid-air. It was really very graceful. He searched the crowd for Haylen and Jack and spied them standing near Lucas.

"You." Lucas pointed at Haylen. "Come up here and find out how this thing works. You found it. I'm sure you know what to press to make it work." Haylen slowly walked up the broken steps of the stage and stopped a few inches away from the globe.

Kar's gaze shifted from Haylen to Lucas. Behind Lucas, a small furry animal hopped towards him. He hoped that Lucas did not sense anything. He wondered what Lillian was up to.

Lucas turned slightly to see what everyone was looking at behind him. A rabbit stood on its hind legs, its left paw slightly in front while its right hind leg stretched out as far as it possibly could. Before Kar could stretch himself to get a better look, the bunny with one ear longer than the other shape-shifted. Lillian appeared and, before anyone realized what she was up to, she kicked the globe with her one giant foot straight out of Lucas' hands.

For a moment Kar thought it would sail across the other side of Mount Footsteps, but it flew straight up past a few shadowy clouds; and as it made its way back to earth, the sun peaked from the horizon, casting a golden glow upon everyone. Having never experienced the concept of slow motion, the Wyckians forever after called it the day-the-morning-came-pretty-darn-slow.

Suddenly the morning rays magically gathered into one large beam and like an arrow on a deadly mission, pierced the globe as it slowly rotated its way back to earth. From the center of the globe multi-colored lights exploded, like thousands of tiny lightning bolts raining down on every Wyckian standing in the field. Lucas screamed in fear as tiny jolts of bright light attacked him.

After the initial screams of terror, the crowd found the tiny bolts ticklish and ran about giggling and slapping themselves as if mosquitoes were on the rampage.

"Make it stop!"

With the grace of an eagle, the dragon flapped its wings and swooped towards the globe as it slowly descended towards the beaten earth. Kar held on tightly as the giant winged creature sent large parts of the already-hysterical crowd to the far corners of the field. Just before the globe made a crash landing, the dragon plucked it up between his blackened teeth and swallowed it whole. A heavy blackness descended on the villages and then, just as quickly, the sun appeared again.

"Now that was a very nice bit of fireworks," a voice yelled out, clapping for good measure. After a dutiful round of applause and cheering, those in the back slowly tiptoed their way back home. Finding that Lucas did not appear to round them up again like lost sheep, they dispersed faster than they had arrived.

Mrs. Beadlepoof tried to snap her fingers but could not escape some of the angry villagers bearing down on her. No one stopped to help her up as they stepped on her to get away. They had no idea that their magical abilities had been taken from them by the globe. They just wanted to get away from a very upset Lucas. He was having a tantrum on the stage. Even the broomsters would not start. Kicking and banging on them did not help either. They all had to walk home.

Haylen and Jack ran to help Mr. and Mrs. Homely off the pyre as Kar suddenly appeared from nowhere to help.

Secret Ingredient popped out of Jack's shirt pocket and yelled, "Hey, watch it! You're shaking me around and you know I hate to be shaken!" They all happily ignored him.

The following week they were given a hero's parade in the EastWyck Village. The town came out cheering and rejoicing, but Lillian was given the pedestal of honor. She stood proudly on a wooden footstool, displaying her one large foot for all to view. Mr. Cartel asked permission to measure it in order to make a wax duplicate for the Wyck museum. Lillian waved it in front of his face and shoved it in front of anyone else who was curious enough to want to take a look. Her family stood, beaming, by her side, showing off their own enormous feet as their chests swelled up with pride.

After things settled down, it took a while for the Wyckians to get used to the idea that magic was no longer a part of their lives. Mr. Tweetle mourned the loss of his bread business, but Mrs. Tweetle was not in the least perturbed about it. She could always bake bread, and teaching children to tap dance was a lucrative business on its own.

Bereft of councilmen and the threat of Lucas' power over them, the Wyckians decided that it was time to take the matters of rule into their own hands.

Their first important bit of duty was putting Mrs. Beadlepoof on trial. Her punishment involved sweeping the Wyck villages of all debris and performing any menial job that was asked of her, like walking the village dogs or cleaning windows. At night, she was locked up in jail. It would last a year and the villagers hoped the punishment would teach her a lesson about putting her nose where it should not have been in the first place. But it did not seem to bother Mrs. Beadlepoof at all. In fact, she was more into the business of the Wyckians than she had ever been, especially when she was asked to clean windows. She had a good peek into everyone's living quarters. As the days passed, she received fewer and fewer requests for house cleaning and was relegated to sweeping up the streets.

Lucas' reintegration into society was not easy. He could not believe that he had lost everything in a matter of seconds. Even his strength had ebbed and he looked like a smaller version of himself. He had returned to a normal thirteen-year-old but soon he was seen talking to himself on the streets and waving his hands about. Everyone thought it was punishment enough. They had their first official village idiot.

Kar sometimes felt sorry for him, which made Haylen furious. She reminded Kar constantly about how Lucas had tried to rob all of them of their one magical ability; but his only response was that it had happened anyway.

Secret Ingredient opened up an information booth on the corner of Padding Lane and Stomping Drive. He charged half a dragon for pointing people in the right direction and two dragons for finding lost items. He took very long breaks and extra long lunches.

There was an all-out search for the Squint twins. They were eventually found a few days after the-morning-that-came-pretty-darn-slow. Someone spied them coming down Mount Footsteps. They had lost fifty pounds between them in the ordeal, but they soon regained it.

Saff Swoonzy, who had been blown off course by Miss Varnus, was eventually found and brought home by the first out-of-town visitor to Wyck.

And the dragon could sometimes be heard snoring somewhere atop of Mount Footsteps, where it had decided to roost for a while.

EPILOGUE

IN THE shadow of Mount Footsteps, Taff Peabrine was tending to his newly assigned flock of sheep. He stretched out under a gnarled willow tree, whose soft branches dipped playfully into a gurgling stream, and yawned deeply. He missed the dog days of old and he especially missed Lillian, who was now a security guard for the Wyck Museum of Ages. He curled up facing away from Mount Footsteps, where the dragon had set up its lair. That was why, later on, he could not tell the astonished Wyckians the exact moment Mount Footsteps and the dragon disappeared. He could only say that when he awoke, it was simply gone.

Meanwhile, in the middle of the forest, far away from the all the noise and rebuilding of the Wyck villages, a golden horse grazed.

About the Author

The inspiration for Christina Waymreen's *SouthWyck* began fifteen years ago with one compelling word: 'Kar', a name meaning 'ocean' in Hawaiian. From this blossomed the story of *SouthWyck*'s Kar, who struggles with magic, heritage, and the future of his village.

Christina likes building fantasy worlds because they are so unrelated to the ever-changing present. Her story is designed to transcend time: If you read it ten years from now or a hundred, it will not make a difference. She loves to enter worlds that belie ours and allow anything to happen.

Also by Christina Waymreen

THE SEEDLESS TREES

www.ingramcontent.com/pod-product-compliance
Lightning Source LLC
Chambersburg PA
CBHW060928180626
46817CB00004B/1437